For a split second I thought about running, but Dunigan filled the doorway as he picked up the unconscious deputy with his handcuffed meat hooks and effortlessly tossed him into the hallway. I'll never forget the hollow clang of the metal door when he shut it, locking us inside the tiny room.

I smashed a red alarm button on the wall behind me just before the giant prisoner slid the heavy metal table across the room as if it were made of plastic, pinning me against the wall. The behemoth leaned on the table and stared at me, eyes wild and grinning maniacally. He took a couple deep breaths and forcefully blew the air and spittle out through his yellowed teeth.

He stood up straight, keeping me pinned to the wall, leaning his girth against the table. I tried to push it away with both hands, twisting frantically, but it was useless against his weight and strength. His grin widened and his breathing intensified as if aroused by my fear. Then he reached toward my head with his two hands the size of catcher's mitts, holding them there a few inches from my head. I turned sideways and pressed my cheek against the wall, keeping sight of his hands with one eye that pulsed with panic. He kept his hands there, close to my face, reveling in the anticipation. I pictured his hands squeezing my head, his thumbs entering my brain through my eye-sockets.

Praise for Good Lookin'

"Todd Bequette, known as a skilled and meticulous criminal defense attorney, fashions those same attributes as a writer with his engaging break-through novel, *Good Lookin'*. Bequette's alter-ego, Joe Turner, expertly untangles what initially looks like an open-and-shut case, guiding us through a series of mysteries along the way that keeps us in suspense even after the verdict is read."

~ Matt Maiocco, Author, *Letters to 87*

~*~

"Gripping characters and an intricate storyline make this legal thriller a compelling read that you won't put down until the final (and unexpected!) denouement."

~ Elizabeth P. Augustin, Writer

~*~

"A highly entertaining, crisply written, and enjoyable book….*Good Lookin'* takes you on a journey through the trials and tribulations of criminal defense attorney Joe Turner as he and his young client, accused of murder, navigate their way through the criminal justice system."

~ Kevin R. Murphy, Judge, Alameda County
Superior Court

Good Lookin': a Joe Turner Mystery

by

T. L. Bequette

Good Lookin': a Joe Turner Mystery

COPYRIGHT © 2021 by Todd Lewis Bequette

Cover Art by *Kim Mendoza*

The Wild Rose Press, Inc.
PO Box 708
Adams Basin, NY 14410-0708
Visit us at www.thewildrosepress.com

Publishing History
First Edition, 2021
Trade Paperback ISBN 978-1-5092-3570-4
Digital ISBN 978-1-5092-3571-1

Published in the United States of America

Acknowledgments

On the pantheon of friendship litmus tests, reading an unpublished first novel falls somewhere between moving day and an early morning lift to the airport. I count myself lucky that so many obliged.

At the top of the list is Alice Piper, who put her Master's in Creative Writing to good use and improved the story immensely. I am also grateful to Catherine Burns, James Burns, Matt Schenone, Cam Peters, Hannah Peters, and my well-read life partner, Helen, for wading through early drafts with helpful critiques.

My editor, Kaycee John, is the best in the business. I thank her for rescuing mine from the ocean of manuscripts worthy of print and for tolerating what I understand to be my serious affliction related to the passive voice. Thank you also to readers Elizabeth Johnson, Robin Johnson, and the team of proofreaders at The Wild Rose Press.

To the extent I have a knack for this, I owe it to my mother's love of books and my dad's ability to spin a yarn. Finally, a special thank you to my son, Ben. He faithfully read every draft, and his outlook on life inspired me to finally put pen to paper.

Chapter One

Leonard Dunigan, the man who would soon be sitting across from me, killed a man with his massive bare hands, squeezing his skull until it caved in upon itself. I began worrying the moment I saw the lone, average-sized deputy sheriff escorting my client into the windowless consultation room. Ever since being appointed to represent him on the murder charge, I had been warned by various members of law enforcement never to be alone with Leonard. Apparently, he had a history of randomly attacking other attorneys, inmates, and guards—people in general.

Today, I needed his signature on a consent form, allowing me to view his voluminous psychiatric records. I'd been assured a deputy wouldn't leave the room.

Dunigan shuffled into the room, both wrists handcuffed in front of him and the chain between his ankle shackles clanking on the cement floor. He wore bright red prisoner sweatpants and a matching shirt. In Alameda County, prisoner clothing came color coded. I could never recall what each color signified but was fairly sure red fell somewhere between insanely violent and sadistic. The deputy, armed with a bigass taser, looked like he worked out. Still, at six feet, seven inches and well over three-fifty, Leonard comically dwarfed his escort.

I watched from my seat at a small table in the eight by ten-foot room as the prisoner entered the room, the deputy close behind. In a surprising show of agility, the gigantic Dunigan spun to his right, struck the deputy's shoulder, and sent him careening into the wall. Before the guard could recover, the prisoner raised both arms over his head and using the handcuffs like an axe, swung downward, a direct hit to the officer's head.

For a split second I thought about running, but Dunigan filled the doorway as he picked up the deputy with his handcuffed meat hooks and effortlessly tossed him into the hallway. I'll never forget the hollow clang of the metal door when he shut it, locking us inside the tiny room.

I smashed a red alarm button on the wall behind me just before Dunigan slid the heavy metal table across the room as if it were made of plastic and pinned me against the wall. The behemoth leaned on the table and stared at me for several seconds, eyes wild and grinning maniacally. He took a couple deep breaths and forcefully blew the air and spittle out through his yellowed teeth.

He stood up straight, keeping me pinned to the wall, leaning his girth against the table. I tried to push it away with both hands, twisting frantically, but it was useless against his weight and strength. His grin widened and his breathing intensified—as did the production of spit—as if aroused by my fear. Then he reached toward my head with his two hands the size of catcher's mitts, holding them there a few inches from my head. I turned sideways and pressed my cheek against the wall, keeping sight of his hands with one eye that pulsed with panic. He kept his hands there, close to my face, reveling in the anticipation of what was coming. I pictured his hands squeezing my head, his thumbs entering my brain through my eye-sockets.

Just as suddenly, he backed away, laughing uncontrollably as he staggered to the other side of the room. I wriggled my thighs away from the wall and collapsed to the table on my forearms, keeping my head up to maintain sight of him. He had his hands on his knees now, his hulking body convulsing with laughter as deputies entered the cell, tasers at the ready. He went down to a knee and sat on the floor in the corner, looking happy and exhausted after a friendly game of sport. In short order, deputies led him away in chains and cuffs, his demented laugh echoing throughout the long hallways of the jail.

I needed a drink.

****

Leaning on my kitchen counter forty-five minutes later, I still imagined Dunigan squishing my head like an over-ripe cantaloupe. I considered the ten-minute walk to Melba's, my local dive bar, but drinking alone seemed more appropriate.

Lately, I'd drastically cut back on my drinking and had to admit I felt better. I slept more restfully now, and it was easier to get my motor running in the morning. Plus, I'd managed to lose some weight. But good God, if there was ever a time when I was entitled to indulge, it was surely in the aftermath of narrowly avoiding a grisly murder. Particularly my own.

It also seemed like since I hadn't been drinking every night, I enjoyed booze more. I'd always found the slow, meticulous preparation of a drink sensual, like really hot foreplay. I placed a plump lime on my cutting board and rolled it back and forth, applying gentle pressure, like the chefs on the food network I always watched on late night TV, usually with a beer and peanut butter sandwich. My steak knife penetrated the fruit, its trickling juice tingling my cuticles as I sliced wedges.

I opened the cupboard above the sink, lifted the beautiful blue bottle of gin down to the counter, and unscrewed its cap, slowing inhaling the botanical vapors. As I splashed two carefully measured jiggers into an icy glass, I idly wondered what it was I smelled. To me, it smelled like pleasure.

I unscrewed the plastic tonic bottle slowly with one hand, feeling its body's firm, fizzing pressure with the other as I controlled its gasping release. I squeezed a lime wedge over the glass and dropped it in. Then I splashed in the tonic and I stirred the drink vigorously, hearing the strengthening hiss in the glass and watching the torrent of tiny bubbles surge upward, ready to tickle my nose with the first sip.

I wasn't sure about drinking more, but I definitely needed to date more.

As I settled into my hideous mustard-colored recliner with my drink, watching sports highlights with the sound down, I thought about today's events. Over the years, I had fielded lots of questions—mainly from my mother—about the safety of my profession given my physical proximity to violent criminals. My standard answer had been that it was never a problem. After all, I was on their side and often the only one standing between them and a lifetime behind bars. It was never in the best interest of the accused to make an enemy out of me.

But that's the thing about murder, I smiled, taking a healthy gulp; nothing about it was ever logical. Not to mention, in dealing with the criminally insane, like Leonard Dunigan, all bets were off. As I recalled his horrible smiling, panting visage, it was clear to me that he killed for the thrill of it. For now, I blinked away the image, took another swallow, and cradled the cold glass close. His face would reappear throughout the evening but soon would begin to blur around the edges until the image disappeared.

Still on my recliner, I was awakened by the bite of melting ice on my chest and the buzz of my phone on the side table. I rubbed my eyes to focus on the text. It was from the Alameda County Court Appointed Program, requesting that I accept the representation of one Darnell Moore, who was accused of murder. I sighed deeply and stretched before collapsing back on my part-time bed.

The Court Appointed Program relied on private attorneys like me to represent indigents in the county whenever the Public Defender's Office declared a conflict of interest—usually because they had previously represented the victim of the current crime. The pay for the appointed cases was not great but in slow times it kept the lights on in my modest downtown Oakland office.

Also, whereas my paying clients tended to commit crimes like drunk driving, financial crimes, or drug offenses, most court appointed clients were charged with murder. While one might assume violent offenders were more difficult to work with, in general, I'd found this not to be the case. Sure, there was the occasional Leonard Dunigan, but for the most part, I seemed to get along with the indigent offenders at least as well as the more white-collar criminals.

The asshole gene cuts across all socio-economic barriers. In fact, some of my most difficult clients have been wealthy men accused of insider trading or money laundering. Perhaps it was because they were used to getting their way or buying themselves out of trouble.

Since my representation of Leonard Dunigan came to an abrupt end less than twelve hours ago, I supposed I would take the case of Darnell Moore.

****

"Hey, you okay? I heard you almost died?" Andy Kopp and I had shared our law office on the fifth floor of a B-level downtown Oakland building for a decade. He was a personal injury attorney, and we spent most of the time in the office insulting each other's clients.

"That's a bit of an overstatement, but it was less than awesome. Thanks for the unusual concern."

"I was worried about your share of the rent."

"Ah, that's more like it," I said as I collected my mail and headed for the door. "Shouldn't you be out replenishing your supply of neck braces or something?"

"Going so soon, Turner?"

"Headed to court. I have the innocent to defend."

"Really? You found one after all these years? Don't screw it up," he called out before our front door closed.

I arrived at the court's master calendar department and took a look at the Darnell Moore file before Judge Kramer took the bench. I read the probable cause statement, where the arresting officer swore the following:

On March 22, 2021, Cleveland Barlow, a known

Cashtown gang member, was shot as he loitered outside his gang hangout at Eighth and Maybeck in west Oakland. Suspect Darnell Moore's car is captured on surveillance entering the intersection seconds before the shooting, then racing away from the scene seconds after. The shooting itself is not captured on video. An eyewitness to the shooting, the proprietor at the E&J Market, chose defendant Moore out of a photo spread as the possible shooter. Defendant Moore is a known affiliate of the victim's rival gang, the IceBoyz.

I approached courtroom deputy, Deputy Posey, a fixture in the department for as long as I could remember. "Hey Paul, can I get Darnell Moore in an interview room?"

He smiled but didn't look up. "Sure. You think you can manage not to make him want to kill you?"

"Funny. Do you think you can manage not to get overpowered by a handcuffed, unarmed inmate?"

He laughed and shook his head. "Booth two."

I grabbed the criminal complaint off the counsel table and glanced at it as Deputy Posey unlocked the side door of the courtroom which led to the interview booth. I noted his rap sheet showed no prior felonies and only a few misdemeanor convictions for drug and theft offenses. His date of birth was in 2002, making him nineteen.

He looked even younger as he took his place behind the thick glass. Standing maybe six-feet-two, with a slender frame, his longish Afro stood on end, making him seem even taller. His light complexion was smooth, without the trace of whiskers on pudgy cheeks.

"Good morning, Darnell, I'm Joe Turner. I'm going to be your attorney if that's okay with you."

"Cool," he said, flashing an easy smile. For a young man who had probably never done more than a few weeks in custody in one stretch and now faced life in prison, he seemed remarkably calm.

I explained that his case would be continued to give me a few weeks to get up to speed on his case, then we'd be back in court to enter a plea of not guilty and begin his defense. He nodded pleasantly, as if I were reviewing his test after geometry class.

"So, Darnell, just to give you a quick summary of the evidence the cops say they have against you…"

"Yeah, I heard all that from the detective," he cut in, his smile widening. "Like I told him, though, I don't know nothing about none of this."

His comment was bad news on two fronts. First, it was apparent that Darnell had not invoked his right to remain silent and had instead attempted to talk his way out of the charges. In addition to never working, it often made things much worse.

Second, I had represented innocent people before. The police were not perfect, and sometimes the District Attorney's Office charged the wrong people. However, a decade of experience had taught me that it was extremely rare that a defendant would be charged with a criminal offense they knew absolutely nothing about.

"So, Darnell, and we can talk about this more when I visit you in the jail, but are you saying you honestly have absolutely zero knowledge about the murder? Who was killed, why they were killed, when, where, and how they were killed?" I wasn't sure why I asked. Just hoping against hope, I suppose.

"Mr. Turner," he said quietly, shaking his head and still smiling. "On Momma's, I for real don't know anything about any of this. Merch." Although I was by no means fluent in street slang, Darnell just promised on his mother's grave and, with the last word, short for merchandise, emphasized his claim.

"Okay, Darnell." I slid my card through a slit in the glass. "I'll continue your case a couple weeks for plea. I'll be out to see you at the jail sometime next week."

On my way out of court, a large, well-dressed African American woman met me in the hallway. "Mr. Turner, I'm Glenda Moore, Darnell's mother." She did not share her son's light-hearted tone. "I know it's early, but how bad does it look?"

"Pleasure to meet you, ma'am," I said, shaking her hand. "It's really too early to say. If you attend next week, I'll be able to at least summarize the evidence against your son."

"I know you must hear this from lots of mothers, but I hope you can believe me. Darnell doesn't have it in him to take someone's..." Her voice cracked, and she looked away for a moment before continuing. "God knows that child can act the fool, Mr. Turner, but he's not a murderer."

"Ms. Moore, I will certainly do my best for your son," I told her, intentionally not responding to her pronouncement of her son's innocence.

On one hand, she was right. I'd heard a similar refrain from several mothers of the accused. On the other hand, it was a somewhat hopeful sign that at least Darnell had been raised in a household with a good mother—not a given for many of my court-appointed clients. Also, I was glad to know that Ms. Moore seemed to grasp the seriousness of Darnell's situation and hoped that she would share that with her son.

Chapter Two
Children are children, but they can spot an evasion faster than adults.—Harper Lee

Oakland, California 2006

Both boys' hands were chafed raw from hauling the rough cinderblocks. Damon was convinced that Danny, the twins' new foster dad, had made up the chore just to be mean. Who ever heard of moving a giant pile of cinderblocks from one side of a vacant lot to the other?

Jesse, the smaller of the twins, was too tired to care. His mind was numb as his spindly arms struggled with the weight of the blocks, his small back bent in half by the time he reached the pile, dropping his burden from ankle level.

Danny was turning out to be a real loser, like all the rest of them. He'd been so nice and happy during the interview at social services. He'd talked about them playing rec league baseball and riding to school in his big shiny pick-up. But what had really gotten the boys' attention was the ice cream.

"So, growing boys need healthy meals, of course," Ms. Caverly the social worker had cautioned in the interview.

"Well, I suppose I eat healthy enough," Danny said as he reclined casually in his chair, hands behind his head as he flexed his biceps. "So long as ice cream is okay once in a while," he added, winking at the boys. The twins had looked at each other with mouths agape, barely able to contain themselves.

The interview had been like a dozen others: enthusiastic with the promise of happy times ahead. Deep down both boys knew that this was all likely too good to be true. They had been disappointed so many times. They were nine now and knew that something always went wrong with foster care. As they had been told over and over, it was difficult to find someone willing to take on both boys even though the pay for the foster parents was double. Still, though, the ice cream comment had gotten them excited and it had been fun to be happy, even for a while.

It was after dark before the oversized pick-up pulled into the dusty lot. Danny motioned for them to climb in the back and flung a plastic bag of fast food at them. They hadn't been allowed inside the cab of the truck since their ride home from social services.

"This sucks, Jess," Damon said, grinning at his use of the grown-up term as he fished a burger out of the bag for his brother.

"Yeah, D, but these burgers don't suck, though," quipped Jesse, following with an infectious giggle.

"Having some chocolate ice cream for desert wouldn't suck either," responded Damon, chuckling before he finished his sentence.

"Nope, having a million bucks wouldn't suck either."

The boys laughed the whole ride home. They had seen a lot in nine years and knew that so long as they had each other, everything would be fine.

Chapter Three

Back at the office, Chuck Argenal, a private eye I used for most cases had made himself comfortable at my desk. "I see reports of your death have been greatly exaggerated," he said without looking up. "I came by to pick up a check."

The initial police reports from the Moore case arrived via email; I sent two copies to the printer. "Lucky for Dunigan the guards arrived when they did. I had him right where I wanted him."

"That guy's big enough to go bear huntin' with a switch." Chuck spoke in a southern drawl of movie lines and country idioms. I usually followed most of it. "So, Joseph, what unfounded charge has been levied against your latest innocent client?" he asked, getting up to leave.

"Only murder." I handed him a copy of the police reports and settled back into my chair. "Darnell Moore. Drive-by shooting in west Oakland. Apparently, there's surveillance of his car driving by as shots ring out. Tentative identification. Sounds gang related. I'll email you the file and get funding."

"Once again, unto the breach!" he said, pausing at the door, eyebrows raised in a question.

"No idea, sorry. Sounds like Shakespeare?"

"Henry the Fifth," he called from down the hall.

Ten minutes later, Andy, my office mate, poked his

head in my office with the unwelcome news that his wife wanted to set me up with her friend.

"Set-ups are a bad idea," I reminded him for what had to be the six millionth time.

"That's what I told her. You're a mess with women."

"Thanks for the support, but here's why it's a bad idea. Say we go out and she thinks I'm a jerk. Then she tells Karen and now I've got two people who think I'm a jerk."

Andy smirked. "I think my wife already knows you're a jerk but go on."

"Worse yet, we hit it off and become a couple. Then inevitably, something goes wrong, and we break up. Now Karen takes her side, of course, and the next thing you know, the two of them are making fun of my annoying habits or my orgasm face or stupid things I said in bed. Then I'm forced into isolation and start drinking too much again."

"I could have gone my lifetime without picturing your orgasm face, but this does sound much worse than I imagined," he said, sounding humored by my neuroses. "And I wasn't aware that you'd ever stopped drinking too much."

"Or say we hit it off then break up, then get back together. Now Karen knows all this stuff about me and now she's already agreed that I was a loser and apologized for ever setting her up with me. Now her friendship with the woman is ruined. It's really a lose, lose, lose proposition."

Andy shook his head. "Two words, Turner. Seek help." He retreated to his office. "I'm going to send you her contact info so I can stay on Karen's good side."

Returning to the Moore case file, I braced myself for bad news, a general mindset I'd developed when reading police reports. They were written, after all, by police officers, in order to justify the arrest of the suspect. As a rule, they weren't filled with evidence of my client's innocence.

The police reports had furthered my skepticism that my newest client knew nothing about nothing. Over the last week leading up to the murder, the Cashtown and Iceboyz gangs had engaged in a pitched battle, turning west Oakland into an urban war zone. Just one day prior to the shooting, notorious Cashtown member Bumpy Lampkin had sprayed the Iceboyz town headquarters with bullets.

Although the reports stopped short of alleging that Moore was a member of the Iceboyz, there were strong indications that he was on the membership path. In his phone, the police had found photos of him posing with other known gang members while flashing their hand signs. In one, Moore posed with a semi-automatic rifle.

I opened the file labeled "Firespotter" a technology utilized by the Oakland Police Department for more than a decade. Using acoustic sensors that blanketed the worst neighborhoods in Oakland, the system identified gunshots through artificial intelligence to pinpoint their location within a 50-foot radius and document the exact timing of the shots.

The Firespotter graphic showed a three-dimensional map of the area surrounding Maybeck and Eighth streets. Twenty-three red circles, each signifying a gunshot, dotted the area just south of the intersection. All of the shots occurred within a five-second span on March 22, beginning at six-seventeen-o-five p.m.

It appeared that the entire Cash guys gang, or whatever they were called, had been expecting an assault and had returned fire. Even in the age of large capacity magazines, the cluster of shots within such a short span of time meant there were probably several shooters.

I opened the "photos" file, bracing myself for gory shots of the victim or worse yet, autopsy photographs. The first was a photo of Moore's car, an olive green 1989 mid-sized sedan seized one day after the shooting when he was arrested. Other photos showed the car's hood to be a slightly lighter shade of green, and both front hubcaps were missing. The car appeared to have been made from spare parts.

The driver's side panel was riddled with bullet holes, the back window, shattered. There were more photos of bullet strike marks inside the car, on the dashboard, and remarkably, on the driver's side headrest. Moore was obviously lucky to be alive. That is, whoever was driving the car was lucky to be alive, I chastised myself.

The next photos were of the residence at 454 West Eighth street. A close-up revealed four different bullet holes in the front door. The front bay window of the Victorian had been shot out. The number of shots fired at the house in such a short duration made me wonder if there was more than one shooter in Moore's car. I didn't relish the thought of trying to get that information out of my client.

Wide-angle photos showed orange plastic evidence markers next to gold shell casings, the part of the cartridge ejected from a firearm when fired. There were two groups of markers, one in the middle of Eighth street and another on the sidewalk in front of the house. Closeup photos revealed ten forty-caliber shell casings in the street, presumably ejected from the murderer's firearm.

With the dinner hour approaching, I didn't want to push my luck with any more photographs. I emailed Chuck and put together an investigation list. He worked better with lists. I often lamented one of the many discrepancies which made criminal defense an uphill battle. Apart from the police department's investigation, the District Attorneys also had inspectors on staff to investigate their cases. They were usually former police detectives with access to all the resources of the Oakland Police Department.

I had Chuck, a former probation officer, who wasn't licensed to carry a gun and still used a typewriter. Still, in the very shallow pool of private detectives, I placed him solidly in the upper third. An aging hippie who wore flip flops twelve months a year, his drawl had a way of putting people at ease in every situation, which often led him to valuable information. He also seemingly knew everyone in Oakland, from barbers to cops to waiters. Mainly, though, he was very entertaining, with a country saying or movie line for every occasion.

I drafted a discovery list for the D.A., which included witness statements, ballistics, and gunshot residue tests on the victim, and Firespotter activity for the area for the forty-eight hours preceding the shooting. I had no definite reason for the last request, but motive seemed to be an important part of the prosecution's case. Maybe there were other shootings to muddy the motive waters.

Chuck's investigation list included an interview with the eyewitness. Tentative eye-witness identifications had a way of becoming much less tentative at trial, and I wanted to speak with the witness before he met with the District Attorney. Because Chuck's technological comfort zone was yet to include email, I planned to call him later and painstakingly recite the task list which he'd write on the well-worn spiral notepad he used for every case. I reminded myself that his entertainment value was high.

****

I drove home, picking up a burrito for dinner on the way. I lived in the Glenview neighborhood in the Oakland Hills. It was a safe area and an easy walk to shops, restaurants, and Melba's.

When I'd bought the place three years ago, aided by a timely inheritance from my favorite uncle, the relentlessly upbeat real estate agent had championed the area's great "neighborhood vibe." I'd only met one neighbor, which was fine, and it wasn't so deep into suburbia that I felt disconnected from the city.

The three-bedroom craftsman, "old world charm and new world amenities", was sparsely furnished. An old oak veneered dining room table served as my home office. Organization not being my strong suit, I hadn't seen the veined surface in months.

I turned off the alarm and fed Alley, my cat. I'd rescued her three years ago, mainly because I was dating an animal lover, but she generally kept to herself and I'd gotten used to having her around.

I kept the pantry stocked with cereal and paper plates. While admittedly not a green option, I had found paper products to be the key to a clean kitchen. I grabbed one for my burrito, a beer from the fridge, and settled into the recliner. I had promised myself to replace the unsightly chair from the moment I dragged it from the basement where it had been left by the previous owner. It was an off-putting mustard color and in order to recline properly—while remaining centered in front of the flat screen—it had to be positioned in the middle of the living room. Now, though, since it had survived the jibes of everyone who visited, I'd become stubborn in my attachment.

Normally, I'd watch a ballgame or a movie, but something about the Moore case stoked my curiosity. First, depending on the strength of the identification, as far as murder cases went, the evidence of guilt was strong but not overwhelming. The Alameda County District Attorney did not often charge an individual with murder unless the evidence was solid. Obviously, they didn't want an innocent person to spend the rest of his life behind bars. Also, there were quite enough open and shut cases to occupy their time.

Here, although it was early, so far there didn't appear to be a confession or video of the actual murder. There didn't appear to be my client's DNA on the victim or vice versa. So, while it didn't exactly look good for young Darnell, he would at least have a fighting chance.

Also, his mother had made an impression. I wasn't quite sure why, but her statement that her son didn't have it in his heart to kill someone rang true. Also, while her son had been far from a model citizen, his lack of prior violent crimes was significant. Over the years, I had noticed that the criminal world was divided between those capable of violence upon another human and those who were not. Of course, it was entirely possible that Darnell just hadn't been caught committing other violent crimes, but something about his persona seemed consistent with his mom's statement.

I slid the surveillance DVD into my laptop and waited for it to load. I continued to be awed by the number of businesses and private residences in Oakland with security cameras. It seemed like eighty percent of the city was blanketed. As had been the trend lately, the footage at Eighth and Maybeck was remarkably clear. Shot from the southwest corner of the intersection, presumably the E&J Market, the video covered the intersection itself but not the residence across the street from the market where the shooting took place.

With a mouthful of burrito, I fast forwarded the video to 6:16:30 p.m. Within ten seconds a green sedan entered the intersection from the south on Maybeck and made a left on West Eighth. Thirty-five seconds later, at the exact time designated by Firespotter, multiple gunshots were heard just before the same car appeared again, this time racing back through the intersection from the west, revealing its license plate as it left the scene going east on Eighth Street. All of the windows in the car appeared to be down, but the interior of the vehicle was not visible.

I closed my laptop and walked to the fridge for another beer, digesting the video. It seemed clear that the fatal shots had come from Moore's vehicle. When shots were fired the car would have been directly in front of 454 West Eighth—where the victim's body was found on the sidewalk.

Also, the car's initial pass through the intersection

was not a good sign. The maneuver was obviously undertaken to ensure the intended victims were loitering in their usual spots, effectively proving the premeditation required for first-degree murder. The car's path also put the driver's side closest to the victims, enabling the driver to shoot out of his window.

My phone buzzed in my pocket. I checked it and saw it was Chuck. "Do we have a fighting chance?" I asked.

"Tough case. Motive, opportunity, maybe an I.D. Looks like he was at least the driver. Maybe plead him to manslaughter if he names the shooter?"

"Don't see that happening."

"I took a look at his rap sheet. If he's the shooter, he took a big leap from misdemeanors to the big time. Maybe a jump-in?"

"Yeah, I thought of that."

Chuck was referring to being "jumped in" a gang. Back in the days of the Crips and the Bloods, it had meant the ritual of severely beating a new gang member as an initiation. More recently, the initiation meant the new member committing a violent offense. "What do you need in the short term?" he asked.

"I'd like to get a statement from the shop owner before the D.A. does."

"Sure. You free today?"

"Yes. Working at home now. Meet at my office at eleven o'clock?"

"See you there."

Though Chuck's sobering assessment depressed me, it served as a good reminder that my gut feeling about my client's innocence would count for nothing at trial.

Even without the benefit of the video, Chuck had been spot-on. If Moore was in the car, the evidence of murder now seemed overwhelming. Even if he was the driver and someone else fired the shots, he could easily be convicted of murder as an aider and abettor.

I crinkled the beer can and tossed it across the room, narrowly missing the recycling bin. It was clear that Darnell had lied to me about most things. I had become well-practiced in truth detecting, owing to years of being lied to by clients attempting to weave a course to freedom through the bars of custody. Darnell's lies were easy to spot and had a naïve quality about them.

More telling than his truthfulness was his remarkable calm in the face of the swirling storm of shit that surrounded him. I had met guilty people who were just as calm, but they fit squarely into the category of sociopaths. Their calm demeanor was less relaxed, their flat affect masking a simmering rage just beneath the surface. I recalled how Darnell's placid vibe had put me at ease during our first chat. It was the genuine article.

The accused who are guilty are never calm. Even if they have a strong defense, they harbor a constant worry that an eyewitness will surface, or someone's smart phone captured their crime. The innocent possesses an inner peace based on the natural order of things. Since they're innocent, nothing will happen to them. Surely the truth will come out, the mix-up will be sorted, and they will go home.

As I pictured Darnell's easy smile warming the glass between us, it was clear that however misguided his belief in the system, his calm demeanor served as a reflection of his innocence.

Chapter Four

Don't worry, though, he'll be as good as new. Boys his age bounce.—Harper Lee

Oakland, California 2006

Damon's mouth watered as he watched Dumbass crack his teeth into the apple again, smacking loudly as he sat on the couch in his tank top, curling his dumbbell and watching his biceps flex.

Danny Dumbass. That's what he and his twin brother had taken to calling him privately.

This one had turned out to be probably the worst foster ever. It wasn't the beatings. They'd had worse than the odd cuff to the head or random punch on the shoulder doled out by Dumbass. The shoulder punches really hurt, and you never knew when they were coming. Still, they weren't the belt or a lit cigarette. And they weren't every night, so you didn't spend all day worrying about them.

But this food thing was turning into a problem.

At home they got ramen noodles for dinner every night while Dumbass wolfed down steaks, burgers, and pizza right in front of them. Once in a while, they could sneak his leftovers out of the garbage, but usually Ramen was it.

"Eatin' better with that foster money," Jesse said under his breath one night.

T. L. Bequette

That comment earned him an immediate knuckle punch to the arm, but later he said it was worth it. The real problem was Dumbass hadn't filled out the free lunch forms for school. Damon had finally gone to the principal's office and taken care of it, forging Dumbass' signature, but they wouldn't take effect for another three days.

Sitting there, hearing the sound of the crisp apple, watching the juice run down the big man's chin, Damon dreaded asking and already knew the answer. "Sir, do you think it would be possible for Jesse and me, to, uh, get some breakfast this morning?"

"Don't they give you food at school?"

"Well, sir…"

"Y'all better get off to school. I ain't taking you today," he said, staring at his biceps as he continued his curls. "Got to work on my guns."

Damon went to the kitchen for a glass of water, then to get Jesse for their walk to school. Every time they left the house, no matter how hungry or sore, their spirits lifted.

On their walks to school, the twins passed a bake shop, its fancy cakes and frosted cookies stacked in the window. They always stopped to stare and inhale the sugary aroma.

"If I had a hundred dollars, I would buy a different cookie every day," said Damon. It had become a game they played every day when they walked by.

"I would build a house out of cookies, so when I wanted one, I'd just break off a part of a wall or a chair," Jesse said, grinning into the window.

"Don't worry," Damon told his twin, as they walked on, "I got an idea for after school. Yesterday on the way home, I seen this waitress outside Vinnie's, throwing away damn near whole pizzas in the dumpster."

"Yeah, pizza sounds good."

"Mean time," said Damon casually, glancing sideways at Jesse with a gleam in his eye, "how this grab you?" He produced a shiny red apple from the pocket of his hoodie.

"Way to go, D!" yelled Jesse. "Old Dumbass won't be chomping on this one."

"No sir, he won't," Damon chimed in, taking the first bite, then handing it to his brother. "No sir, he will not," he repeated softly, savoring the victory.

Chapter Five

I was squirting mustard on my hotdog from the cart outside my office when Chuck pulled up in the immense mid-'70s jalopy he called Ma. One of the ugliest cars on record, all signs of the make and model had either rusted or fallen off long before Chuck acquired it for two hundred fifty bucks and a set of used golf clubs. The lone exception was the faint scripted "ma" on the console, the letters imprinted on the hard vinyl by part of a long-departed insignia.

Once burgundy, it was now multi-colored, with faded streaks of pink on the hood and orange rust spots around the wheel wells. An absurdly long car, the tatters of its black vinyl roof blew in the breeze, a bad haircut atop the wreck.

Chuck said he kept it because he didn't care if it was burglarized, which made sense as much time as he spent in the sketchiest parts of Oakland. "Hey, watch the interior," he warned, eyeing my snack.

"Yeah, sorry. I should have noticed you just had it detailed. I love how they infuse that aroma of smelly socks."

"Ma's still purring like a kitten," he said, patting the cracked dashboard as we set off for the E&J Market.

West of downtown, the fast pace of the city abruptly gives way to a sleepy residential dystopia.

Garbage is strewn over sidewalks, and black wrought-iron bars on the brightly colored Victorians lend an undercurrent of tension. Paradoxically, churches dot the landscape. For the most part, the streets are empty, save for the occasional gathering at a corner market.

On the way, I ate my hotdog and reviewed the police report documenting the "tentative" identification of Moore by the witness, the proprietor of the E&J, one Vardan Bedrossian. The identification wasn't recorded, which was annoying, as was the officer's decision to characterize the witness' statement as a "tentative" identification.

According to the reports, Mr. Bedrossian had pointed to two photos—one of Moore and one of a "filler", indicating that the two photos most resembled the shooter. So in fact, this was not an identification, tentative or otherwise. Indicating that a photograph looked like the suspect is a far cry from saying "I think that's the guy."

I had yet to receive the witness' taped statement, which I presumed would cover his description of the shooter and his vantage point. Today, I was curious to ask Bedrossian where the shooter was seated in the car.

I recognized the intersection from the video as Chuck parked his submarine in front of the store. The E&J was a converted one-story, two-bedroom brick home. On the porch, in a high-backed chair to the left of the front door, sat a distinguished looking black man in a fedora. He sat ramrod straight, his left hand resting on the handle of an ornately carved cane, the sleeve of a green cardigan sweater hanging from his forearm.

The window to the left of the front door had been boarded up and painted black. "E&J Market" covered the width of the boards, the white letters hand painted and unevenly spaced. The front door, covered in a metal grate, was open.

With a nod for the man on the porch, I climbed up four steps to the front door. Up close, I saw he was quite old. His expressionless face of hardened leather stared straight into the street.

I paused briefly at the door and turned back to see the view of the street before following Chuck inside. Directly across the street was 454 West Eighth, part-time hangout of the victim's gang, Cashtown. The home was a blue and white Victorian in disrepair, its intricate molding along the roofline chipped and falling away. The railing of a terrace hung from the second story, partially obscuring a broken bay window. A wrought iron fence encircled an overgrown yard littered with fast-food wrappers, bottles, and probably syringes. In front of the house on the sidewalk, a reddish-brown shape stained the sidewalk, no doubt Cleveland Barlow's last resting place.

Homicides had become so common in Oakland, there was a protocol for cleaning blood off of public sidewalks. Whatever chemical they used changed the color of the stain but never removed it completely.

Inside the E&J, the store was windowless and dimly lit, with three aisles of mostly liquor and snacks on shelves that nearly reached the low ceiling. Hanging from the ceiling along the back wall, video screens showed an area inside the store entrance and the front counter.

"What you need, guys?" The man behind the counter spoke with a heavy accent, east European, by the sound of it. He looked to be in his sixties, short and stout with a black buzz cut and a moustache that covered most of his face. "You want cigarettes? Liquor? What you need?" he asked, smiling beneath the moustache as we approached.

Chuck took the lead. "Mr. Bedrossian?"

The smiled disappeared as his eyes narrowed. "That's me. What you want? Who are you?"

"Sir, I'm Chuck Argenal. We'd like to speak with you about the shooting that occurred here recently."

He paused, his eyes darting back and forth between us. The wheels were turning. Finally, he took a step back and leaned against the wall behind the counter, folding his thick, hairy arms across his chest. "You want to speak," he said, sticking out his chin, then with a subtle shrug, "So speak."

We stepped aside as a customer entered the store and approached the counter, placing a tall can of malt liquor on the counter and gesturing for cigarettes. The transaction complete, Bedrossian resumed his mulish pose.

I hadn't necessarily anticipated cheerful cooperation, but the hostility was unexpected. "Sir," I began, "we were just hoping to get a better understanding of…"

"You guys don't show badges. So not cops." He spoke quickly, in short, staccato bursts with a tight edge to the tone. "Not cops. That means on the other side. I talk to police. That's it," he said, punctuating his last two words with the safe sign. "Guys. Sorry for rude, but…"

His eyes shifted past us to the front door, and his eyes widened, a huge smile spreading over his face. "Holy shit!"

He threw his hands over his head and began speaking in his native language. Chuck and I stepped aside as he danced from behind the counter to meet a young man in army fatigues. The men embraced heartily and exchanged cheek kisses before hugging again.

Chuck and I stood awkwardly until the young man caught my eye. "I'm Rocco," he said without the trace of an accent as he extended a hand. "I just arrived from Afghanistan."

"This my son. He fights for America," the elder Bedrossian said proudly. "Haven't seen in more than one year." Still beaming, he grabbed his son's face again and kissed him.

"Okay, Dad." He smiled sheepishly and said something to his father in their language. "We are Armenian. He gets emotional."

"Thank you for your service," I said. "Did you just arrive from the airport? Can I give you a hand with some luggage?" I looked for a reason to hang around a bit, thinking maybe we'd have more luck with Bedrossian with his son around to explain our intentions.

"No, I'm good, thanks," he replied, quizzically, no doubt wondering who the hell I was.

"Okay, then. We don't want to spoil your homecoming," I said awkwardly. "Mr. Bedrossian, if it's okay, I'll leave a card."

"Okay, thanks." He took it without looking at me, still smiling and staring at his son.

On the way out, I noticed bullet holes and strike marks around the door frame of the market and more on the boarded-up window. I wondered if any of them were fresh and made a mental note to request discovery of all reports of shooting at the location in the past few years.

Back inside Chuck's heap, he laughed at my lame attempt to ingratiate myself. " 'Hey, you don't know me from Adam, but can I give you a hand with your luggage and maybe join in the family celebration?' "

"It was worth a try. The son was at least civil. And by the way, who travels half-way around the world with no luggage?"

"Boy, his dad is tougher than a two-dollar steak, operating a business in this neighborhood. Got the feeling he kept a sawed-off shotgun under the counter."

"Might make sense to make a run at him in a week or so. Maybe get the kid to mediate."

"I also wonder about the dime store Indian on the porch. I'll bet he doesn't miss much."

"Did you get a look at the security cameras?"

"Read my mind. I'll subpoena the video footage. Might shed some light on his vantage point. He sure couldn't have seen the shooting from inside the store."

Chuck turned up his favorite Kansas City blues, swaying with the beat as the big car surfed through the pothole-ridden streets of west Oakland. I called the jail to schedule a visit with Moore for the following afternoon.

****

The North County Jail in downtown Oakland is a relic. Built in 1945, from the street the eight-story structure resembles a beige tombstone. High up on the structure, rows of narrow vertical windows encircle the building like arrow slits for archers. The jail houses eight hundred inmates in half as many cells, all either

31

serving a sentence or awaiting trial. Among law enforcement and inmates alike, it is known as the Dungeon.

Inside the jail lobby, rows of seats are bolted to the floor, their fabric torn and frayed. Pay phone stalls line the walls, their phones long since removed. An old television, deeper than its screen is wide, sits dormant on a shelf in the corner above two vending machines.

I exchanged my bar card for a badge on a lanyard that read "Maximum", turned over my cell phone, and followed the deputy through a metal detector redundantly labeled "Secure Area." No matter how many times I'd entered the bowels of the jail, I was never prepared for the smell. It was as if body odor and disinfectant formed a fist and punched my face.

Built before electronic locks, every door in the facility is made of gray metal bars, straight out of the old west. Consequently, intermittent clangs of the heavy doors echo throughout the cement walls of the building.

It was my first trip inside a jail since the Dunigan fiasco, but it barely crossed my mind. Darnell Moore had been one of the most cheerful and friendly murder clients. Even if things deteriorated rapidly, I was pretty sure I could protect myself from his spindly frame.

I was greeted by Deputy Spriggs, a veteran of the Dungeon. He led me down an impossibly long hallway that was a study in monotony. The hallway floor, like all those throughout the jail, was unfinished cement, the windowless walls and ceiling of the hallway, painted gun-metal gray. In the distance, the hallway shrank in size until it disappeared, creating the impression that my walk would eventually suffocate me in grayness.

After what seemed like a quarter-mile, Deputy Spriggs arrived at a barred door on the right and opened it with a comically large key. I took a seat at a table inside the eight by eight converted cell and waited for the arrival of my client.

Ten minutes later, resplendent in red and white striped jail togs reserved for gang members, Moore bounced into the cell as if arriving at a party. "Hey, Mr. Turner!" He greeted me enthusiastically as the deputy uncuffed his hands. "I really appreciate you coming. How are you?"

How am I? Well, not in jail, I wanted to answer. Instead, I said, "Good. How are you holding up?"

"I'm good. I'm eager to tell you what I know. In the court interview room, you know, I didn't feel like it was totally private."

This was a very good sign—a tacit acknowledgement that he'd been less than forthcoming.

"I'm happy to hear that, Darnell. I've copied the basic police report for you." I slid the half-inch stack towards him. "I've redacted the names and addresses of your family in case the report falls into the wrong hands."

"Good lookin'."

'Good lookin'. One of my favorite street terms, both in sentiment and economy of words. Shortened from "good looking out," it's a concise expression of thanks for looking after another's well-being.

"Why don't you tell me a little about yourself so I can get to know you."

"Sure. I grew up in west Oakland, but we moved around a bit. I graduated from Franklin High three years ago. I stay with my mom and my little brother."

33

"How old is your brother?"

"Ray is fourteen. He got a scholarship to go to a prep school back east next year. I forget the name of it."

"That's impressive."

"Yeah," he said, broad smile on his face. "He paid attention a little better than me in school."

"Were you working at the time you got arrested?"

"I was doing warehouse work, but I got laid off."

"Okay," I said, shifting gears, "About why you're in here. Can you start by telling me your activity on the day of the shooting? That would have been last Sunday."

"Okay, let's see." He stared at the wall, somewhere above my head. "So, from what I remember, I had been out the night before, getting my groove on with the ladies," he said, flashing his smile, "so I slept 'til about noon. Then, I just chilled with some friends and that's about it."

You've got to be kidding.

"Darnell," I said calmly, conscious of maintaining my composure, "in order for me to do my job and help you, I need to know the facts. I know we just met and I'm a white guy in a suit and you have no real reason to trust me. The problem is, I'm all you got."

"Mr. Turner, believe me, I know you're on my side. I just truly don't know anything about that murder."

I stared at the floor for several seconds and decided to cross examine him. Maybe I would trip him up or at least show him the hopelessness of his position.

"Darnell, why don't we try it this way. Do you have any idea why your car, a very distinctive looking green mid-sized sedan made from junkyard spare parts was at the scene of the murder when it happened?"

"Hey, who's side are you on?"

"Why was your car there?"

"People borrow my car all the time. If that car was at the scene, I wasn't in it."

"Is there more than one key?" I started asking questions at a fast pace, deliberately giving him no time to think.

"No. I lost the spare."

"You usually keep the key with you?"

"Always in my pocket or in my bedroom, why?"

"You were home?"

"Yes, sir."

"So your mom can verify you were there all evening."

"I'm not sure she was home."

"Well, it was Sunday. She was probably at home at six on a Sunday night, right?"

"I don't know."

"Do you own a gun, Darnell?"

"No, sir. I've never touched a gun."

"Other than the semi-auto you were posing with in that photo, you mean?"

His smile faded. "We was just messing around. I don't own a gun."

"So when I get the search warrant inventory, it won't list a gun found under your bed?"

"No."

"Who borrowed your car last Saturday evening?"

"That I couldn't tell you."

"They had to get the key from you, right?"

He paused. He was stuck and he knew it. "Man, you got me all confused."

"Do you know who might have wanted to kill Cleveland Barlow?"

"No, I don't even know that dude."

"Not even someone in Iceboyz?"

He was shaking his head now, frustrated. "What? I don't know about no Iceboyz."

"Darnell, please. If you live in west Oakland, you know Iceboyz."

"I didn't say I didn't know the gang."

"Five seconds ago, you told me you didn't know about the Iceboyz. In the last minute, you've lied about someone borrowing your car, never touching a gun, and being clueless about the Iceboyz. You are wasting my time, kid."

He paused again, retreating to his well-practiced smile, but it looked forced. "Mr. Turner, this case against me is just circumstantial, right?"

Standing to face away from him, I didn't want to yell at him on day one. I was afraid I'd found Darnell's misplaced confidence in the strength of his defense. There are two types of evidence: direct and circumstantial. The law treats both types exactly the same. The problem, however, was that somewhere along the way, circumstantial evidence had become synonymous in non-legal circles as inferior or weak evidence.

I hit the buzzer to summon the deputy and retook my seat across the table. "Here's the thing," I began in a more relaxed tone. "There are two ways to prove that it's raining outside. The first is for someone to testify that they were just standing outside, and it was raining. The other is to come into court wearing a raincoat and carrying a wet umbrella. Both ways work.

"So it's true that so far, no one has said they saw you shoot Mr. Barlow. However, the jury will learn that you had motive, and that someone shot him who looks similar to you and was driving your car."

"But. Mr. Turner, I didn't do this!" he pleaded as my escort arrived.

For the first time I heard a tinge of panic in his voice. At least I had accomplished that.

"You know, Darnell. I actually believe you."

I stood and walked out, leaving him there alone with his thoughts.

Chapter Six
I think there's just one kind of folks. Folks.—
Harper Lee

Oakland, California 2006

"You two are too young to look that tired."

The twins followed the raspy voice over the short picket fence where a well-dressed black man leaned on a cane while watering a dry patch of grass in front of a market. The boys stopped walking and smiled wearily as the man put down his hose and moved closer.

After school, Damon and Jesse took a walk down Maybeck Street to explore the railway yard two blocks off their regular route home. It was Friday and if they avoided home for a while, Dumbass would probably be gone drinking when they got there.

"Long week?" the stranger asked. To the boys, his tone was kind and matter of fact, without a hint of subterfuge.

"Yes sir, I guess so," Damon answered.

"Well, one thing I know for sure," the man said, rubbing his wizened face, "after a long week, sometimes something sweet helps." He fished in the front pocket of his pants, then reached over the fence. Two pieces of butterscotch candy rested in the center of his palm.

The twins looked at the candies, their gold

wrapping shimmering in the sun like jewels. "Go on," the man said. Damon and Jesse looked at each other, each asking for permission with a smile.

"Thank you," said Damon, taking the candy and giving one to his brother.

"Yes, sir. Thank you, a lot," added Jesse with enthusiasm, his eyes glued to his candy as they walked away.

From that day on, the twins had a new route home on Fridays. He was always out when they walked by, either on the market's porch or in the yard waiting for them. They would talk about their week at school and listen to the nice man with the soothing voice, fancy canes, and limitless supply of butterscotch candy.

Usually, they would enjoy their treat on their way home, letting the sugar dissolve on their tongues, then chewing the wrappers until the last of the flavor was gone. Sometimes, they would wait until later and enjoy them as a dessert after their ramen. The twins came to savor their weekly treats and chats with their new friend.

Chapter Seven

The moment I emerge from any jail, particularly
the Dungeon, never fails in its invigoration. Even
though I've never been locked inside against my will,
there is still something very liberating when free air
fills your lungs.

Today was no different, and I decided to skip the
BART train and enjoy the twenty-minute walk home.
I'd been trying to choose that option more often lately.
With my reduction in alcohol intake and occasional
trips to the gym, if I squinted at myself in the mirror,
some slight definition began to appear.

I had inherited my dad's height and according to
my mom, his rakish good looks. Since law school,
though, my athletic frame had gradually melted away.
Blessed with mom's metabolism, I would never be
heavy, but the years of beer and brats had left me
rounded and soft.

While walking, I reviewed the latest emails to
come in on my phone. Chuck's name appeared first. I
called him first. "What's up?"

"How did the visit go?"

"Complete waste of time," I said. "He don't know
nothing about nothing."

"You know what you got, right?"

"I have a feeling you're going to tell me."

"What we got here is a failure to communicate."

"A movie line for all occasions. See ya."

The following morning, I massaged my hamstrings as I read the sports section over coffee in my office. I was sore from my walk, which was pathetic. The Moore case was in court this morning and I'd come in early. I needed a life. Maybe I would call Andy's wife's friend.

Just then my partner walked in and stopped outside my door. "Did you call Edna? Karen is all over me."

"No, but I might," I answered while reading an email from Deputy District Attorney Nathan Didery who informed me he had been assigned the Moore case. "Wait, her name is Edna?"

"Yeah, the name doesn't scream super-hot, but Karen says she's a catch."

"Wait, those were her words? 'Edna is a catch?' She might as well have said she has a great personality."

"So, you're seriously not going to call her because of her name? That's shallow, Turner, even for you."

I gathered my files for court and paused at the door. "So, you're honestly telling me you believe there's a chance she's attractive?"

"Of course not," he scorned. "Her name is Edna!"

On the short walk to court, I stopped for a hotdog, a reward for my morning's exercise, and digested the news of my opponent. Nathan Didery was a competent trial attorney and a straight shooter. However, dealing with him could be exhausting. Nicknamed "Jittery Didery," he was perpetually nervous, constantly double and triple checking things he worried about—which turns out to be everything.

My hamstrings barked as I ascended the steps to

the Alameda County Superior Courthouse. Of all the courthouses in the bay area, my home court was my favorite. A ten-story stone edifice with a steepled roof, it overlooks Lake Merritt, the nicest feature of downtown Oakland.

Since the visit with Darnell, I'd wondered if I'd been too harsh. After all, he was nineteen years old, had already been in custody for longer than ever before, and now faced the unspeakable prospect of a long life behind bars. Over the years, it had occurred to me that young men and women sentenced to life endured more severe sentences than older convicts simply because they began their sentence at a younger age. Anyway, by the time I was across from him again, I'd decided not to grill him further. He would open up when he was ready.

After a cordial greeting, I explained to him that we would enter a plea of not guilty today and address his speedy trial rights. Darnell had a right to a preliminary hearing—a hearing designed to make sure there was at least enough evidence to have a trial—within ten days. He agreed to waive that right—"waive time" in attorney parlance—to give me time to prepare, investigate his case, and to hopefully convince him to tell me what he knew.

"Mr. Turner?" he said, as we wrapped up our brief meeting.

"Yeah, Darnell?"

"I wanted to apologize about, uh, you know, saying I don't know nothing about the Iceboyz. Of course, you know, everyone knows about them," he said sheepishly. "I hang with them sometimes."

It was true that in substance, his admission was insignificant. He had apologized for the most obvious of his many lies. Still, it was a start. I appreciated the gesture and told him so.

Out in the courtroom, I got my first load of Jittery Didery.

"Hi, Joe. Good to see you," he said quickly in a nasal tone, seemingly short of breath. His gray suit hung off his rail-thin frame, which seemed in perpetual motion, a bundle of nervous energy. He wore his black hair in a buzz cut, his sharp features and wire-rimmed glasses connoting a frenetic insect.

Before my lips could form the first words of my return greeting, he continued, in a torrent. "So, I understand your client will enter a plea today. I, uh, was wondering, of course, I was just wondering, if, if, if you've spoken to him about whether he would waive time? Of course, as I'm sure you are aware, I certainly hope he does but I'm..." He stopped only because he had run out of breath in mid-sentence but reloaded quickly. "I'm certainly mindful that he has his rights," he said, extending both arms toward me with palms out to illustrate his point, "but obviously I'm, of course, you know, very hopeful."

In fairness, the concern was shared by every District Attorney who prosecuted major felonies. If a defendant insisted on a preliminary hearing within ten days, the Court would calendar it in one week's time, leaving the prosecutor with a Herculean task on a strict deadline. Obviously, though, some dealt with the stress better than others.

The sadistic part of me wanted to keep him twisting in the wind for a few minutes, but I actually felt like the poor guy was close to requiring medical attention.

"He'll waive time, Nathan," I said calmly, and saw the relief wash over him.

Sighing deeply, the prosecutor steadied himself against the rail surrounding the jury box. "Thank you, Joe."

Judge Murphy ascended the bench below the giant American flag that hung from the ceiling in every department in the courthouse. When my late father had served as the county's District Attorney, the judge had been his second in command.

"Mr. Turner, do you have a matter that's ready to call?"

"Thank you, Your Honor. People v. Darnell Moore. Mr. Moore is present, in custody."

Darnell was ushered into the courtroom through a side door and stood next to me at the counsel table where he confirmed to the judge that he was waiving his right to a preliminary hearing within ten days. The Court set the preliminary hearing out two weeks. I told him I would see him soon, dreading another trip to the Dungeon.

****

As I slid the disk into my computer, I felt the same queasiness that always accompanies listening to my clients' interrogations. Moore appeared in the interview room at the Oakland Police Department that I'd seen so many times before. The room was ten by ten, with a table and three chairs, two for officers on one side, one for the suspect on the other.

Moore was placed in the room at two-fifteen p.m. on Thursday, after being arrested at his home that morning, three days after the murder. He stayed in the room alone for nearly five hours by himself. An officer came in to check on him once. I fast-forwarded over the video of him sitting in the chair, then laying his head on the table trying various positions to get comfortable as he dozed off. It is common practice for police to interview suspects when they're exhausted.

The time stamp at the bottom of the screen read 7:09:10 p.m. when two plain-clothes detectives entered the room. Probably starting their shift, the clean-cut men wore ties and empty leather shoulder holsters. The scene looked right out of the movies, missing only the single light bulb hanging from the ceiling.

In most interrogations, the moment of truth comes early on, when the Miranda warnings are given. After hearing of his right to remain silent and right to an attorney, the suspect either insists on his right to counsel before speaking, effectively ending the interrogation, or more commonly tries to talk his way out of his predicament. I knew the path Darnell had chosen, if only because there were still forty-seven minutes left in the video.

After eliciting some basic identifying information about Darnell, Detective Bosco, a twenty-two-year veteran of the Oakland Police Department, proceeded to give a clinic on how to convince a suspect to waive their Miranda rights.

"Mr. Moore," he began, accentuating the Oklahoma drawl that made him sound more honest. "Christ, can I call you Darnell? I feel like I should because I got a son your age."

"Yes."

"Here's the deal. I'm gonna be straight with you. I'm looking at you, reading your rap sheet. A few theft offenses. Misdemeanor drugs. Petty shit, right?"

"Right, that's the thing, though…."

"Let me finish, Darnell, then I'll let you talk. Anyway, I got a snapshot of you on one hand, but then I'm looking at what happened." The detective paused, shaking his head, as if actually confused. "This is a cold-blooded drive-by murder in the middle of a gang war. It just don't add up. Anyway, I'm hoping that you can make some sense of this for me."

"Yes, sir, I can," began Darnell, already sold on the idea of explaining that this was all one big mistake.

"Now, before you start, there's one more thing," he said, rolling his eyes. He addressed his partner on his right, who was already smiling, well-versed in his partner's spiel. "I swear, sometimes I think this job is nothing but paperwork," the detective said, producing a form labeled "Miranda Waiver" from a drawer in the table.

"So, Darnell, we got to tell you that you don't have any obligation to talk to us. And I need to read you what's on this form. It says, 'you have a right to remain silent,'" the detective read, noticeably quickening his pace. "'You have a right to an attorney. Even if you can't afford an attorney one will be provided. Anything you say can be used against you in court.'" Bosco put the form on the table and removed a pen from his front pocket and held it in front of him.

Darnell took the pen but hesitated slightly.

"So, Darnell, here's the thing," the detective continued. "You have every right not to talk to us. If that happens, we'll just process this case as a murder, and you'll be in front of a judge first thing Monday morning with a lawyer." Darnell shifted in his seat, no doubt thinking about the awful prospect of a weekend in jail. "And to be honest, my partner here didn't want to give you that opportunity." The partner, still in character, now sat sternly with his arms crossed. "But if you want to tell your side of the story, this is your opportunity."

Inevitably, Darnell took the pen and signed, now poised to do irreparable damage to his defense.

"Have you called yet?" Andy called from his office and I was happy for the distraction.

"No, I haven't called Edna," I said, emphasizing her name.

"So," he paused, appearing in my doorway, "even though I'm categorically opposed to this idea and the last thing I want to do is subject anyone to your dumpster fire of a love life, I feel like if I don't tell you, I'll be violating some sort of man code."

"Yes? Out with it."

"Okay, I happened to see a photo of Edna last night in Karen's phone." He stared hard at me and began an exaggerated deliberate nod. "You should call."

"Really" I said. "Edna. Who knew?"

"Yeah," he laughed, retreating to his office.

Well, this put things in a whole different light. Meaning, I'd have an entirely different set of reasons why to worry about calling. I stretched in my chair and returned to Darnell's interrogation.

For even the most experienced criminal, Detective Bosco was a formidable challenge in the interrogation room, or "the box" as cops referred to it. Darnell, for all his street savvy and personality, would prove no match.

For example, Darnell fell victim to the entirely reasonable assumption that during interrogations, the police were prohibited from lying to suspects. In fact, nothing could be further from the truth. Countless times, I'd seen officers extract confessions by lying to one suspect about his partner in crime's statement. "So Bugsy, your partner Slick just told us you guys robbed the bank. He says it was all your idea."

I remember my dad telling me one tale about an interrogation when he was a young Deputy D.A. He and a detective convinced a less than intelligent suspect to undergo a polygraph examination. They set up with the accused's back against an old copier and affixed random cords and wires to his arms with Velcro and tape. Each time he would deny committing the murder, another cop would surreptitiously hit the copy button and the machine would produce a single piece of paper that read, "*lying*" in bold letters.

The detectives sat patiently as Darnell began with his transparent spiel about having no idea what was going on. I cringed as he chuckled nervously, claiming that when he was arrested, he had assumed all those unpaid parking tickets had finally caught up with him.

When he finished, the detectives sat quietly until their suspect squirmed in his seat. "So, Darnell, your car's on video doing the drive-by on Monday and there's a witness who says you were the shooter."

"That's impossible," Darnell said, shaking his head. "I wasn't even in the area. I was home all day."

"So, here's the thing, Darnell. It's possible the witness is mistaken. It's actually hard for me to believe that you were the shooter, given your background. But for you to say you weren't even there is simply not being truthful."

The detective produced documents and placed them on the table facing their suspect. I couldn't see detail on the video, but they appeared to be city maps overlaid with colorful symbols and graphics. "Darnell, do you know about cell phone tracking?" The young man shrugged slightly, staring at the table. I could see his wheels turning and I groaned audibly, knowing what was coming.

"Darnell, your phone—the one that was on you when you were arrested—was within at least a block or two of West Eighth and Maybeck at the time of the shooting. That is not open to debate." In fact, there had not been near enough time since Darnell's arrest to generate a cell phone tower analysis. It would take at least a week just to subpoena the records from the cell phone provider. Who knows what documents were on the table—perhaps a cell phone report from a prior case or maybe they were entirely falsified?

"Like I said, Darnell, I don't think you were necessarily the shooter, but I know you were there, and I think you know who else was in the car."

By now, the smile was gone from Darnell's face and he mumbled, "I guess I might have been in the area, but I don't know nothing about that shooting."

Moments later, the interrogation ended. Darnell had stopped responding to questions and the detectives left him staring at the table. The cell phone hadn't told the detective if Darnell was at or near the scene of the crime, but now the suspect himself had done so.

I paid some bills at my desk, wondering about Edna. I hadn't dated in almost a year since a torrid fling with an old college friend ended in catastrophe. The nervous excitement of something new felt good. On my drive home, I practiced the voicemail I would leave, trying to sound casual and confident.

My phone rang, and Chuck's voice interrupted my rehearsal. "Hey Joe, have you seen the surveillance video?"

"Briefly. Why?"

"There's a red muscle car parked at the northeast corner of the intersection. A blond guy gets into the car as Moore turns left—"

"Hey!"

"Sorry, as the *suspect* turns left on West Eighth Street. He's still in his car after the shooting as the car drives away."

"I missed that. Sounds like he might be a witness."

"Yeah, but you can't make out the license plate without enhancing the video. I'll send it to our guy."

"Thanks. Sometimes you're like a real investigator."

"I resemble that remark. How did the kid do in the box?"

"Well, let's see, Bosco tricked him into saying he was nearby when the shooting happened but had nothing to do with it."

"Let me guess. He told him he was visible on surveillance?"

"No, it was the old fake cell phone records trick."

"Of course."

"Hey, I know how you hate technology, but is there any way I can email you the latest. I got Moore's interrogation, and the autopsy report just came through."

"Sure. My nephew is in town and he's busy unlocking the mysteries of the computer."

"Beautiful. You'll be joining the twenty-first century any time now."

"You seem particularly whiney, even for you."

"Chuck, if you hadn't noticed, this case is sinking like a stone."

"This is the life we have chosen."

I was sure it was a movie line but wasn't in the mood. "See ya."

At home, I thought about calling Edna while I poured a glass of Pinot Noir. Recently, I had rediscovered wine after not drinking it in a decade or so. I had hung with a crowd in law school that drank a lot of wine, I suppose to seem sophisticated. The trouble was, all we could ever afford were barely drinkable, so I'd sworn off all wine after I graduated.

Recently, though, I'd tried a glass that bore no resemblance to the old law school swill, so I had gotten into wine again. That is, I'd gotten into drinking wine. I still didn't know much about it.

I realized I was thinking about wine to avoid calling Edna. Maybe I should text. No, horrible idea, Joe. Maybe your first date should be a video chat, so you'd never have to interact in person.

I poured another glass of Pinot. It was Friday, after all, and I did like the way red wine made me feel somehow more relaxed than whites. Stop stalling, you sackless wonder. It was just a message. Andy had mentioned that Edna usually worked late, and it was only five-fifteen p.m. so I was sure to get her voicemail.

I wondered where she worked. I realized I had no idea. For all I knew she was a D.A. That could be awkward, but not really. Some of my best friends were prosecutors. My mind conjured a quick fantasy involving an empty courtroom with me having sex with a woman who looked like a model on the counsel table.

My own screaming voice inside my head finally shook me from the daydream. "Joe, pick up the phone!"

I found her contact in my phone and pressed the call button.

"Hello. This is Eddy." Shit. She answered. "Hello?" she repeated.

"Hi, Edna. This is Joe Turner. I'm sorry. So, um," I said stumbling over my words. "I didn't expect you to answer." I wanted to kick myself.

"If you'd like I can hang up and you can leave a message?"

I laughed. "No, I think I can manage."

"So, you must be the attorney that Karen told me about."

"Yes," I answered, regaining composure. "I can imagine how unbelievable it must be that I talk for a living."

"Not at all. I probably threw you. I go by Eddy," she said smiling through the phone in a warm voice. "All this is pretty awkward. How about coffee tomorrow."

"Tomorrow. Tomorrow? Great. Sure." Why was I saying everything twice?

"Okay, there's a place called Papillon on Piedmont Avenue."

"I know it well. Sounds great." Stop saying great, you moron.

I'm sure sensing that I was in no condition to decide, she kept taking the lead. "How about ten-thirty a.m.? Does that work?"

"Gr…Good. Yes. I look forward to it."

"Me too, Joe. See you tomorrow."

After we hung up, I slowly lowered my head in my

hands, finally releasing my death grip on the phone. "Good God, Joe," I said to myself aloud, sighing deeply. "You've got to get a hold of yourself."

Chapter Eight
It's not time to worry yet.—Harper Lee

Oakland, California 2006

Damon was surprised to see the same CASA worker across the desk for his monthly meeting. Their Court Appointed Special Advocates, volunteers who were assigned to each foster child, usually lasted less than six months, but there was Happy Cheryl again. That was the nickname the twins had given Cheryl Swillinger because of the giant smile that was always plastered on her face every minute of the day.

They liked the meetings because there were usually cookies. And even though Happy Cheryl spoke to them like they were five years old, she was nice enough. They'd learned over the years not to trust any of the social workers. He and his twin wanted to stay together in the same house, and it seemed like all they ever did was try to find ways to separate them.

"So, how's it going in your new home?"

"Fine, Ms. Cheryl," he said, eyeing the open package of macaroons on the table.

"So, how's Jesse doing, Damon?" she asked, pushing the cookies toward him.

"Thank you, ma'am."

"Sure, do you remember my question?" she said after a time, smiling as Damon chewed half a macaroon and shook his head.

"How is Jesse doing?"

Antenna up, he shrugged. "He's okay, I guess."

"Well, I just talked with Jesse a little and he seemed kinda down. Really down, actually."

Damon shrugged again. Here we go, again, he thought. "Seems okay to me."

Actually, Jesse had been real quiet lately. Damon could still make him laugh once in a while, but it seemed like he didn't care about anything. He also missed the long talks with his brother at night. Dumbass made them sleep in separate rooms. He said it was because they were too noisy. Since his bedroom was on the other side of the house, Damon figured it was just because Dumbass liked to control everything.

"Can you think of anything that's bothering him?"

Let's see, Happy Cheryl. Maybe it's because we don't have enough to eat, and we have to work every weekend while Dumbass drinks beer and lifts his precious weights. Not to mention worrying about the next time he'll knuckle punch our shoulders.

He rubbed his shoulder absentmindedly and shrugged again.

"Nothing?"

"Ms. Cheryl," Damon said, trying to sound grown-up, "the only thing me and Jess really worry about is being separated again."

"Okay, sweetie. Hey, what do you guys have planned for the big day tomorrow?" He looked at her with a blank stare. "July seventh? Mean anything to you?" she joked.

"Oh, yeah." Damon smiled. He had not thought about their birthday in a while. "Yeah, I'm sure we'll have something fun planned."

The conversation moved on to school. Damon would eat another cookie before he left and stuff four more in his jacket pocket for Jesse's birthday present. That would cheer him up.

Chapter Nine

I've always had anxiety when it came to the opposite sex, owing mainly to a fear of being rejected by a partner, often without regard to how I felt about her. Romantic rejection is just so personal. It's not a bad grade on a paper or a lost court case—or even specific criticism of a personal trait by a friend.

Rejection in matters of the heart is an all-encompassing disapproval of me as a human. So I worried.

From my first crush on Stacie Wilson in the fifth grade, I worried about my haircut, then my complexion, then my car. As an adult, my worries ran the gamut from my body, to body hair, to being perceived as too snarky or negative. Sex was the big one, with all its accompanying extra pressures.

With Eddy, I knew her looks would rachet up my stress. Even without Andy's endorsement, I could tell by her voice. Or so I thought, anyway. At least I'd survived the phone call. I'd worry about our coffee date in the morning.

I poured another glass of wine, boiled water for pasta, and opened the Moore autopsy file on my laptop. The absurdity of distracting myself from the stress of a casual coffee with a homicide case wasn't lost on me. Apparently, I was just that crazy.

The gruesome autopsy photos would have to be

reviewed, but they could wait with dinner on the way. The coroner's report would be bad enough if the summary on page one was any indication.

On March 22, 2021, Cleveland Barlow was in front of 454 West 8th Ave. in Oakland when he was shot twice by an unknown suspect. When paramedics arrived, Barlow was lying prone on the sidewalk with blood and brain matter behind his head. He was rolled into a supine position for assessment and found to be pulseless, apneic, and with negative heart tones. Paramedics responded and determined death after attaching ECG pads. The hands were bagged for GSR.

An autopsy was performed. The body was opened via the usual Y-shaped incision. Other than the gunshots, there were no internal abnormalities. The pathologist determined the cause of death to be two gunshot wounds, one to the chest and one to the head. The chest wound was through and through. The death was determined to be a homicide.

The pathologist really went out on a limb as to the cause of death. I noted that either the shooter had apparently been a very good shot or very lucky. Shooting from a vehicle with presumably one hand on the steering wheel, the gunman had managed to pull off two kill shots, as the report opined that independent of each other, either of the two gunshots would have been fatal.

The wounds were further evidence that assuming Darnell was the driver, he was not the shooter. To pull off this marksmanship while driving the car seems even more unlikely. On the other hand, there were ten forty-caliber shell casings documented in the tech report, indicating the shooter had probably emptied a standard ten-round clip. In that light, maybe the ratio of two kill shots out of ten wasn't that impressive. The D.A. would certainly argue that blind luck played a role.

The report also listed every bruise and abrasion on Cleveland's body, no matter how slight. I always thought this was a needlessly intrusive exercise, but I supposed once the body is cut open, everything is relative.

Struggling to stay focused, I skipped to the description of the path of the bullets. The gunshot wound to the head "entered the right side of the frontal cortex two and a half inches above the right orbit," essentially the upper forehead. The bullet "travelled generally toward the back of the head, down toward the bottom of the head at a thirty-degree angle before lodging at the base of the skull."

This downward angle was interesting. A shot fired out of a car window at a pedestrian certainly wouldn't be angled downward. The report also described the gunshot wound to the chest as angled downward. This wound was "through and through," meaning the bullet entered and exited through the body.

I pulled up the photos folder on my laptop and opened the file containing photos of Moore's car. The car had a sunroof, and I'd seen a few drive-bys where they had been used by the shooter. This might explain the angle. "Damn it, Darnell," I mumbled to myself. "You've got to come clean at some point."

I got up and I took the pasta off the stove top and I grabbed the jar of red marinara sauce from my pantry. Given the images in my head, I opted for some butter and parmesan instead and poured the last of the wine. I would sleep soon with jumbled thoughts of Eddy and brain matter careening off my skull.

****

"You must be Joe. I'm Eddy Busier," she said, removing dark cat's eye sunglasses to reveal pale blue eyes. Her cute upper lip peaked in the middle, showing perfect teeth. I'm certain my eyes were wide, my mouth agape.

I had entered Papillon a nervous wreck, arriving twenty minutes early. I had seen the tall blonde walk in but dismissed the possibility that she was Eddy. I didn't date women like this. Hell, movie stars didn't date women like this.

She wore skinny jeans and knee-high boots that showed off long athletic legs. Some sort of cashmere poncho thing showed off her breasts, suspiciously ample given her slender waist. I hoped I'd chosen the blue oxford without the mustard stains.

"Hi, Eddy. Nice to meet you."

"I see you have coffee. I'll just go get some."

My focus remained glued to the jeans as she walked away. Good, I thought. Time to recover. I wanted to murder Andy for significantly underselling Eddy. Then again, I didn't know what I would have done differently. I was a solid seven and she was a fucking runway model!

Okay, Joe, breathe. What was that persona I'd read was attractive to women? Mild indifference. Yeah, good luck with that, Turner.

Why I stood when she arrived back at our table I'll never know. My parents had burned outdated and overly formal manners into my brain as a child, but I hadn't done it in years.

"Wow. What a gentleman," she said, her pink

shiny lips forming a wide smile.

"I have no idea what I'm doing," I said, smiling at myself. "Suddenly, I'm having high tea with the royals."

"No, it's very nice," she said, laughing. "And nobody knows what to do in these situations."

"I agree. Let the awkwardness begin," I said, feeling better about myself. "And I'm sorry, did you say Busier?"

"Yes, rhythms with Hoosier."

"Got it."

"So," she said, clasping her hands in front of her. "It's probably appropriate for me to ask about your work," she said, rolling her eyes. "So," she continued with theatrically feigned interest, "Joe Turner, please tell me about your work."

"Actually," I deadpanned, "right now, I'm sort of between jobs." I smiled only after a few seconds of awkward silence.

"Darn you!" she laughed. "You got me. That was actually quite good."

This was actually going incredibly well. Her unattainable beauty had somehow relaxed me. I had nothing to lose. And by the way, I thought, psyching myself up, my mom says I have rakish good looks. "As I think you know, I'm a lawyer."

"Yes, Karen mentioned that. Criminal defense, right?"

"Yes. And you?"

"I'm a shepherd," she said with a straight face. And that's when I knew. Apart from her breathtaking beauty, it was then that I knew that Edna Christine Busier was the woman for me.

"Your job must be fascinating. How honest do you suppose your clients are about their, um…"

"Crimes?"

"Yes. I was going to say activities."

It was a good question. "Often times not very. But I've gotten pretty good at telling when they are lying. At least, I think so."

The next hour flew by. As we chatted comfortably, making each other laugh, I gradually grew less self-conscious about the gap in our attractiveness delta. I learned that she was an archaeologist. I knew nothing about it, but it seemed like about the coolest job ever.

As if I wasn't smitten enough, I thought I detected a British tone to her speech. Not an accent, but more the way she emphasized words in a sentence. And even when I'd made boneheaded comments, she'd laughed them off and made me feel okay. "An archaeologist? Wow. So like, digging," I'd heard my inner idiot say, cringing.

But we'd both started laughing immediately at the stupidity of the comment, and Eddy pulled out a fake notebook, mouthing, "Knows it involves digging. Check."

When it was time to go, I desperately wanted to ask to see her again. I thought she was even pausing, hoping I'd mention it.

"Well, Joe, see if you can tell if I'm lying."

"Okay, I'll give it a shot."

"I'd like to see you again."

"Well, Eddy, we just met, but so far you don't strike me as evil and sadistic."

"Well, thank you."

"So I'd be delighted to see you again," I said,

failing to rein in my goofy smile.

"Good. I really had fun. Talk soon," she said, getting up to leave.

"Me too."

I walked home on cloud nine, reliving every line of our conversation and making plans to get in shape. Tomorrow I'd stress about when to text or call, but for now I was determined to revel in my bliss.

Back home, I made coffee—I didn't recall actually drinking any with Eddy—and enjoyed what I vowed was my last bowl of Frosted Oaties for a while. Having been denied sugared cereals growing up, I'd made up for lost time as an adult. But now, it was time to make some changes.

I was aware that my dietary and exercise trends had usually tracked my relationships. I also knew that my usual pattern of setting unreasonable expectations combined with my lack of discipline inevitably led to a quick burnout and eventually, regression. Last time, I didn't get past day one, the five-mile run rendering me barely able to walk the next day.

This time would be different. I was in decent shape already, and I'd be smart, easing into regular workouts. It all seemed so simple from the comfort of my recliner, I thought, feeling a nap coming on after the sugar high.

Later, though, I would manage a run around the neighborhood after a reasonable number of pushups. Eight, to be exact. Afterwards, wobbling up my stoop to find Alley at the front door, I knew I'd be sore tomorrow.

I cracked open a beer and sat at the dining room table, the open coroner's report where I had left it. I flipped through the rest of the pages. The most depressing part for me was always the painstaking documentation of the victim's clothing and personal effects. The victim wore a summer camp T-shirt and new blue and gold basketball shoes. He had a movie stub and subway ticket in one pocket, a wallet containing twenty-one dollars in the other. He wore a retainer on his teeth, two friendship bracelets on his left wrist, and a Saint Christopher medal around his neck.

Somewhere in the description, as was usually the case, the victim laid out on the cold metal autopsy table became seventeen-year-old Cleveland Barlow, who was going to miss the last train home.

****

The next morning, I opened the search warrant file on my laptop. After Darnell's arrest, Detective Bosco had drafted a search warrant for the Moore residence and an affidavit, summarizing the evidence against his suspect in a sworn statement. The detective brought the affidavit to the judge on night duty, who signed the search warrant.

Most Sundays found me walking to a local park with the paper and an everything bagel. Today, though, I was drawn back to the Moore case. To date, at least as far as I knew, I'd never lost an innocent client to life in prison, and I didn't want Darnell to be the first.

Besides, I needed something to occupy my mind to keep me from firing off a text to Eddy first thing in the morning. While I had given up on appearing mildly indifferent to her, I still recognized the advantage of showing some restraint.

I reviewed a supplemental police report which documented Darnell's arrest. He'd been home in bed when the arrest team showed up at six o'clock a.m., the hour intentional so as to catch their target at home and asleep.

Understandably, arrest details in homicide cases were forced to assume the worst—an armed gunman who would resist. That meant the team surrounded the family's apartment with a SWAT team and announced their presence on a loudspeaker, ordering every occupant out of the house.

At least Darnell hadn't run from the police. Not only would it have been another piece of difficult to explain evidence, his cooperation meant that there had been no need for the concussion grenades or smoke bombs. I imagined the horror and confusion of Darnell's mother and his little brother, forced into the street in their pajamas.

I glanced at my phone and checked my messages for the third time. Enough was enough. I'd already drafted the text last night, aiming for just the right note, somewhere between over-eager and apathetic.

—*Hi Eddy. It's Joe. I really enjoyed myself yesterday and I'd like to see you again soon. I'm not in trial, so my schedule is flexible*—

I pushed send. Looking back, I supposed, it was a little embarrassing that I'd worked on it for over an hour, but I was satisfied.

I knew the timing of my text to Eddy had something to do with avoiding the next document on my screen, the Search Warrant Inventory. While the police didn't always find incriminating evidence when they searched my clients' homes, the first time the searches were helpful to the defense would be the last.

The first fifteen items were more photos of Darnell with members of the Iceboyz flashing gang signs, posing with large amounts of cash and various semi-automatic weapons. I knew a jury would find item sixteen particularly incriminating. Seized from Darnell's bedpost, it was a blue baseball cap emblazoned with "KC." The cap, favored by Iceboyz members, denoted a "Cashtown killer", referring to Cleveland Barlow's gang. I couldn't wait for Darnell to explain how he was actually a Kansas City baseball fan.

Then I scrolled down and implausibly, things got much worse. Found in a shoe box inside a hallway closet was a SLAZIK 27 handgun. I hated guns but out of necessity had gained a working knowledge of them. I knew it was a semi-automatic handgun but didn't know if it shot forty-caliber bullets. I assumed the worst and quickly word-searched the gun.

Amazingly accurate and controllable, the SLAZIK 27 puts ten rounds of forty-caliber ammo at your fingertips in a package small enough for a pocket or ankle holster.

I went back to the report to see if there were any bullets left in the gun. No, none in the chamber and the clip was empty. "Of course it was empty, ladies and gentlemen," I heard Didery telling the jury, "because Darnell Moore had fired all of his bullets at West Eighth and Maybeck."

I stared at the screen and for the first time was ready to admit to myself I was wrong about Darnell Moore. The voice in my head telling me Darnell was not capable of killing another human being was now a faint whisper, drowned out by a roaring stadium.

I breathed deeply and assessed. Darnell's car was on video, its occupants committing the fatal drive by shooting. The shooter, according to a witness, looked like Darnell, and he had admitted "probably" being in the area at the time of the shooting. He was a gang member with motive to kill a Cashtowner like Barlow and was found in possession of a weapon of the same caliber that had been fired at the murder scene.

I was mad at myself for being conned by someone so young and inexperienced. I remembered how cool and relaxed he was the first time we met. Just as he had planned, I had mistaken the self-assurance as proof of his innocence.

More than that, I had been stubborn. I made snap judgments all the time. This guy's a jerk, that guy's honest. Come to think of it, I had just made a very exciting one yesterday morning. I was generally fairly accurate, but not perfect. This time, though, in the face of an avalanche of evidence to the contrary, I had maintained my obstinance.

I needed to blow off some steam and decided to go for a run. It usually helped me think, and two consecutive days would probably tie my all-time record. Following my typical path, I headed east through the quiet streets of my Glenview neighborhood, uphill into the Oakland hills.

As my lungs began to burn, the pain and fresh air improved my perspective. The case was not about me. It was not about me being duped by a teenager or being too stubborn to admit it. I grimaced at my selfishness and recalled other unflattering examples of my trait. I'd caught myself after trial losses lamenting my trial record while my client was led away in handcuffs.

With that, I focused on defending Darnell Moore. His guilt was not for me to say. The discovery of the firearm had obviously been a severe blow. However, forty-caliber handguns were extremely common in Oakland, right up there with nine-millimeters as the city's most popular, based on my unofficial survey.

However, it was the potential for even more devastating evidence that had me worried as I mercifully turned downhill to jog home. Assuming sufficiently intact bullets could be recovered from the crime scene, ballistics tests could prove whether or not they were fired from Moore's gun. While the current state of the evidence was quite grim, a positive ballistics finding would be game, set, and match.

I turned off my brain for the last half mile and arrived at home exhausted and sore but proud of my effort and in a much better frame of mind. I felt like pizza but didn't want to undo my progress.

My cell phone rattled on the kitchen table where I had left it. The text was from Eddy.

—Hi Joe. I had a very nice time with you as well. Does Thursday work? I have the day off—

I was ecstatic. Although she'd seemed sincere when she'd said she wanted to see me, there was a part of me that wondered. Part of it was my last serious relationship, ending as it had in such a spectacular inferno of deception. Part of it was Eddy herself and her stunning beauty and charm.

But she had texted after all.

I called the pizza place but ordered salad. I would end up filling up on peanut butter sandwiches and beer, but I was proud of the initial thrust. I shut my laptop for the night and turned on a ballgame, determined to maintain my good mood. In the back of my mind loomed the anxiety of date number two, but that could wait.

I reclined and washed down peanut butter with a caramel stout. I looked at her text again. Not just a nice time. She had had a very nice time.

Chapter Ten

Real courage is when you know you're licked before you begin but you see it through to the end no matter what.—Harper Lee

Oakland, California 2006

"Hey, Messy." The big kid they called Stoney gestured toward a mud puddle. "You and your smelly brother's drinking fountain is over there." Damon usually stuck close to his twin during recess, but Jesse had wandered off to the drinking fountains.

"What a surprise," Stoney's friend jeered, "Messy's wearing the ratty orange shirt again. The one he blows his nose on."

Damon began hustling toward the fountains where a crowd was gathering. He and Jesse had heard the taunts of "Dirty Damon" and "Messy Jesse" before, but they had become more common lately, and he could tell his brother was ready to snap. As Damon approached, he heard calls of "fight" and saw the jostling circle of kids that always surrounded a playground scuffle.

Damon shoved his way through the crowd to find Jesse on top of the bigger boy, raining fists on him in a wild fury. Damon pulled him off, bear hugging him from behind as Jesse continued to flail in the air frantically, desperate to inflict more pain. Damon held him there as the crowd gradually dispersed, leaning against the wall of the school, feeling his brother's heart pound through his shirt.

"I ain't never seen you like this, Jess. You okay?" he asked cautiously after he had finally released his hold.

Jesse's red and tear-streaked face turned toward his brother, but he didn't answer. Damon stood there, stunned as the recess bell rang, his brother's face singed into his memory.

He knew Jesse's every look. They were his own identical facial expressions, after all, so he had recognized every smirk, eye-roll, and variation on a smile, no matter how subtle or fleeting. But this was different. Although Damon had never seen it before, the look was unmistakable. He could even feel the expression himself, twitching somewhere just beneath his own face.

As he watched him walk away, he wondered about the source of his twin's pure and perfect rage.

Chapter Eleven

"Yes!" Andy punched the air as he walked into my office.

"Oh, not many things make my partner that happy. What is it this time?" I asked. "Long term disability, brain injury?"

"Nah. Broken arm—but—tada!—the client is a surgeon. Hello, lost wages!"

"Ah, my partner the bottom feeder, preying on the misfortune of others."

"To the contrary. Unlike you, I right the wrongs of society. You defend the wrongs of society."

"Whatever gets you through the day."

"Hey, I heard you have another date tomorrow."

Up to now, I'd resisted the urge to ask Andy if Eddy had mentioned me to Karen, so I was happy he brought it up first. "Yeah, and by the way, you didn't tell me she was a ten. Be honest, in the looks department, aren't we on much different levels?

"You guys are on different planets."

"Again, your support warms my heart. Do you have any intel for me?"

"Apparently, against all odds, she likes you well enough."

"What did she say?"

"She said you seem very nice and funny, but you talk about yourself a lot."

His words hung in the air. I felt ill and put my face in my hands. I knew I'd been a babbling idiot. Then I looked up to find Andy's grinning mug. "Just fucking with you."

I looked around to find something to throw at him but, like all good PI lawyers, he'd already run for safety.

I had spent Monday and Tuesday putting out fires in other cases and had just started digging back into the Moore case. Chuck planned to meet me in the office later today, and Rocco Bedrossian was bringing his dad in for an interview.

I put in my headphones and opened the 911 call.

"Operator, what's your emergency?" I heard excited indecipherable phrases in a foreign language.

"Hello, sir? What your emergency? Do you speak English?"

"Oh, yes. Sorry," Vardan Bedrossian began in his familiar accent. "I was excited. I speak English." He was breathing heavily into the phone, clearly upset.

"What's your emergency?"

"There's been a shooting."

"Where?"

"At West Eighth and Maybeck in Oakland. There's a person lying in the street."

"Are you safe? Is the shooter still there?"

"No. Shooter drove away."

"Did you get a look at the shooter?"

"Yes. Young black man."

"Did you see the car?"

"Please come. The boy is in the street."

"Sir…"

The line went dead.

I switched files, opening Bedrossian's recorded statement at the police station.

"This is Officer Zuckerman. I'm here with Mr. Bedrossian. It is March 24, 2021. We're here at the Oakland Police Department. The time is one-twenty-four p.m. Sir, what did you observe on Monday?"

"I was alone in the store."

"Okay, sir," the officer said slowly, perhaps sensing a language barrier, "I'd like to know what you saw on the day of the shooting."

"Yes. I was sweeping near the front door. I opened the front door to sweep the dirt outside. I heard the sound of screeching tires. I looked up and saw a car in the street, firing at the house across the street."

"Can you describe the vehicle?"

"I don't know cars."

"Big car, small car? Color?"

"It happened very fast. I was focused on the shooter."

"Who was shooting? The driver or a passenger?"

"The driver, yes. The passenger, I didn't see."

"Was there a passenger?"

"I didn't see for sure."

"How about the driver?"

"He was like the guys in the photos."

I took off my headphones. This was interesting. Bedrossian had already seen the photo lineup when he described the shooter. I wondered if it hadn't been for Bedrossian's comment if I ever would have found out.

The officer continued, undeterred. "White guy? Black guy?"

"Black guy. Light skinned black guy. Young. Maybe twenty."

"Any facial hair?"

"I don't recall any. No."

"Ever seen this guy before that day?"

"No. First time."

"Anything else?" The officer paused, waiting for a response. "Okay, it's one-thirty-seven p.m. We're all done."

I reclined at my desk and digested Mr. Bedrossian's identification of Darnell, such as it was. First, he had witnessed a shooter on the move. It stood to reason that the shooter was turned away from him, toward his targets. Even if he had his eyes on the road, the view was, at best, a profile.

His description thereafter to the 911 operator had been of a young black male. Given his knowledge of the neighborhood, Bedrossian could well have guessed that without ever seeing the shooting.

After the police had captured Darnell's car on surveillance video, they had placed his Department of Motor Vehicles photo in a photospread next to five other young light-skinned African American men with little to no facial hair. Bedrossian had circled Darnell's photo and one of a filler. Other than the general similarities, the filler and Darnell didn't really look much alike.

Although the identification procedure was not recorded, which was unusual, the officer had at least quoted the witness verbatim in his report.

"This one and this one. These look the most like the shooter."

All in all, Bedrossian added something to the prosecution's case, but not much. Certainly, it could not support a guilty verdict alone. Of course, it didn't need to add much, given the video, the motive, the gun, and Darnell's admission to being in the area.

My phone buzzed.

"Hi, Rocco. You guys on your way?"

"Very sorry, Joe. I couldn't convince him to come. I talked to him about the importance of letting you talk to him. To me, what you said makes perfect sense. The last thing we want is for him to make a mistake and put away an innocent kid. But he's just very stubborn."

"Yeah, I get that, Rocco. Thanks for trying. So, it's safe to say he'll be at the preliminary hearing?"

"Yes. And frankly, I'm not thrilled about it. It could be very dangerous for him, especially when I'm overseas. Luckily, this time when I heard about the shooting, I had some leave coming and I needed treatment on my leg. Will the preliminary hearing be open to the public?"

"Yes, unfortunately, it is."

"Well, sorry he wouldn't speak to you. I think, in his mind, he's just been at war with these gangs for so long. It's almost like he sees the Court as an opportunity to stand up for himself."

"I completely understand, and if he wants to testify, he should. I just want him to be accurate. Anyway, thanks for trying. Tell your dad, if he changes his mind and wants to talk, he can give me a call."

"Will do. Oh, and Chuck dropped off a subpoena for our surveillance video inside the store. I'll dig it up and email it to you."

"Thanks, Rocco."

I texted Chuck.

—*Never mind. The tough Armenian cancelled*—

****

"I should warn you, if there was an Olympic Team for mini-golf, I'd pretty much be the captain," she said playfully.

"Well, you may get your shot. Wasn't ballroom dancing an Olympic sport once?" I asked, handing her a plastic cup of white wine.

"Are you good?" she asked, selecting her putter from the bin.

"At ballroom dancing? Yes, very accomplished. Why, care to make it interesting?"

"Yes," she said. "What are the stakes?" she asked, raising one eyebrow as her face was suddenly close to me. Then her soft, full lips were on mine, our mouths open, tasting wine. It happened right there on the first tee at Big Al's Arcade and Putt Putt as the faint sounds of the arcade chimed in the distance.

"Well, we'll have to think of something." I said, smiling my utter happiness into her blue eyes.

Although I had sensed definite chemistry on our first date, I had been really too anxious to enjoy it. Today, though, it was intoxicating, and I could tell she felt it too. On a perfect spring day, we strolled around in the sunshine, drinking white wine from red cups while we talked, laughed, and putted under bridges and through clowns' mouths.

I learned that after graduating from college, two years behind me in school, she'd worked as an archaeologist for a land use company in Australia for ten years. Now, she was doing consulting work while getting her doctorate at Cal. She was raised in San Diego, where her parents still lived. I talked about my job, including my current frustration with my most recent client.

"It must be challenging for you, getting young black men to trust you. Do you usually break through?"

"I don't know if we ever achieve trust. But usually they realize they need to be honest with me, if only for self-preservation purposes. Nice shot by the way," I said, while thinking "nice ass, too."

"It must be rewarding if you're able to save an innocent person from prison."

Who was this beautiful woman who kept saying the right things? Half the time when I mentioned my profession, I got some version of, "I know it's necessary and all, but I couldn't do your job." It was a nice way of saying, "I could never stoop to your level of utter moral degradation and by the way, how do you sleep at night."

"Well, usually it's more like saving a slightly less innocent person from quite so much prison time, but yes, it can be rewarding when it works out," I said while lining up a putt.

"So, do you believe this guy, Darnell."

"I'd like to believe him, but I'm not sure."

"Hey, what about that magical power of truth detection you told me about? Gun to your head," she giggled. "Did he kill the guy?"

"Well, you know," I said, smiling at her joke, "people don't kill people, puns kill people."

"That's truly awful, and you're dodging the bullet, I mean, the question," she said, suppressing a laugh. "Well? Guilty or not?"

"Not," I said, surprising myself, "but I'm not sure about this one." I ran down the evidence against him in a few sentences.

"Ouch. I see what you mean."

"By the way," I said, "we've come to the final hole and although I'm far ahead, I'm willing to let this be the deciding hole."

"What game have you been watching, Turner? I have a comfortable lead, but okay, this can be the decider."

"I knew there had to be something wrong with her," I said under my breath, loud enough for her to hear. "She's a cheater."

"Whatever," she said, pushing me toward the tee box. "Oh, and loser buys dinner next week."

"Great," I said, controlling my enthusiasm, my mind doing a touchdown dance while I lined up the putt.

Eddy positioned herself facing me. "Don't get distracted, Joe," she whispered in a sultry voice, while shaking her sandy blonde hair out of a bun and kissing the air between us.

"Really shameless behavior by Busier here at the hallowed grounds of Big Al's. One wonders if she may be suspended from competition," I said in my best announcer's voice. Then I watched my putt roll up the ramp and straight into the dragon's mouth. "Yes!"

"Impressive, but I can still tie."

"So, Eddy," I asked casually, as she addressed the ball, "do you inhale or exhale when you putt?"

She smiled, but maintained focus, and her putt found its mark. "Wahoo!" She raised her putter in triumph. "Good match, Turner." she said, high fiving me, keeping hold of my hand as we strolled to the parking lot, where we'd met after my afternoon court appearance.

"So, I guess we split dinner. Does Wednesday

work?" she asked as we arrived at her car. "I'm going to England for work for two weeks on Friday, and I'd love to see you before I go."

"Sounds great."

"Perfect. I'll cook."

"That sounds wonderful," I said, taking her in my arms. "And by the way, brilliant getting the kiss out of the way earlier. Err, not that I wanted it out of the way, but…"

"I know what you mean," she said giggling. "Genius move by me, getting that horrible thing out of the way." She leaned in and I pulled her against me as our lips met again, inhaling scents of jasmine and really fresh laundry.

"I had a great time, Joe. See you in a few days."

"Me too. Goodnight, Eddy."

I picked up a half-baked pizza and was still smiling when I got home, taken aback by my grinning mug in the oven door. Things seemed to be progressing rapidly with Eddy, and I wondered whether I should guard against getting carried away. Our relative attractiveness was still a mental hurdle.

Maybe I should be cautious, but for the rest of the night, I reveled in the memory of the best date of my life.

****

After a Friday morning run, I stopped by the office to meet with a new DUI client. After an uneventful interview, Chuck called.

"Hey, Chuck, what's shakin'?"

"You're in a suspiciously good mood. Wouldn't have anything to do with a certain someone?"

"It might."

"Please tell me she has no connection to the case."

"Good God, no. I've learned my lesson on that front."

"I got the enhanced video back and ran the plate. Would you believe our star witness was driving a stolen car?"

"The way this case is going, yes. Yes, I can. Can you see his face clearly enough for an ID?"

"No. Looks like a dead end."

"Shit. Well, I'm off to visit our hero soon. I'll try to talk some sense into him."

"If he doesn't settle, he's dumber than a bag of hammers."

Thirty minutes later, I was strolling through Friday's farmers market on the busy streets of downtown Oakland on a sun-splashed spring afternoon on my way to the North County Jail. Even entering the dank lobby, I felt a heavy lid slam shut on my senses.

As I waited for my client in the interview room, I thought about my answer to Eddy's question about his guilt. Part of what made me cling to my belief in Darnell's innocence was the psychosis that accompanied every case. Most of those accused of murder are guilty. For the most part, the police aren't in the business of arresting innocent people, and by the time the case is filtered through the District Attorney, the odds are good they've got their man.

So, when a defense attorney comes upon someone who is factually innocent, it is a rare and noteworthy opportunity. Rather than defending "because everyone deserves a defense," now we are on the side of justice. It is infinitely more fun to defend the innocent and argue a worthy cause. So far, my gut had trumped logic in the Moore case, but I was aware that my psyche also had a rooting interest in his innocence.

Soon, I was sitting across from Darnell. He was still upbeat, but gradually I could tell the place was wearing on him. His eyes were sad, his smile, fatigued.

Inmates had told me it wasn't just the sensory deprivation that came with incarceration. It was the tension and fear that accompanied every waking moment. A very high percentage of the inmates in maximum security were prone to violence when they lived in the outside world. Add in the frustration and depression of confinement, and the results were predictable.

"Hi, Darnell. How are you holding up?"

"Cool."

"I wanted to prepare you for the preliminary hearing. It's a hearing designed to see if there is enough evidence to have a trial. The standard of proof is very low, so I anticipate the District Attorney won't have a problem meeting the burden of proof."

"Yeah, I've been hearing that in here from some of the old-timers."

"Just remember not to talk to anyone about the facts of the case."

"Yeah, I know."

"Okay. So, they found a gun in your closet."

"Yeah, I figured they would."

I breathed deeply, remaining calm. "Darnell, you sat in that very chair not two weeks ago and assured me that you didn't own a gun. I'd really appreciate it if you could be honest with me."

"But that's not my gun. I said so."

"So, whose was it? Your church-going mother or

your brother the prep school scholar?" I yelled, no longer the least bit calm. "You know what, Darnell, believe it or not, I actually believe that you didn't kill anyone!" I only paused to catch my breath and kept yelling. "I think the witness is full of shit. I think you're a want-to-be gang member, and I don't think you have the skill, let alone the balls to ride through an intersection and execute two kill shots! But I'll tell you what, Darnell, if you keep lying—to me, to the police and to the jury, then you better get used to places like this and worse!"

I stood and stretched. His eyes were wide, and I could tell my tirade had rattled him. "Mr. Turner, can I say something?"

"No, listen up. I'm done fucking around." I spoke calmly but my tone was serious as I sat down and faced him again. "The gun evidence is not good, but it could get a lot worse. The D.A. will run ballistics tests to determine whether the SLAZIK found in your closet is the murder weapon. They could be running the tests as we speak. Right now, the case against you is strong. If you come clean about your role, at least we'll have a fighting chance at trial.

"However, listen carefully, Darnell. If it turns out that your gun was the murder weapon, you're cooked. You will be convicted of first-degree murder, and you will spend the rest of your life in prison. If that's the case, we need to cut a deal now. Given your youth, I might be able to get you twenty if you plead to voluntary manslaughter. You would be eligible for parole after fifteen."

I paused, letting the information sink in. I was less than optimistic that the D.A. would make that offer, but

I needed to start the conversation with Darnell in case it was a possibility.

"So, Darnell, it's time to tell the truth. Was the SLAZIK the murder weapon?"

He had recovered from my rant and was leaning back in his chair with his arms crossed, cocky smile in place. "You got a little fire in you, Mr. Turner. I'm glad to see that. But twenty years?" He laughed and shook his head. "I definitely am not feeling that."

"Darnell, please answer the question."

He paused, enjoying his moment of control. "No," he finally said. "That gun was not the murder weapon. I promise you that."

"Okay, Darnell, I hope you're right," I said, getting up to hit the buzzer. "I'll see you in court."

Chapter Twelve
Before I can live with other folks, I have to live with myself. —Harper Lee

Oakland, California 2006

"Well, if it ain't dirty and smelly."

Damon had seen Stoney and his group gathered by the railroad tracks, a block from school, and he knew Jesse had too. Their leader sat on a guardrail, grinding a fist into his palm.

The image of Jesse's face, twisted with rage, had stayed with Damon throughout the day. Now, as they approached the group of bullies, he felt the look forming on his own face.

"I could smell you two a blocks away," Stoney chirped, hopping down from his perch.

Jesse closed the gap. "Want another ass-kicking?"

Jaw set, Damon clenched his teeth in hatred for their tormentor. His twin's look had taken hold. Suddenly, he felt himself propelled in front of Jesse, face to face with the bully. His first blow was instinctive, a forearm to that pudgy smirking mug.

Damon hesitated for an instant, as if he had watched someone else deliver the strike. Then he breathed deeply, feeling himself surrender to his inner soul, and it all came thundering out—the pain, hunger, and sorrow—all of it released in an unrelenting fury upon his target.

When it was Jesse's turn to pull him off, Damon staggered away, exhausted and confused.

Soon, the twins were walking home, side by side. It was Friday, but they didn't feel much like a butterscotch candy.

Chapter Thirteen

I took in a ballgame with some college friends on Saturday, straying from my recent trend toward healthy eating with too many brats, nachos, and beers. After a sluggish start to Sunday morning, I managed a painful run, then settled in to prepare for Darnell's preliminary hearing on Tuesday.

I was hoping the enhanced surveillance video would reveal an open sunroof in Darnell's car, bolstering my theory that a passenger shot from that location. I recognized that it was possible for my client to be convicted of murder even as the driver, but it would at least give us a fighting chance.

By fighting chance, I actually meant a snowball's chance in hell. I didn't relish the sight of young Darnell on the stand, thinking he was being charming and persuasive, spinning some unbelievable tale. *"I was just driving through the enemy's neighborhood on my way to get a smoothie when this passenger I'd just met stands up through the sunroof and starts firing."*

Unfortunately, despite at least two dozen rewinds, staring at the video from every angle, I couldn't say if the sunroof was open or not. I remained more convinced than ever the shooter was there, though. It would explain not only the downward angle of the shots, but their accuracy. I also knew, though, that whether or not Darnell was a hard-core gang member or just someone on the periphery, there was very little chance of him naming the shooter. Doing so would not only put him at risk but his entire family as well.

The enhanced video made the mystery witness across the street more visible. It was now clear the car thief wore a white T-shirt with "Gaels" emblazoned across the chest in blue, the mascot of local Saint Mark's College. Still, the facial features were too blurry to make out.

One thing was clear, the Gaels fan had certainly witnessed the shooting from the perfect angle. From his position across the street to the east of the victim, he was surely in a position to see the source of the gun shots as Darnell's car approached from the west. Immediately after the shooting, the driver's side of Darnell's car would pass within ten feet of him as it entered the intersection and drove past.

I made a note to check the jail log for arrests for auto theft in the past two weeks. It was a long shot, but maybe the guy had been unlucky enough to get arrested for the stolen rental he was driving.

My phone buzzed with an email alert, and without looking I knew it was Didery, in fine form a full three days before the preliminary hearing. Last night, the Deputy D.A. had left a voicemail, asking me to stipulate to the cause of death at the preliminary hearing. It was common courtesy in cases like this one where the cause of death was not in dispute, as it would save everyone the time of having the coroner testify.

I had forgotten to return Didery's call, and he had followed up with an email and a text earlier in the day before I had gotten out of bed. I sent an email on my phone confirming the stipulation. Before I put it down, it buzzed a text from Eddy.

—So if the victim was shot in the eye by your client's Slaezik, would he need Slaezik surgery?—

—That's a loaded question. Looking forward to Wednesday. Let me know what to bring—

On the way to the office, it was Didery again, calling at eight-fifteen a.m. He was quickly becoming a pebble in my shoe and we were nowhere near trial.

"Hi, Nathan. The stipulation is fine. I emailed. Sorry for the slow response." *...to your email at eight o'clock p.m. on Saturday night.*

"That's okay. I appreciate the email. I answered with an email early this morning. I was just wondering if you had gotten it yet."

"No, I'm just on my way into the office. What's your email say?"

"I just forwarded the written stipulation. I was hoping you could sign it and send it back."

"Um, I guess I can, but why do you need it in writing? I'm going to stipulate." I knew the answer was he was just being "Jittery Didery," thinking of what he'd do if I changed my mind. He acted like one of those OCD types with contingency plans for meteor showers and alien landings.

"Well, I just think the better practice is to memorialize it now out of an abundance of caution. Wouldn't you agree?"

Again, I was reminded of one of his annoying eccentricities. He was constantly asking for agreement, as if daring someone to call him on his neuroses. "Okay, Nathan," I said, sighing into the phone, "when I get to the office, I'll see when I get to it."

"Thank you. Also, my inspector has obtained

surveillance videos from various businesses in the area around the time of the shooting." I cringed. I had expected it from a D.A. as thorough as Didery. He was hoping to catch a clear video of Darnell behind the wheel. "Nothing important, but I'm emailing you the videos."

"Thanks, Nathan." I breathed a sigh of relief as I pulled into the office parking lot.

Inside, I greeted Lawanda, the part-time assistant Andy and I shared. Retired from a long-time secretarial job at an insurance company, she had accepted the position on the condition that she not have to perform certain tasks, some of which were classically secretarial in nature. Still, she was reliable, good on the phones, and Andy and I enjoyed her occasional reference to herself in the third person as in, "Now, Joe, you know Lawanda doesn't do filing."

At my desk, hoping to avoid more calls, texts, or emails from Didery, I got his stipulation out of the way, then checked my phone.

—*Thanks for asking. If it's not too much trouble, please bring a mustard green and kale salad, a side dish—preferably roasted vegetables with a Romesco sauce, a cheese souffle, and any custard-based dessert—*

—*Well played, Madam. Lol—*

I opened the surveillance videos, suddenly in a much better mood. Even though Didery had said they were uneventful, I needed to see for myself.

Seven different businesses had provided surveillance tape starting from an hour before the homicide. I began fast-forwarding through the videos, my eye out for Darnell's green sedan, but my mind elsewhere. In video number five, something else caught my eye.

It was a bright red muscle car turning into a gas station only two blocks from the crime scene. The car parked in front of a pump, and out walked the driver, passing directly in front of the surveillance camera, his face in full view. I paused the video with him centered in the shot. Slender and smallish, he looked to be in his early twenties. He was fair with blond, medium-length hair, and fine features. He wore a white T-shirt that read "Gaels" in blue letters.

"Hello, murder witness," I said to myself, celebrating a minor victory. I knew it was entirely possible that the witness may tell Chuck that the shooter was his acquaintance, Darnell Moore. If that were the case, we would send him on his way. I was always a little uncomfortable with that course of action, but not only was it legal, it was required of a zealous advocate. The law required only notice to the prosecution of witnesses you intended to call at trial. If the Gaels fan identified Darnell, he would be the last witness I would call.

Still, given the current state of the evidence, the discovery was something. Now, to identify the witness and find him. It was a situation like this in which the police enjoyed a huge advantage. With access to a huge database of mugshots, facial recognition would solve the problem in minutes.

Instead, I turned to Chuck, who knew a lot of people in Oakland. As an ex-probation officer, he also knew a lot of people on the wrong side of the law.

Eddy's name appeared on my phone with a text.

—*Bring the wine and your sexy self*—

Still smiling a goofy smile, I cut the still shot and texted it to Chuck.

—*Hi Chuck. Here's the mystery witness up close. Recognize him?*—

—*No, but I know a few hundred cops I can ask. If the guy's a regular customer, someone will recognize him*—

—*Thanks. I'll give you a call after the prelim tomorrow*—

—*Have fun storming the castle*—

The preliminary hearing in the People of the State of California v. Darnell Moore had been assigned to Judge Ed Hazelton in Department 6. Appointed to the bench in 1984, he was still spry at seventy-eight years old. Never accused of overworking himself, he often wore jeans and a polo shirt under his robe. "Judge Haze," as everyone called him, was efficient in moving cases through his department.

"Hi, Joe, c'mon in," he said, peeking out of his chambers as I entered his courtroom. "I see you're appointed. Thanks for taking the case. We're low on qualified defense attorneys these days." Judge Haze had worked under my dad at the District Attorney's Office and had only recently stopped chiding me about switching to defense after a few years in the D.A.'s Office.

The reality was that defense suited my critical nature. Also, I knew my father would have approved as he always spoke highly of defense attorneys and their crucial role in the system. As a District Attorney he had taken pride in fairness and often quoted Blackstone's "It is better ten guilty escape than one innocent suffer."

I suppose the real reason for my switch to defense

was that I drank too much as a young prosecutor. I probably still did, but back then I drank to escape memories of witnessing my dad's murder, and it had been affecting my performance. There'd been rumblings within Human Resources, and in the end, it had seemed prudent to part with the office on my terms.

I was mildly surprised to see Didery already in chambers. It was technically inappropriate to speak with the judge about the case outside the presence of your opponent, but it didn't bother me, and Judge Haze made his own rules. It clearly bothered Didery, though, as he stood quickly as I entered. "Joe, I hope I'm not being inappropriate. Judge Hazelton asked me to, uh—"

The Judge interrupted the prosecutor with a dismissive wave. "Joe doesn't care. Nathan was just getting me up to speed on this case. Don't suppose your guy would take a second and call it a day?" He was asking if my client would plead guilty to a second-degree murder. His sentence would be fifteen years to life.

"Not at this point, Judge. My client is nowhere near that decision." I had thought about that as a potential outcome, but not only wasn't Darnell "feeling that," there were too many unknowns for me to recommend the deal.

"Okay, well it was worth a try. Let's get this show on the road then. I've got an appointment after lunch, so let's wrap this up before the noon hour." Didery shot me a look of disbelief. Not surprisingly, he had planned a thorough and lengthy preliminary hearing.

Out in the courtroom, we took our seats at the counsel table, and Darnell was soon escorted into the courtroom, squinting under the bright fluorescent lights.

For inmates who attend court, their days start at four-thirty a.m. and it looked like Darnell had been sleeping on the cold cement floor of the holding tank just outside the courtroom.

Didery's first witness was Oakland Police Department Sergeant Robin Severson, the officer in charge of the crime scene. The Sergeant sat with perfect posture in the witness chair in her black uniform, her hair pulled back in a tight ponytail. She was all business in describing her activities at the crime scene.

"Upon my arrival, the victim was being attended to by paramedics. I posted officers on the perimeter down West Eighth Street and around the intersection of Eighth and Maybeck. Once the crime scene was secured with police tape, I approached the victim."

"What did you observe?" asked Didery from the podium.

"The victim was laying in front of 454 West Eighth Street perpendicular to the street with his legs on the street, his torso on top of the curb, and his head on the sidewalk. There was a copious amount of blood. He was nonresponsive. Appeared to be suffering from a gunshot wound to the head and another to his chest area. He was pronounced dead at the scene."

"Did you eventually learn the name of the victim?"

"Yes, the victim was identified as Cleveland Barlow."

My client leaned over to me and whispered, "Hey, ain't that hearsay?"

I was impressed but would later explain to Darnell that since 1990, officers could testify as to hearsay in preliminary hearings.

"What did you do next?"

"I radioed for a homicide detective and organized the techs."

"Did you observe evidence of gunshots being fired at the scene?"

"Yes, there were ten forty-caliber shell casings scattered on the north side of the street, the side nearest the victim's body. There were also numerous shell casings of various calibers in the yard of the residence and in front of the house on the sidewalk, near the victim. Also, there appeared to be bullet strike marks on the door and door frame of the residence."

"No further questions."

"Mr. Turner, do you have any cross examination?"

The judge's look said if I did, it had better be brief. I really didn't have any questions I needed answered, but I felt compelled to let my client know I was at least paying attention. "Thank you, Your Honor. Officer, you also bagged the victim's hands for gunshot residue testing, correct?"

"Yes, sir."

"And did you eventually learn the results of those tests?"

"Not yet. The lab hasn't gotten to it yet."

"Thank you. No further questions."

Mindful of Judge Haze's schedule, Didery did his best to streamline his case. After laying a foundation with the officer who obtained the surveillance video, he played the footage on the court's giant video screen.

Next came Officer Zuckerman, who testified that the suspect's vehicle seen in the video was registered to one Darnell Moore and showed the Court photographs of the bullet holes in the car. He also testified about Darnell's admission that he "might have been in the area around the time of the shooting." Again, for my client's benefit, I cross examined on the length of time Darnell was kept in the interrogation room and elicited his numerous denials before his eventual admission.

At eleven o'clock, Didery called Mr. Bedrossian to the stand. The D.A. could have elicited the witness's statement through the officer who interviewed him, but I was thankful for the opportunity to hear the witness's testimony first-hand before the trial.

Outside his market, Bedrossian seemed less confident. His eyes scanned the courtroom, taking in his surroundings as he walked toward the witness stand and took the oath.

After a brief introduction, the witness told the Court of his activities just prior to the shooting. "I was alone in the market, sweeping," he said, his accent producing an 'sv" sound at the word's beginning.

Judge Haze frowned and sat up in his chair. "I'm sorry, sir, you said you were sleeping?"

"No, sweeping. With broom," the witness answered, pantomiming the motion with his hands.

"Apologies, Mr. Bedrossian. Please continue."

"I opened the door to sweep out and I saw a car driving toward my market."

"Was the car travelling away from Maybeck or towards it."

"Fast, toward Maybeck."

"Can you describe the car?"

"It was a green boxy car."

Darnell shot me a glance. He was definitely paying attention, noticing the witness's improved memory since his interview with the police.

"What else did you observe?"

"The car screeched to a stop. I heard gunshots. Many gunshots, then the car sped away."

"Were you able to see how many people were in the car?"

"I only see the driver. If there were others in the car, I did not see."

"Did you see anyone actually shooting a gun?"

"Yes, the driver was firing lots of shots."

"Were you able to see the driver's face?"

"Yes. I saw his face from the side. I saw his—" the witness paused as if trying to recall something "—I saw his profile." This was going exceedingly poorly. All this case needed was an identification to have to overcome.

"So, you saw a profile of the driver's face?"

"Yes. Profile."

"Mr. Bedrossian, do you see the person you saw behind the wheel in court today?"

The shopkeeper stared straight at the prosecutor. "Yes, the defendant." I looked at Didery. The answer didn't seem to surprise him.

"Please point to where he is seated and describe an article of clothing he is wearing." Bedrossian pointed to the defendant without looking at him. "He's wearing red and white striped clothing."

"Your Honor, may the record reflect the witness has identified the defendant, Darnell Moore?"

"The record will so reflect."

"No further questions."

"Mr. Turner, cross examination?"

I was torn. On one hand, I wanted to save my best cross-examination of Bedrossian for the trial. On the other hand, I wanted to let him know that the trial would not be a pleasant experience. Also, I needed an outlet for my frustration. "Good morning, Mr. Bedrossian. You called 911 after the shooting, didn't you?"

"Yes."

"I'm curious, initially you were speaking in your native Armenian language, correct?"

"I haven't heard the tape but sometimes when I'm excited, I revert to my language."

"Do you recall what you said?"

" 'Oh my God.' 'Jesus Christ.' Things like that."

"I understand. Now, you told the Court that the person that shot out of the car was, quote, 'the defendant,' right?"

"Yes."

"And you knew when you walked into court that the defendant would be the guy seated next to me in jail clothes, correct?"

"Yes."

"Did someone tell you that, or did you just figure that out?" The witness looked at Didery, who was stone-faced but no doubt feeling a migraine coming on. If the witness said Didery told him, it would be very bad for the prosecutor.

The witness refocused on me. "I figured out that he was the defendant."

"Are you sure about that?"

"Objection, argumentative."

"Sustained. Move on, Mr. Turner."

"So anyway, Mr. Bedrossian, before you even walked into the courtroom, you knew that you were going to identify the defendant?"

The witness crossed his arms defiantly, gaining

confidence. "I saw him in court here, and I recognized him."

"When you saw the driver of the car, you said you saw his profile. Just so we're all on the same page, that means you saw his face from the side view."

"Yes."

"When you saw the defendant, you say he was shooting."

"Yes."

"And he was shooting toward a house that was across the street from you, correct? He wasn't shooting up in the air or firing blindly out his window, was he?"

"No."

"No, you saw him aim the gun in the direction of the house, correct."

"Yes."

"And he must have been looking where he was shooting, correct?"

"Yes."

"So, if that was the case, Mr. Bedrossian, the driver of the vehicle would have been facing away from you, correct?"

The witness knew he was trapped. "I saw his face. It was him."

"Mr. Bedrossian, if the driver of the car was aiming at the house across the street while he fired and looking where he was shooting, then how did you see his profile?"

"I saw him."

"Before today, did you ever tell anyone that you saw a profile of the shooter?"

"I don't recall."

"Sir, before today, had you ever used the word,

'profile'?

"Today, I see him. Now I am sure it is him."

"No further questions, Your Honor."

I would save Bedrossian's prior statements as the main ammunition at trial. I was still convinced his identification wouldn't hold water at trial, but it was still another piece of evidence to be explained.

Judge Haze looked at the clock on the wall. "That about wrap it up, Mr. Didery?"

"Your Honor, I did have two witnesses I wanted to put on."

"Counsel, approach," the Judge said, waving us to the bench.

"Nathan, you're beating a dead horse here. What other possible evidence could there be that this kid's the shooter? Who are your other witnesses?"

"I have a cop who found a gun in his bedroom and a gang expert," said Didery, intent on resuming with the dead horse beating.

"No, I've seen enough. Step back."

The judge then undertook the formality of ruling there was enough evidence for Darnell to face the charge of murder and set a trial date six weeks out.

When I rose to leave the courtroom, I noticed Darnell eyeing three young men in the back row. Two carried Kansas City baseball caps, dead giveaways for Iceboyz. If these were Darnell's friends, he had no need for enemies. All three were glaring at him—mean-mugging, as Darnell would no doubt describe it.

I walked back to the office, feeling sorry for my client. I couldn't imagine his predicament. Name the real killer and risk his life and his family's; remain silent and spend a lifetime in prison. I snickered inwardly, realizing my assumption that Darnell was not the shooter. I couldn't seem to make up my mind about this kid.

After a brief stop at the office, I drove home and went for a run in the bright afternoon sunshine. So far, by focusing on the Moore case, I'd managed not to worry too much about the third date with Eddy and all that would likely come with it. In a word, sex.

She did invite me over for dinner, after all. Since she was flying on Friday, she may have scheduled Wednesday in case I spent the night. Then again, she would probably schedule Wednesday whether or not I was spending the night because she would likely be busy the day before she travelled. But it was the third date. Wasn't sex on the third date a thing? But she didn't really strike me as a conformist, anyway. I pulled into my drive, shaking my head. "Glad you're not overthinking it, Joe."

Chapter Fourteen

You never really understand a person until you consider things from his point of view… Until you climb inside of his skin and walk around in it. —Harper Lee

Oakland, California 2006

Damon never forgot the night he lost his brother. Recently, Jesse had become more and more quiet, staring off into space for minutes at a time, almost unresponsive. Even the jokes that always worked to cheer him up were met with silence. He stared through his twin with hollow eyes.

One night, missing their late-night talks, Damon got up for a drink of water with thoughts of sneaking into Jesse's room. A couple times, he tried tapping lightly on Jesse's bedroom door, but his brother must have been asleep.

From the kitchen, he heard footsteps in the hallway and peered down into the darkness. Dumbass blocked the hallway, as his hands struggled with something. "Get your ass back to bed."

Something told Damon not to retreat. Something, or someone was behind Dumbass, struggling to get past, blocked by the big man's girth. Of course, deep down, he knew who it was, but his mind tried desperately to blur the image.

"Damon!"

His brother's plaintive cry sprung him into action. Without thinking, he raced through the dark hallway toward Dumbass.

The blow to his head came out of nowhere, striking him on his left ear, sending him into the wall. Damon got to his feet and staggered onward, only to be pushed to the floor again, landing on his face. Rising up, he watched Dumbass shove Jesse into his bedroom, then go in after him.

Before the door closed, Jesse suddenly appeared in the gap, wedging his shoulders through the jamb, struggling like an animal to get out.

It was at this moment that Damon saw an image that would haunt him for the rest of his life—his brother's delicate face etched in terror just before he was pulled back into the room. Damon rose to his feet and lunged for the door, but it slammed shut and locked as he arrived.

He pounded on the door, screaming until he collapsed, fists raw, his nose bleeding from the fall. He stayed there at the base of the door all night, listening to the awful grunts, bed squeaks, and whimpers of his twin.

Chapter Fifteen

It wasn't that I doubted my sexual aptitude. I wasn't going to author an addendum to the Kama Sutra, but I knew all the basics. And God knows when it was good, I enjoyed it as much as the next guy. For the most part, I had gotten over the giant chasm in our relative attractiveness. Couples like us were out there. Usually it was when a beautiful woman was with a super wealthy guy, but they were out there.

Still, the prospect of first-time sex had always made me anxious for fear of failure or rejection. Not that I had performance issues that required medication—not yet anyway. And while I was never thrilled with the appearance of my naked body, that wasn't it either.

It was just that it was all so personal. For me, the actual nakedness was a metaphor for the absolute exposure of all things private. The first time involved sharing all of your most personal needs and peculiar preferences with someone who was usually a relative stranger. Enjoyable sex did, anyway. My stress was the reason why the term sexual encounter was descriptive. Sex shouldn't be an encounter, like confronting a strange dog in your driveway.

And that was the dilemma. I felt like to succeed in the endeavor—to give and receive pleasure—meant exposing everything. And if we were not a good match—if she didn't like the way we fit together or my scent or what I said, if I talked too much or kissed too much or hadn't shaved enough of my body—then we would both know it. I'd be lying there, my failure naked and exposed.

So, it was with these thoughts bouncing around my brain that I climbed the hill in the charming Rockridge neighborhood and arrived at her townhouse, holding a bottle of Pinot Noir.

She greeted me with a kiss on the lips. "Hi there!"

"Hi. What a place," I said, still looking at her smile. She wore an off-white top that sort of wrapped around her perfect breasts and hung vertically to a cool turquoise belt buckle and faded jeans. On second thought, I was far from getting past the gap in our looks.

"I feel like I need a decorator. Nothing really matches, but it's comfortable."

If this was just "comfortable," I shuddered at the thought of her seeing my recliner. Her home was bright, with high ceilings, shiny parquet floors, and colorful artwork. There were comfortable looking overstuffed sofas on area rugs—real adult furniture.

"Wow, Carnegie Slopes," she said taking the wine. "I love the winery. Have you been?"

"No, Sonoma?" I asked, following her to the spotless modern kitchen.

"Yes, it's on the coast. It's beautiful. In fact, look at this," she said setting two stemless wine glasses on the counter that were emblazoned with Fort Carnegie Winery. "This is the winery that makes the wine. It's a good sign for us."

"Yes, well, you said you were making lasagna and

I thought the notes of dried sage and orange peel would pair well."

"Is that right?" she asked, laughing.

"Yeah, that and I liked the label."

"So, I have something to ask you, Joe Turner?" she said, with a cautious smile, pausing to gage my reaction as she handed me a wine opener.

"Sounds serious, maybe I'd better pour the wine first."

"Okay, good idea. Here's to sage and orange peel," she said after I had poured.

"So, what's on your mind? Is this about my three children? My time in prison?" I asked, taking a seat opposite her on a kitchen stool.

"Well, here's the thing. I've gotten to know you a little bit, now..."

"Yes," I said filling up the pregnant pause.

"And I have a feeling that you might be a little nervous about tonight." She smiled and paused again. "Being the third date and all?" she asked raising her eyebrows.

"Ah, yes. The third date and all of its various...accompaniments?"

"Accompaniments, exactly."

"I'm assuming you're referring to the tradition of the third date baking competition?"

"You goofball," she laughed, pushing me playfully.

"Okay, seriously," I said and took a healthy drink of the wine. "Yes, not to be presumptuous, but you'd be right to say that I may be a tad bit nervous about the expectations."

"So, here's what I think, Joe Turner."

"Yes, Eddy Busier?"

"By the way, isn't my name awful?"

"No, Busier is a great name."

"Very funny. My dad was Ed and so was his dad."

"Got it, but you were about to tell me something."

"Okay, I think that I'm also nervous about it and if it's okay with you, I'd like to just enjoy tonight without that pressure." She took my hand in hers. "So maybe we could agree not to do it tonight but sometime soon when it's right?" Her blue eyes looked at me hopefully.

"I think that is a fabulous idea," I said, smiling.

She came off her stool and into my arms. "Really?"

"I do. Turns out you know me pretty well."

"Oh, I promise I'm going to," she whispered before our mouths met for a kiss that started soft and turned deep and passionate.

"You know what?" I said, still holding her close. "You can probably guess."

She thought for a second before her blue eyes twinkled. "Yes! When it happens, I don't think I'll be nervous either."

From there, the evening was a dream date. We drank wine, ate lasagna, and sat on her couch, filling the gaps in our knowledge of each other. I described the seminal childhood event of seeing my father murdered. She shared that she had an older sister who worked on the stock market in Los Angeles and a twin sister who was a therapist in Seattle.

"But don't get any ideas."

"What do you mean?"

"I thought twins were every guy's dream."

"Not me. I can barely keep track of one body other than my own."

"Good to know. More lasagna?"

"You know, my first instinct was no, but since you're not going to see me naked, why not? It's delicious."

"See, another benefit to my decision, although I'm thinking maybe we should strip for each other now and get it over with?" she said with a gleam in her eye.

"And still not have sex? No, hard pass," I said, laughing. Beauty, brains, and a slightly wicked streak. I liked so many things about her.

"How's your friend, Darnell, doing?"

"It's rough sledding." I told her about Bedrossian's identification at the preliminary hearing.

"So, he was in all likelihood at the scene, driving his car, had a motive because of the rival gang, and now there's an ID? Yikes."

"And owns a gun that shoots the same caliber of bullets that killed the victim."

"Are those popular guns?"

"Apparently popular for killing humans, yes."

"Well, that's something."

"Yeah, but for some reason I think I'm back to believing him."

"Well, someone once told me you're very good at spotting a liar. Oh, wait, that was you."

"Very funny, Busier. I stand by my history of accurate truth detection with a few notable exceptions."

"Have you made any progress with him trusting you?"

"Zero."

"How about you, Joe?" she asked, turning to face me on the couch, putting both hands on mine. "Are you a trusting person?"

"Sometimes too trusting, I think."

"Uh oh, sounds like some serious scar tissue, Turner. Karen said your last relationship ended badly."

"It was a bit of a catastrophe."

"Can I ask what happened?"

"I made the mistake of getting involved with someone who was related to one of my cases."

"Eww. Sounds messy. Not the defendant, I hope?"

"God no, but it was a tire fire." I poured the last of the wine in her glass.

"Well, I promise," she said smiling, "I was nowhere near West Oakland at the time of the shooting."

"Good to know. So how about you? Any serious relationships in your past?"

"Yeah, well, the trip to Australia wasn't entirely career based."

"I'm picturing a tall and tan professional sailor with an irresistible accent. I want to punch him."

"Well, you're right about the accent, but that's it. And feel free to punch away."

Our conversation was interrupted by periodic episodes of kissing and touching that made me question the no-sex mandate. Still, I knew it had been the right call. We were learning about each other, inside and out. Between the first kiss and tonight's pronouncement, I had learned that she wasn't afraid to make a decision. She possessed a rapier wit and great listening skills, recalling details of Darnell's case. She also seemed to like it when I kissed her neck.

"So, I'm off to London on Friday for two weeks," she said when it was time to walk me to her door.

"Do you go often?"

"A few times a year so far. That's where our parent

company is based. Have you ever been?"

"Yes, I did a semester abroad in college. It's where I picked up the language."

She laughed. "What am I going to do without you for two weeks?"

"Well, I know I'll be thinking about what we'll do when you get back."

We kissed again, and I could have floated home.

****

The timing of Eddy's trip, if she had to go, couldn't have been better. Trial was not far off, and the Moore case needed my undivided attention. I had spent Thursday transcribing the interviews of Darnell and Bedrossian. I could have paid for them to be transcribed, but I had found that it helped me learn their content inside and out if I did it myself.

Now, in my quiet office I could think the case through. Ideally, rather than just telling the jury that Darnell wasn't the murderer, I would have an alternative explanation for the jury. The time honored SOMDI defense. Some other mother did it. Of course, that would require actual evidence, which, in turn would require Darnell to point me in the right direction.

Barring that, I would divide and conquer. Taken together, the evidence against Darnell was strong. His vehicle was used in the shooting, and he had all but admitted being in the area. He had motive to kill, advertised as it was by his Kill Cashtown cap. He had been caught with a gun that matched the caliber of the murder weapon and had been identified by an eyewitness as the shooter.

I would have to attack each piece of evidence individually. Anyone could have driven Darnell's car and committed the murder. In fact, what murderer in their right mind would use their own car? And while it was true that the Iceboyz had motive to kill Cashtowners, would the gang rely on Darnell, who hadn't committed a violent act in his life? Or was it more likely that one of the other violent gang members with the popular forty-caliber handgun had committed the crime? That left Bedrossian, who had failed to describe even one attribute of the shooter only minutes after seeing the assailant speed through his field of vision while facing the opposite direction.

I called Chuck for an update. "Hey, any progress on getting the surveillance tape from inside the E&J?"

"Not yet. Bedrossian says there may have been a problem with the camera."

"That sounds fishy."

"That's what I thought, too. Maybe see if we can get the D.A. interested?"

"Good idea. Also, don't forget to contact the dime store Indian."

"Okay, it's on my list. At least we know where to find him."

"Thanks. See ya."

Chuck's idea to see if Didery would subpoena the surveillance video from inside the E&J was a good one. While technically the defense had the power of subpoena, a District Attorney subpoena served by the police tended to get better results. First, though, I decided to call my new friend, Rocco, and ask him directly about the video.

"Rocco, if there's something your dad doesn't want seen, like selling alcohol to a minor, I understand. I'm willing to watch the video inside your store. I just need to do my due diligence."

"I understand. I don't think that's it, but I'll take a look at it. I think there's a problem with the formatting. I'm sure it's retrievable. Pops isn't exactly a genius when it comes to technology."

"Okay, thanks. And what do you know about the old guy who was sitting on the porch at your market when we visited?"

"Yeah, that's Elijah Jakes. He's sort of a fixture in the neighborhood. Actually used to own the E&J before he sold it to my dad."

"Is that his usual spot?"

"He's been there every day since I've been back. Good friends with my dad. He's actually learning my dad's language."

"I wonder if he was on the porch when the shooting happened?"

"I would be surprised if he wasn't. Want me to ask him?"

"That's okay, thanks. I think Chuck's going to speak to him."

As I was saying goodbye, Andy wandered in holding his face in his hands.

"What's new, partner?"

"I just got Ludlow'd," he muttered, rubbing at his temples. "Lost a summary judgment motion. Case dismissed in a case where damages were going to be mid-six figures."

"Ouch."

Andy's verb choice indicated his courtroom defeat had come at the hands of one Douglas Ludlow, renowned for his reputation as the least intelligent judge in the county. After managing to squeak by the bar exam on his third try, he had been hired by the District Attorney's Office and then rapidly appointed to the bench based on his father's considerable influence in California politics.

"Any chance to appeal?"

"Unlikely. Oh well. So much for early retirement," he said, pausing on his way out. "How's Eddy?"

"Out of the country for two weeks. Any feedback on my third date?"

"Besides your exceedingly small penis, no."

"Nice try, Andy. Hey, what language is spoken in Armenia?"

"Armenian? Is that a language? Why?"

"I need a translator."

A word-search showed the answer was Armenian and Russian. I found an Armenian interpreter through a translation service and sent them a copy of Bedrossian's 911 call. I spent the rest of the afternoon staring at the more than a hundred color photos of the crime scene, trying to re-enact the shooting in my mind. While I still didn't think Darnell killed Cleveland Barlow, there wasn't a shred of evidence to the contrary.

At six-thirty p.m., I rubbed my tired eyes and clicked to the last photograph in the file. It was a booking photo of the defendant, taken soon after his arrest. He looked young and scared.

On the drive home, Chuck called. "No luck with Elijah Jakes. I would have had a better chance with an actual wooden Indian. He literally walked off the porch and disappeared into the store when he saw me coming, then snuck out the back and left."

"Unbelievable. Chuck, we're officially in crisis mode. Trial is scheduled to start in a month, and we don't have a defense."

"You'll think of something."

"What? Like Jakes and Bedrossian decide to shoot the kid at the very instant Darnell is barreling though the intersection. Their shots go through the passenger window of Darnell's car, out the driver's window, somehow missing Darnell, and kill the victim?"

"I love it," he said, his laugh coming over the waves. "I'd pay to see you sell that to a jury with a straight face."

"Don't laugh. You may get the chance. See ya."

Despite my characterization of my theory as wacky, Bedrossian, the long-tormented market owner had crossed my mind as a possible suspect. It would explain his rush to blame someone else. Also, I wasn't sure his bullets would have had to travel though Darnell's windows. Maybe he could have shot over the top of the car, or slightly ahead of it.

But I would still have to explain the immense coincidence of the timing of Darnell's dash through the intersection, not to mention all the other evidence pointing to his guilt.

I got home with every intention of burning off my frustration with a run, but a ballgame was on and a few gin and tonics would have the same effect. I exchanged texts with Eddy, wishing she was with me on the recliner. At some point I realized I had forgotten to eat and slapped together a peanut butter sandwich. Soon, I stumbled off to bed, the Darnell Moore case flushed from my mind, at least for a night.

The morning was unkind, but after coffee and cold pizza, I was ready for a run, returning to find an email from Didery. Did this guy ever stop working? Attached to the email were the recorded jail calls of Darnell, from the first date of his incarceration to the present. I cringed. Not only was there a good chance there was something incriminating in the calls, the task of listening to the calls meant hours, even days of tedium. The fact that I could listen while watching a game or running helped, but still the task was one of my least favorites.

No matter how many times I warned my clients against talking about their case on the phone, it was astounding how many defenses had been torpedoed with an admission on the phone to a friend or loved one. Every inmate phone call was actually preceded by a recording. So often did inmates disregard the warning, my defense attorney friends had joked that the warning message should add, "Begin your confession at the sound of the tone."

One memorable client, accused of possession of a firearm, told his friend to be sure and "hide the, uh, biscuit in your car." Not surprisingly, when the gun was found in the car, the jury had cracked the code and convicted in less than thirty minutes.

I wanted to get through Darnell's calls so I could devote time to more important matters, like figuring out what in the hell I would tell the jury. Throughout the next week, his conversations with his mom and brother became the soundtrack for most of my waking hours.

Against all odds, by week's end, I had eavesdropped on roughly three quarters of the calls without hearing my client utter a single incriminating statement. For the most part, he continued to sound like the confident, upbeat kid who was sure he would be out of jail any day.

I was at my kitchen table paying bills when Eddy's name appeared on my phone. Not wanting to bother her on her trip, I had managed to only respond to her texts, though I'd been daydreaming about her more than I cared to admit to myself.

—*What's up, counselor? I've been thinking about you*—

—*Me too. Was just picturing you on a dig. I believe that's the terminology?*—

—*Yes. More impressive than your first comment about my field. "Wow. So like, digging." What were you picturing on the dig?*—

—*Nothing too specific. Just you in a hard hat and hot pink string bikini with a rolled-up map in one hand and a whip in the other*—

—*Lol. Yeah, not very specific at all. How'd you guess my dig attire?*—

—*Just lucky. How's the trip going?*—

—*Okay, lots of boring meetings but I love the city. I do miss you. Feel free to text me once in a while*—

—*Okay, I didn't want to bother you, but I will. I can't wait to see you*—

In the office on Monday, a ballistics report arrived in the mail. Pulling open the manila envelope, I braced for the news that Darnell's gun had been the murder weapon. It wouldn't be the first time one of my clients had been shot down by his own gun.

Juries love scientific evidence because it is visual and easy to understand. Every handgun is manufactured with its own unique rifling, which refers to the markings etched inside a firearm's barrel to impart a spin on the bullet for accuracy. The rifling leaves the same unique imprint on bullets. Similar distinctive markings are left on shell casings, the brass jacketing of the bullet that is expelled from the gun when fired.

Firearm examiners can test fire a suspect's weapon into a water recovery tank to obtain comparison bullets and shell casings, then compare them to those recovered from a crime scene under powerful microscopes. The report documented the bullets dug out of the front door of 454 Eighth Street. I flipped hurriedly through the lengthy report to the conclusion.

None of the 4 bullets examined were of sufficient quality for comparison purposes.

Surprisingly, only the bullets and none of the ten shell casings found in the street had been examined. Also, only the four bullets dug out of the front door and door frame had been recovered. The ten shell casings meant ten rounds had been fired. One left at the base of Cleveland Barlow's skull still left four bullets unaccounted for.

I double-checked the crime scene photos. The shell casings, which were ejected to the right of the handgun, were scattered within a radius of twelve feet near the middle of the street. I printed one wide angle photo and I drew a line from the front door where the bullets were recovered through the location of Barlow's body into the street.

As I suspected, the line ran to a location in the street just to the left of the shell casings. That meant that all the rounds were fired from roughly the same location. The bullets that missed Cleveland Barlow had lodged in the door. So where were the other five bullets?

Overall, I was pleased there was no ballistics match to Darnell's gun. On the other hand, I was certain

Didery wouldn't overlook testing the shell casings for long. I shut the file and tidied up my office for a meeting with a new client—a college friend whose son had been running a drug store out of his high school locker. My phone buzzed. It was Eddy.

—*Tell me something I don't know about you, Joe Turner*—

—*When I'm alone in my car, I sing off-key and practice impersonations. Your turn*—

—*I eat more peanut butter than any other food*—

—*Me too! Chunky?*—

—*You calling me chunky?*—

—*Ha-ha. No, and not plain either*—

Chapter Sixteen

I was born good but had grown progressively worse every year.—Harper Lee

Oakland, California 2006

The boys sat at the kitchen table, wondering what was going on. Cooked hotdogs with canned chili beans and potato chips sat on paper plates in front of them, along with cups of cold milk, items usually reserved for Dumbass' morning cereal. Damon eyed his hotdog, salivating.

"Eat up, boys. Your friend, Cheryl Swillinger is coming by for a home visit. Should be here soon."

Then it all made perfect sense. A visit from the social worker was behind the dinner. Damon smirked at Jesse across the table, but his twin was staring off into space again.

It had been three days since that awful night when Damon lay on the floor outside his brother's room. Jesse had barely said a word since. Damon stopped tapping on his door at night. He thought about telling Ms. Cheryl but he knew Jesse would never forgive him if they were separated again.

He had to do something.

Damon was about to squirt ketchup on his hotdog when Dumbass snatched it out of his hand. "You don't put ketchup on a hotdog, dummy. Here you go," he said, smothering the dog with mustard.

Damon stared at his ruined hotdog. He felt the tears coming. He didn't cry much, mainly because it always made Jesse cry, too. But sometimes things just built up in his head until there was no more room and the tears spilled over. Not today, he thought, wiping his nose on his sleeve. He wouldn't give Dumbass the satisfaction.

He'd wait until after dinner, after Happy Cheryl had asked more stupid questions, passed out candy, and went home. Then, he'd curl up on the floor with a blanket. He slept there now because his bed squeaked too. He'd lie there and let the tears spill over until his throbbing head pounded away the images of his brother suffering.

The next day was Saturday, and the boys found themselves pulling weeds in the lot behind the house. Dumbass had come outside in the hot sun for long enough to tell them where to take turns dumping a wheel barrel full of weeds in a ditch at the back of the property.

"You boys need to work smart," he said, sipping his beer then cooling his forehead with the icy can. "You gotta plan your work and work your plan." He smiled stupidly, proud of his saying.

"Plan your work and work your plan," Damon repeated after Dumbass was out of earshot. "That's probably the dumbest thing I've ever heard. Even for Dumbass, that's dumb."

Jesse looked up from his weeds. It looked to Damon like his twin was planning something but then he went on weeding.

"Hey Jess, you wanna run away from here?" he asked, nibbling on a raw onion he'd found in the yard.

Jesse looked up again. For the first time in a while, Damon felt his twin's steady focus. His eyes were bright and clear. "No, D, I don't want to run away," he said with deadly earnest. "I'm gonna kill him."

Chapter Seventeen

Since Eddy wouldn't return until Friday, the week dragged on with more jail calls echoing in my earbuds while I scoured the police reports, looking for a break in the case. Thursday morning found me in the master calendar department for a scheduled pretrial conference. Theoretically, it was an opportunity for the defense to negotiate a plea bargain. But for the Moore case, it was a date to let the judge know that there would be no settlement.

It was the reason why murder cases went to trial more often than other cases. Didery knew he had a strong case, so he had made clear that his best offer would be fifteen years to life in prison on a plea to second degree murder. Since Darnell had made clear on several occasions that he "wasn't feeling that", there was nothing to talk about.

"Hey, Joe," Jittery said, "I left some discovery at the front counter of our office for you."

"Okay, thanks." I wondered why he hadn't just brought it to court. "Is it particularly voluminous or...I was just wondering why you didn't bring it."

"Oh, uh, well, I prefer that you get it from the office. That way, you can sign for it and we can file stamp your signature. More of a, you know, reliable system, wouldn't you agree?"

"Yeah, and while you're at it," I wanted to tell him,

"maybe have the front desk get a urine sample and a DNA swab just in case someone has stolen my identity." But I dutifully signed for the reports at the D.A.'s Office. They turned out to fill a banker's box. I lugged it back to the office, inhaling a hotdog on the way.

At my desk, I opened the discovery box. The gunshot residue report was there, documenting the tests performed on the victim for the tiny particles that are deposited on the hands of someone who fires a firearm. I flipped to the conclusion: "There were no findings on either specimen." Both of Barlow's hands tested negative for gunshot residue.

Barlow may have been armed. If so, one of his fellow gang members would have likely taken his gun after the shooting. Still, the fact that he hadn't gotten off a shot made his murder all the more cowardly.

The remaining contents of the box consisted of hundreds of pages of police reports, all documenting shootings by the Cashtown and the Iceboyz gangs in the past year. I put it aside to read later, assuming the shootings would be used by Didery to solidify the gang-related motive for the murder.

My phone rattled on my desk.

—*Hi there. I'm flying back tomorrow. You free Saturday?*—

—*Yes! Safe flight*—

The phone was still in my hand when Chuck called.

"Hey, Chuck, what's new?"

"We got a break. An old friend from the Probation Department recognized our witness. He's a two-bit mook named William Wendell. Mainly into drugs and petty theft offenses. Hangs out at Bushrod, but he's due for a check-in with his probation officer today at two o'clock."

"Look at you, Chuck, getting all sleuthy on me."

"Yeah, well, even a blind squirrel finds an acorn once in a while."

"Well done! Pick me up whenever you're free?"

"See you in fifteen."

Chuck and I sat inside his bucket of bolts eating hotdogs, idling in front of the probation department, waiting for Wendell's arrival. Our plan was to catch him on his way out afterward. The fact that he wasn't in custody meant he had not been busted for driving the stolen car, so we had some leverage if we needed it.

At two-ten p.m., our guy was hustling inside the front door of the building, wearing the same St. Mark's T-shirt he had worn in the video. He emerged twenty minutes later, walking quickly away from the building, shoulders hunched, his hands jammed deep in the pockets of his jeans.

As he moved down the sidewalk toward Chuck's car, he looked this way and that, as if scanning for danger. As he neared, Chuck got out of his car. I crumpled my wrapper and did the same, regretting the second hotdog.

"Hey, can I bum a light?" Wendell asked Chuck in a raspy voice, holding a cigarette between his fingers.

"Sure. You're Wendell, right?" The young man peered over his cupped hand with startling green eyes, eyeing Chuck silently as he returned the lighter and frowned into a long drag. He appeared to be in his early twenties. His shabby clothing hung from a thin frame. Up close, his freckled face was lined and weathered from too much time in the sun.

"Who wants to know?"

"We're defending someone accused of murder and think you may be a witness."

He looked at Chuck, then me, digesting Chuck's answer, then pushed past us on the sidewalk, walking away.

"You're on Jennings' caseload, right?" Chuck called after him, referencing his probation officer.

Wendell stopped in his tracks five yards away. His head sunk to his chest, and he continued to face away from us for several seconds, rubbing his closely cropped blond hair with one hand. Finally, he turned and sauntered back to us, looking around, furtively. "Look, I don't need any trouble," he said, his face grimacing as he puffed his cigarette. "Meet me at Slim's," he said, gesturing to the hamburger spot down the block.

"Okay," said Chuck. "And we know about the car, so you need to be there."

"I'll be there," he said, tossing his cigarette on the sidewalk and walking away.

We watched him scurry off, head tucked between his shoulders and darting glances in all directions, as if afraid of his own shadow. "Well, we knew our witness wouldn't be the pope," I remarked, as we followed him across the street toward Slim's.

He took a seat at a corner table, his back to the wall. He was already ordering when we walked in. "So, you think I saw something," he said after we were seated, and the waitress had disappeared.

"Look, Wendell," I spoke up, noticing the pungent funk of body odor and pot for the first time. "We're not here to fuck around. We know you saw the shooting at Eighth and Maybeck. We need you to tell us what you saw. If not, we'll give the video of you driving the stolen car to your probation officer."

"Wow, the dweeb is playing hardball," he said sarcastically. He sat back and smiled, savoring his rare position of power. He sized us up for several seconds, looking back and forth between us, wearing the seasoned smirk of a street hustler. This kid had been around, for sure, and he was considering all his options.

"Look, assholes," he said, eyes darting around the room. "Do I look like a fucking idiot? This is Oakland. I grew up here. If I play ball and identify some gang member, my ass is dead. You think I can't do six months in jail? That ain't shit." He put two bony elbows on the table and rubbed his forehead with both hands. I got the sense he was thinking about being in jail, away from his drugs.

"Tell you what," Chuck said, "I have a photograph of our client. If you look at it and tell us he's the shooter, you'll never hear from us again. But if you know he wasn't the shooter, then we'll need you to cooperate."

He stared at the table, rubbing a hand over his scarred knuckles. "Cooperate how?" he asked, shaking his head, his face etched in dread.

"You'll be subpoenaed to testify about what you witnessed."

He put his face in his hands and sighed deeply, then looked up when the restaurant door opened. I got the sense he could list its occupants from memory. "Okay, listen. I'll look at your picture, but I ain't eye-deeing nobody. I ain't no snitch."

Chuck took the booking photograph of Darnell from his shirt pocket and laid it on the table. Wendell sat up straight and looked over our heads, his green orbs scanning the room. He glanced down at the photo for less than a second before pushing it toward us. "Ain't him."

"Just to clarify," I said, feeling a surge of adrenaline, "you're saying—"

"He ain't the shooter," he spat between clenched teeth, looking me in the eye.

"Here we are, young man." The waitress arrived with a double cheeseburger and a plate of home fries. "Will you gentlemen be dining with us?"

"No, thank you. We're going to get this for him and be on our way," I said, wanting to get away from the odor.

"Suit yourself," she said on a shrug. "You can pay up at the cash register."

We exchanged contact information with Wendell while he eyed his food.

"You don't suppose you could, uh, spare any cash?" he asked tentatively as we got up to leave.

"Sorry," I answered, wishing we could. "You're a potential witness."

"Well, do you think I could maybe order more food?" he asked hopefully, talking through a mouthful of cheeseburger."

"Sure. Enjoy it."

Back in his car, Chuck made some notes from the interview on the well-worn spiral notepad he always kept in his back pocket. "Now we're getting somewhere," he said, closing the pad.

"He sure didn't take long to look at the photo."

"I noticed that too. Seemed certain. And boy was he nervous."

"More nervous than a long-tailed cat in a room full of rockin' chairs," Chuck added, thickening his southern drawl as we pulled away from the curb.

"Your supply is endless, isn't it?"

"I got more than you can shake a stick at."

"Wendell does make Didery seem placid by comparison. Years of drug use, you think?"

"Maybe just raised on concrete. Life on the streets of Oakland will do that to you."

After Chuck dropped me back at the office, I wrote a memo to the file about our interview with Wendell and drove home with a new outlook on the case. I knew we were a long way from Wendell providing helpful testimony in court. Just getting him to court would be a challenge. Still, things were looking up.

I worked out, made pasta for dinner, and watched a ballgame, with thoughts of tomorrow's date with Eddy dancing in and out of my mind. Despite my declaration to the contrary, I was certain my anxiety would make a strong appearance at some point. For now, though, I sipped a glass of Pinot Noir and dozed off, thinking of her faded jeans, infectious laugh, and whiffs of jasmine and fresh linens.

With no courtroom obligations on Friday, I organized the ever-expanding Darnell Moore file and I played nine holes with Matt Eisner, my former mentor in the D.A.'s office. He had been a good friend and colleague of my father. Twenty-five years later, we were playing golf once a month, with the loser buying the pitcher of beer.

"How goes the Moore homicide?" he asked, as I

lined up a putt on the last hole.

"First, you're not going to distract me," I said, eyeing my seven-foot putt. "This is for the win. And second, why would you refer to it as the Moore homicide? No respect for the presumption of innocence."

"Okay, what would you call it?" he asked in the middle of my backswing and watched as my putt skirted the edge of the hole.

"Your cheating knows no bounds. And of course I'd call it the Barlow homicide, out of respect for the victim."

He lined up his own putt to win the match, grinning with one eye on me. "Don't worry," I said with mock indignation, "I would never stoop so low as to talk in your backswing."

I cleared my throat instead, and we split the cost of the pitcher.

After a restful night's sleep, my phone rattled on my nightstand.

—*Drinks this evening? There's a great dive bar near my place*—

—*Sounds great. Can't wait to see you*—

****

Even as I climbed the steps to her front door, I was excited but confident and serene. This was weird. Momentarily, I contemplated being nervous because I wasn't nervous.

On each of our three previous meetings, the first sight of her beauty had caught me off-guard. As I stood there, gazing at her now in her doorway, I wondered if it would ever go away.

She was smiling at me, wearing a T-shirt knotted at

her waist, linen pants with a draw string, and blue canvas sneakers.

We hugged, a long embrace before we kissed. "I really missed you, Joe."

"Don't act so surprised," I joked. "I have a way of worming my way into your heart."

"Sounds sort of disgusting, but I know what you mean."

We held hands on the walk to Bill and Nick's, a neighborhood bar in the heart of Rockridge. On the way, I noticed for the first of many times the looks I got when I was with her. Other guys on the street would stare at her, which was to be expected. Then they would look at me, almost certainly thinking something like, "How can I be like that guy so I can be with someone like that?" Or perhaps, more like, "Him? Are you kidding me?" I didn't really care.

Over Dark and Stormies, we talked about her trip and our favorite parts of London. I was beginning to realize that she was rising quickly in the company, recently promoted to the grandiose title of "Vice President of the Americas."

"The Americas. How very arcanely British. How does it feel to be the V.P. of entire continents?"

"Pretty damn good. Central America is a pain once in a while, though. Actually, the lecture in London made me miss academia. I think I'll get a resume out to some colleges. Speaking of work, how's Darnell's case coming along."

"A bit better." I told her about the meeting with the latest witness.

"You know," I said finishing my second drink, "given how you handled our first kiss, I was sort of surprised you didn't decide to meet me at the door today in a nighty."

"Don't think it didn't cross my mind." She gestured at my empty glass. "You want another?"

"No, thanks. I have my, um, performance to think of."

"I'm assuming you're referring to the scrabble game we have planned later?"

"Of course."

We walked back to her home arm in arm as the sun began to dip, casting a glow on our path as we turned east and uphill. She leaned back against me at her door, pressing her curves into me. I held her there, smelling her hair.

Inside, she led me into the bedroom by my belt buckle. She lit two candles on either side of her bed and closed the shades. She removed something from behind her head and shook sandy blonde curls past her shoulders to her breasts, bursting beneath the blue T-shirt. I stepped out of my shoes, prying them off with my toes so I could keep watching her.

I started to unbutton my shirt. "Wait, am I misreading this?" I asked, playfully.

"No more jokes, Turner," she whispered, pulling her shirt over her head.

Then our bodies and lips met, kissing gently at first, then with eager tongues, breathing each other in with short breaths. Our hands were on each other now, mine moving down past the small of her back, caressing her curves over the smooth linen pants, pulling her firm body against me. Fingernails traced over my bulge as I found the drawstring, her pants falling to the floor.

She unbuckled my belt, pulling me to the bed,

where she sat looking up at me with pouty blue eyes. She flipped her hair behind her shoulders. Her hands slid down my thighs, springing me free. Then I felt her soft mouth around me, a murmured groan escaping my lips. "Eddy, wait," I gasped, feeling the first surge of ecstasy building.

She sucked hard once more before letting go, slipping out of her panties as she reclined on her bed. I lay atop her, kissing her lips, then moving down to her supple, round breasts. She was panting now as I trailed kisses down her stomach, my hands on her hips, feeling them grind against me.

"Joe," she gasped, and I felt her fingers under my chin, gently moving my face back up toward hers. "I want you," she whispered between pants, guiding me into her slowly. My hands pressed up from the bed, her hands on my hips as I arched into her. Her lips parted in a delicate gasp of pleasure as I began to thrust harder, her hips rocking under me to our shared rhythm.

She pulled me down to her, her nails on the back of my shoulders as I nuzzled through blonde waves, tasting her soft neck. She straightened her thighs against mine, and I pressed into her firm breasts, both desperate for total contact between our bodies. Our rhythm quickened. Our panting bodies writhed as one, finally exploding in ecstasy, then collapsing together.

Chapter Eighteen
Shoot all the blue jays you want, if you can hit 'em, but remember it's a sin to kill a mockingbird.—Harper Lee

Oakland, California 2006

"Plan your work. Work your plan." He recited the mantra over and over as he strode purposefully toward the house. They were working in the back again, this time digging holes for fenceposts. He had told his twin he was going for a drink of water from the hose at the side of the house.

He waited eight days for his opportunity. Eight long days and eight horrible nights. He knew there was a good chance that Dumbass would be asleep, liking as he did to nap on weekends in the late afternoon. And there he was, as he approached the sliding glass door, lying on his back on the recliner, snuffling that sickening snore. One hand rested on his belly, the other hung to the floor where a can of beer was sweating on the hardwood.

He knew his precious barbell would be there where he kept it, against the wall next to the cinderblock and plywood shelves where he kept his DVDs with pictures of naked people on them. Bending at the waist, he carefully rolled the foot-long weight from the wall. Then, placing his small hands between the black metal disks on the cool chrome bar, he lifted, his back bowing above the weight. It was heavier that he imagined, but he managed to straighten and bring the weight to his chest. All the physical labor had made his slender arms hard and wiry.

"Plan your work. Work your plan," he whispered to himself.

He balanced on rubbery legs, struggling to control his breathing, edging close to the blue corduroy of the recliner. The next part would be tricky. He needed to jostle Dumbass awake. It was risky, but he needed to see the fear in his face.

"Work your plan," he whispered again.

Then he bent his knees and hoisted the barbell above his head like an axe, one weight in front of the other. His arms quivered under the strain as he nudged the beefy arm that hung to the floor with his knee. The big man stirred slightly but didn't awaken. Another nudge with his knee. His shoulders were burning now. Finally, the eyes were opened, staring expressionless for a few seconds before recognition began to wash over his face. The eyes narrowed into a frown, then widened slowly. It was the look of fear he needed.

His quivering arms brought the weight down with all his strength, the awful face below him disappearing behind black metal with a dull crack. Then he was raising the weight again glancing down at the face, now red and gurgling. The weight was lighter above his head now, crashing down again then lifting to reveal more blood and distortion. His small chest was heaving but he couldn't stop. Not yet.

"Work! Your! Plan!" He blew out the words in heavy breaths, one for each strike.

The face disappeared slowly; the outline of its features barely visible now as the weight found a softer target with every blow. Finally, the face he hated was gone. The bloody barbell thudded to the floor. He picked up the cell phone off the coffee table and bent at the waist, his hands on his knees, catching his breath. His vision blurred by tears, he collapsed to his knees and dialed 911 with small shaking fingers.

Chapter Nineteen

On Monday afternoon, I appeared at the arraignment on the new drug case, then sat on a bench in the hallway outside the clerk's office, where courtroom assignments for trials were posted a month prior to the first day of trial. As I waited to find out which judge would preside over the Moore case, my thoughts drifted to Eddy. On Saturday, we had held each other for hours talking and laughing before getting up to eat peanut butter sandwiches. In the morning, we had made love again, then walked a block to get coffee.

"Coffees for Joe and Eddy? Joe and Eddy," the barista had called out over the din of the customers, bringing a smile to our faces. I couldn't stop thinking of her—her smile, her wit, her body, the way she made me feel.

The trial assignment sheet appeared on the glass door of the clerk's office, taped from the inside. I traced down the list of trials, listed alphabetically, until my finger stopped on Darnell Moore, then across the ledger to the right. I blinked in disbelief. The trial would be heard by none other than the tower of incompetence himself, Douglas Ludlow.

For years, Ludlow had been stuck hearing traffic and small claims cases, where his ineptitude could do the least damage. Recently though, he started making noises about handling more serious matters. Finally, the presiding judge relented, assigning him civil cases. Now, having assuredly made a mess of things there, he had been cast out by the civil division. I had heard rumors that he would be assigned criminal cases but giving him a homicide case was unconscionable.

"Hi, Joe." The voice over my shoulder took a second to register as I contemplated the bad news.

"Oh, hi, Cheryl," I said, finally turning around. "Sorry. How's my favorite social worker?" I'd met Cheryl Swillinger when I was a young D.A. assigned to the juvenile division.

"Work is as depressing as ever, but I'm engaged!" she said, flashing a ring as she hustled down the hallway.

"Congrats, even though you're marrying a D.A.," I called after her.

My eyes returned to the assignment sheet, hoping I had read it wrong, but no luck.

Later that afternoon, the assignment would be formalized in the master calendar department at a readiness conference. I called Matt Eisner. As second in command at the D.A.'s Office, he might have the juice to get the case re-assigned.

"Hey, Matt. What the fuck. Dudlow for the Moore case?"

"Yeah, I saw that. Brutal."

"Matt, we both know he'll be way out of his depth. Does he know it's a homicide case?"

"I doubt if he's bothered to read the assignment list. He's currently at a political fundraiser, schmoozing with the same idiots who put him on the bench to begin with."

"Anything you can do? This is a fucking joke."

"Not a chance, Joe. Sorry. He's whined for years and finally got his way."

I sighed. "Okay, thanks." I grabbed a hotdog from the stand outside the courthouse and walked into the chaotic master calendar department. The bailiff let me in the lockup to speak to Darnell.

"Hey, Mr. Turner, have you seen my mom in the courtroom?" It was the first time he had greeted me without a smile.

"No, they haven't let family members in yet."

"If she comes, I need you to tell her to be careful. Some people in here are thinking I'm going to snitch, …just tell her to watch herself." His voice was shaky.

"Will do."

"Also, do I have to appear in the courtroom?"

"No, I can waive your appearance. Listen, Darnell, PC is an option for you in there," I said, getting up to go.

"No, I'll be cool," he said, forcing a smile.

Entering protective custody, or "PC" was a big step for an inmate who grew up in Oakland. The protection of being housed separately from the general population was thought to be its only benefit. Given the logistics of housing, there were fewer privileges and free time. More importantly, it was tantamount to an admission of snitching, which would stay with you forever, in or out of custody.

Back in the courtroom, Chuck was there to drop off subpoena returns. "Moore's friends are here again, mean-mugs in place."

"Department 11 is now is session. Please be seated." The bailiff's baritone quieted the courtroom as Judge Kramer took the bench with his robe open, wearing khakis and an oxford. A former Public Defender, Kramer was smart, fair, and known for an absolute intolerance of bullshit.

"My reporter has been at it all morning. She won't be reporting this unless anyone has an objection." With that, the judge began calling the calendar, assigning cases for trial to begin in one month's time.

"May it please the Court, Nathaniel Winston Didery for the People of the State of California, Your Honor," announced the prosecutor as if addressing the House of Lords. "The People announce ready for trial, Your Honor."

The judge raised one eyebrow above his reading glasses. "Did I mention we weren't on the record?" he said under his breath, smiling.

"Joe Turner for Mr. Moore, Your Honor. I'll waive his appearance. Ready for trial. May we approach briefly." I didn't expect Judge Kramer to change the assignment, but I had to try.

The judge covered the microphone as Didery, and I arrived at the bench. "Joe, I'm pretty sure I know what this is about. Unfortunately, I can't help you."

"I figured, Judge. It's just that it's a homicide case," I said, hearing myself whine.

"I understand. Mr. Didery, your position?"

"Your Honor," Didery began, rod up his ass firmly in place, "I don't believe it's appropriate for me to weigh in on this matter."

Judge Kramer blinked slowly. "Sorry, Joe, you got the short straw. My hands are tied."

"Okay. Thanks, Judge."

Didery and I retreated to our podiums. "People v. Moore," the judge announced. "Trial assigned to

Department 27, Judge Ludlow. June 7, nine a.m."

I was thinking of Eddy again on the walk to my car through the dark courtroom parking lot when the three young men I'd seen in court suddenly appeared from the shadows and moved into my path.

"Yo bitch-ass client best hold his muthafuckin' mudd, yo. He about to get wrecked," said the short one in the middle, spitting out the words from under the flat brim of a blue Kansas City cap.

Finding little comfort in the fact that I was neither a Cashtown member nor my bitch-ass client, I took a big step in retreat. "I can tell you that Darnell has no intention of—"

"Shut the fuck up, snitch-piece," he barked, and moved towards me, gesturing with one hand inches from my chest, the other inside his pea coat. "I'll cap your ass, too, for shits."

Having obtained a masters in street lingo over the past ten years, I knew that he had warned Darnell against snitching and had threatened to shoot me, the mouthpiece for snitches, just for fun. I stepped back again, this time silently with my open hands facing him, the international symbol for "Please don't fucking cap my ass."

The aspiring rapper continued. "Tell bitch-ass D to keep names out his mouth or I'll kite his ass. Back door parole coming, know what I sayin'?" Then, turning to go, he added, "If you a dump truck and he gotta do all day, then he gotta do all day, yo."

"Snitches get stiches, yo," the one on Pea Coat's right chimed in, earning a glaring rebuke from the leader, I assumed for his unimaginative comment that closed the curtain on the performance.

Again, I knew very well what Pea Coat had referred to. He could order a hit on Darnell from outside jail using the kite system—a network of passing "kites" or notes inside the jail, usually with the cooperation of prison guards. "Back door parole" was the humorous but dark term for dying in prison. He added that if I were "a dump truck" or an incompetent attorney and Darnell had to "go all day" or serve life in prison, then he would just have to do exactly that.

****

In the following weeks before the trial, I holed up in my home office, also known as my dining room table, outlining cross examinations, clipping video, and drafting *in limine* motions.

Eddy and I had seen each other twice more since our first night together, each date ending in her bed, each time better than the last. Now motivated to look better naked, I was running and working out daily, finding the exercise a welcome break from the trial preparation. Currently, she was in Los Angeles for a wedding. We'd texted frequently.

—*If you need me to jump out of a cake for the bachelorette party, remember I'm available*—

—*Really, is that a side hustle of yours?*—

—*That and underwear modeling?*—

—*Lol. Thanks anyway but I think I'll keep you for myself*—

—*How does the bridesmaid dress look?*—

—*Every bit as bad as I predicted. Who chooses purple? We look like giant grapes*—

—*You aren't exactly shaped like a grape*—

—*Off to the rehearsal dinner. I miss you*—

—*Miss you too*—

I noticed a voicemail forwarded from my office and listened.

"Mr. Turner, oh God, Mr. Turner, please help me." It was the quaking voice of a hysterical Glenda Moore, Darnell's mom. "The jail called and Darnell was attacked. Oh, God." She paused to sob. "He's in the infirmary but they won't give me any other information. Please help me. Please, Mr. Turner."

I showered, changed, and drove to the jail, calling Mrs. Moore on the way with a promise to report back on Darnell's condition. After my parking lot visit from the Iceboyz, I had reported the threat on Darnell to the watch commander at the jail. Realistically, I knew if Darnell was a target, there was not much the guards could do to protect him.

Seeing inmates in the infirmary was less of an ordeal than regular visits. Since the pandemic, the jail had begun moving the hospitalized inmates to an interview room at the front of the jail, partitioned with heavy glass and equipped with telephones.

As I waited for Darnell's arrival, I considered his impossibly bleak predicament and felt sorry for my client. He could continue to refuse to name the shooter and likely spend the rest of his life in prison. Or he could snitch, and if the D.A. believed him, accept a plea bargain that would still have him in custody for at least a couple decades, time made infinitely worse by a daily fear of being killed. And oh, by the way, even if he has decided not to snitch, the gang may kill him before the trial anyway just in case he changed his mind.

He was rolled into the interview room in a wheelchair. Remarkably, a smile played at the corners of his mouth.

"What happened, Darnell?"

"Got shanked by some punk." He shrugged, his right hand subconsciously holding an area below his left ribs. "That's all."

"Well, obviously, your family is very worried. I really think you should consider entering protective custody."

He smirked and shook his head slowly, as if to say, "You'll never understand."

Switching gears, I told Darnell about finding Wendell and asked if he had thought about testifying in his trial. Generally, I believed it was in a defendant's best interest to testify. Otherwise, the jury would no doubt consider his silence as evidence of guilt, questioning why someone accused of a crime would not take the opportunity to deny it.

In most homicide cases, a defendant's testimony was a bad idea because on cross examination, their normally extensive record of past violence could be recited to the jury. Darnell didn't have this problem. In fact, his lack of any prior violence was a plus. On the other hand, I shuddered at the prospect of him sticking to his complete denial tale while attempting to explain away the mountain of evidence to the contrary.

"Nah, I don't think me testifying would go very well," he said glumly. He sighed deeply and shook his head again, smiling a sad smile. I had seen it too many times. The yoke of custody was taking its toll, its weight slowly wearing away his youth, quietly dimming his outlook and suffocating his hope.

"Hey," he said, as my door buzzed open, "could you, uh..." His voice trailed off as he stared at the floor. He looked up with moist eyes. "Could you tell my mom I love her?"

"I sure will. Take care, Darnell."

****

A week before the start of trial, I was in Didery's office to finalize discovery and share statement transcriptions. We had exchanged witness lists earlier, mine now including Wendell.

I noted that Didery had included Rocco Bedrossian in his. He probably planned on using him to authenticate the video tape obtained from his father's store. It was a shameless ploy. Didery knew that if given the chance I would stipulate, or agree to the videotape's authenticity, but he would much rather have the handsome guy serving his country be part of his case.

"So, I ran the rap sheet on your eyewitness," the D.A. said, smiling across his desk at me, failing to contain his glee.

"Yeah? Extensive, I'm assuming?"

"Fairly. He has a prior murder conviction as a juvenile."

I was shocked with the news. "What? Murder?"

"Yeah," Didery nodded, opening a folder, and scanning its contents. "William Jesse Wendell. Born July 7, 1997. Apparently killed his foster dad with a barbell when he was ten."

Chapter Twenty
With him, life was routine; without him, life was unbearable.—Harper Lee

Oakland, California 2006

Jesse was sitting calmly on a foot stool next to the recliner when the police arrived, his white T-shirt splattered in crimson. He had already hugged Damon goodbye. They had said goodbye before, but they both knew this one was different.

Damon sat on the couch, tears streaming down his face. He wanted to say something to Jesse before he was led away by the police. He wanted to say he was going to find themselves a good home where they could play on baseball teams and eat hot pizza from a restaurant and watch cartoons on Saturdays. But he knew it wouldn't help. He knew what his twin was thinking. He always did.

Chapter Twenty-One

"This is starting to piss me off, Chuck," I said, turning on the blue tooth on the way back from the driving range. "I'm starting to think the Bedrossians are playing games." It's not like I thought the store video would show old man Bedrossian hiding his submachine gun under the counter. At this point, it was just the principle of the matter.

"I know what you mean, Joe."

"I'll have Didery drop a subpoena on them."

"Any luck speaking to Mr. Jakes?"

"Actually, I just got off the phone with him. He's not exactly enthusiastic, but he's agreed to an interview in your office after court on Tuesday."

"Great."

"And I served Wendell with a subpoena for trial. He was higher than a hawk's nest but promised to appear."

"I have my doubts."

"Me too, but the threat of jail can be very persuasive."

"See you tomorrow."

We were two days from the start of trial, and the video was one of several minor loose ends bothering me. I also hadn't heard back from the Armenian translator, and there was no sign of the ballistic results on the shell casings. It still seemed inconceivable that

Didery had neglected to have them tested, but I couldn't ask him for fear he would be spurred into action.

—Are we still on for tonight? Can't wait to finally see your place—

Shit! Eddy's text caught me off guard. I hadn't cleaned in…well, ever.

—Absolutely—

—Is 6 ok? I can bring a pizza.—

It was four-thirty p.m. Maybe enough time.

—Sure. I'll order the pizza. Great place in my neighborhood—

I pressed send as I walked in my front door. A quick survey told me there was not nearly enough time. The cleaning crew came once every two weeks—a mandate by my mother after her first visit. They kept the place clean enough. I just had an issue with tidiness.

I prioritized and got to work. Clean sheets on the bed. Suits hung up. All clothing not in drawers, which appeared to be three quarters of my wardrobe, piled in the laundry room. I'd sort dirty from clean later. Same with the towels strewn about the bathroom and bedroom.

After the third trip to the recycling bin, I was ready to admit a flaw in my extensive reliance on paper plates. The plastic blue container was full, and I still had four grocery bags filled to the brim. I looked around the neighborhood from the side of my house. Satisfied the coast was clear, I dumped the remaining bags in the black container reserved for garbage.

Sue me, recycling fascists.

Next, I vacuumed out the recliner, collecting a startling amount of food. Apparently, the big chair had been a bridge too far for the cleaners. I wiped down the kitchen then began collecting glasses and cups from every room in the house. I had entirely too many of these. Perhaps a move to plastic was in order, but then again, the recycling issue—a decision for another time.

I raked beer bottles off various tabletops throughout the house and made three more trips to the garbage bin. Alley came inside and promptly sprinted back out, clearly freaked out by her changed environment.

I caught sight of my embarrassing five-pound weights. What, Joe, the seven and a half pounders were too heavy? I rolled up my exercise mat and stowed it with the weights in, where else, the laundry room. Note to self: Do not open laundry room door. From there, my efforts were mainly cosmetic. The liquor bottles back in their cabinet for the first time in years. Alley's bowl off the kitchen counter. At least thirty editions of the New York Times out to the garbage.

I looked around. It definitely had that only-recently-cleaned-up look, and the dining room table I used as my desk remained covered six inches deep in case files, books, and sports pages. That would have to remain, as most of the case files were active, and I had a good idea of the contents of the various piles.

I showered and hustled to the corner grocery. Eddy was teaching me about wine, and I wanted to impress her. She pulled into my drive as I was walking up my stoop.

"I love this neighborhood," she said. "And what a cute house!" I sensed relief in her voice. After seeing her digs, I had tried to lower expectations as much as possible.

"Thanks. C'mon in."

She walked in after me and took it in. "It's charming," she said holding back a laugh. "And there's your recliner, as advertised. What is this decorating style, Joe?"

"I'd say sort of a post-modern rustic grunge."

"Looks like you've had a few working lunches lately," she said, gesturing to the buried dining room table.

"Such a smart ass, Ms. Busier."

"Just getting started early on my campaign to shame you into buying some furniture. It could be a really great place." She kissed me after I had set down the grocery bag.

"What's in the bag?"

"Wine. Trying to impress you."

"Oh wow. Port Lancer Pinot. This is good stuff, Joe. Very well done."

"Thanks. I was torn between that and a strawberry wine from Kentucky."

"Can I get the tour?"

"Sure," I said leading her down the hallway. "Spare bedroom on the right. I assume that's where you'll be sleeping."

"We'll see how good the pizza is. I was going to bring one from Zach's."

"Laundry room is there. I wouldn't open that. And in here is where the magic happens," I said, pushing open my bedroom door.

She spanked me. "Very funny."

"I'll order the pizza," I said walking back to the kitchen. "Hey, want to see the Moore video?"

"Absolutely." I started my video on my laptop and left it on the dining room table.

We talked about the trial over pizza and wine. She had a great memory for facts and seemed to know the case as well as I.

"So, from the photos, it sounds like Darnell is in a gang, but is it weird that he's never committed a violent crime?"

"It is weird, and it's one of the reasons I can't see him murdering someone. I have a feeling he's all hat and no cattle." Chuck was rubbing off on me.

"Probably the reason why the gang is afraid he'll snitch."

"Exactly."

"The D.A.'s theory will likely be that this shooting was Darnell's test to officially be in the gang."

"Yes, I've heard the Iceboyz have very high standards for admittance. Letters of recommendation are important."

I laughed. "You are the second funniest person I know."

"Yeah?" she said sliding closer to me on the couch.

"Seriously, Eddy," I said taking both her hands in mine. "Thank you for caring about my work. It means a lot to me."

Her azure eyes rested on mine for several seconds. "This is pretty good."

"Yeah," I said unable to contain my smile.

"You know, the tour of your bedroom was pretty brief," she whispered, her hand sliding to my thigh. "I think I need another."

"Does this mean the pizza was up to your standards?"

She tilted her head under my face and kissed my neck as I inhaled a rush of arousal. "No," she said, kissing me again, "I just want you."

****

I sat at my computer early on Monday morning, eating cold pizza and daydreaming about Eddy. Coffee and the Sunday paper in bed had been followed by another round of slow, warm rhythm, our familiar bodies communing on their own, seeking and revealing with nuance, texture, and changing pressures. Subtle glances and carefree murmurs of desire escaping moist mouths, heightening the ache beyond our quivering reach before we had surrendered together in tangled bliss.

I shook myself from my sensual trance and refocused on my task. I had decided to draft a Motion to Suppress the gun found in Darnell's house. Like most search warrants, the warrant had authorized the search of Darnell's bedroom as well as common areas in the home. Other bedrooms were off-limits.

The gun had been found in a shoe box inside a hallway closet. Photos of the gun and the shoe box revealed the closet also contained a vacuum cleaner and what appeared to be several women's jackets. If I could convince Ludlow that the closet was not a common area but instead the private closet of Darnell's mom, he might exclude the gun from evidence. The motion was not based on sound legal theory, but with Dudlow making the decision, anything could happen.

I printed the motion, dressed, and decided to walk to court. Never one to work harder than he had to, I knew Dudlow would spend the first day essentially planning the trial's schedule, so I stepped out into the late spring air carrying only the Motions *in limine* around my shoulder in my leather satchel. With the smell of fresh-cut grass in the air, the day reminded me of the promise of baseball's opening day. All of the teams were undefeated, and hope was in the air. Darnell, in the eyes of the law, was innocent, at least for now.

As I rode the elevator to the fifth floor, I resolved to stop referencing the judge's nickname in my mind, lest I call him Dudlow in person. Inside Department 27 at eight-fifty a.m., I quickly scanned the courtroom for Jesse. He had been subpoenaed for today. It was likely an early hour for him, but still I wasn't optimistic.

I was not in the least surprised to find Didery sitting ramrod straight at the counsel table. Three boxes —what I assumed was his entire case file—were stacked to his right. A clean legal pad was directly in front of him on the counsel table. Above it one black pen rested, centered and precisely parallel with the notepad's top.

We exchanged greetings, and I took my seat to his left at the counsel table. We both wore dark blue suits and white shirts, his rigid with extra starch. After twenty minutes of waiting, I took out my motions. "Here you go, Nathan," I said, sliding copies of my motions down the table. "We may as well have something to read while we wait."

"Um, I would rather, uh, wait until you've filed them with the clerk. That way we can exchange file-stamped copies, wouldn't you agree?"

"Uh, sure." This guy must squeeze out shits the size of marbles. After another ten minutes of sitting in silence, I carried my motions to the clerk's desk with a wry smile. "Morning, Cherlynn. Apparently, I need to file my motions."

"Hi, Joe," she said, rolling her eyes. A statuesque African American woman in her forties, Cherlynn Robinson was regarded as the most competent clerk in the courthouse. Her pairing with Ludlow was not an accident. Many times, I had witnessed her deftly "reminding" the judge of things that had never crossed his mind in the first place.

As I waited for my motions to be file stamped, I heard a door close, signaling the judge's arrival in his chambers, nearly a half hour late. Seconds later, the clerk's phone rang. "Gentlemen, the judge will see you now."

I followed Didery into chambers. It was richly furnished with burgundy leather sofa and chairs atop a Persian rug. The dark wood-paneled walls were decorated with golf memorabilia and photos of the judge with various political luminaries. Behind his desk, covering most of the wall, hung an enlarged photo of the judge taking the oath at his swearing-in ceremony. The shot taken from below, a soaring tribute to the jurist's grandeur.

A large, ponderous man in his late fifties with longish hair of a suspicious shade of auburn, I had never seen him out of his robe, which he kept zipped tight, his fleshy jowls spilling over his collar. He sat at his ornately carved cherry wood desk, barely looking up from a law book as we entered.

"Good morning, Judge," said Didery about to approach the desk for a handshake.

With a dramatic wave, Ludlow stopped Didery cold, a traffic cop's signal as his eyes remained glued to the page. I was skeptical about the level of the judge's concentration, having heard him enter his chambers less

153

than twenty seconds ago. Ludlow slowly took off his reading glasses and held their edge to his lips while reclining in his massive leather chair to frown at the ceiling.

"Well this was quite a show," I thought to myself, now thoroughly convinced he was acting. Didery and I stood awkwardly for several more seconds as the judge did his best to impress us with his spoon-bending concentration.

"Fascinating reading," he finally said. "Truly fascinating legal concept. Sorry fellows, I tend to get wrapped up in the law."

"What was it, Judge?" I couldn't resist.

"What's that?"

"What was the fascinating legal concept?" I asked, hoping I sounded genuine.

"Oh, uh, no matter. Let's get to the matter at hand," the judge replied gruffly, suddenly in a hurry. "I assume you have some *in limine* motions to file today?"

Didery and I explained that we both had standard boilerplate motions. In the way of actual decisions, the judge would have to exercise his dizzying intellect to decide which of Darnell's prior theft convictions would be admissible should he decide to testify and which of the grisly photos of the victim's dead body would be excluded as more prejudicial than probative. The only hearing required would be in ruling on my motion to exclude the gun.

"Gentlemen, I expect the gun issue to be fully briefed," the judge said with emphasis. This was code for, "In your briefs, please assume I know nothing about the law," which I had done.

"Yes, Your Honor," Didery and I replied in unison,

exchanging knowing looks.

"Any issues with witness availability?"

I explained that I was still tracking down an Armenian translator and would add him to my witness list as soon as I knew his name.

"Okay, I'll hear the motion tomorrow morning, then we can begin jury selection. I'll be on the bench to put this on the record in a few minutes."

Back in the courtroom, Darnell had taken his seat at the counsel table, watched closely by the bailiff, Deputy Hartag, a short man who took his job of protecting the public very seriously. Nicknamed "Hard Ass", he sat behind the defendant at his desk, his hand resting on his holstered pistol.

I was happy to see Darnell dressed in civilian clothing for the trial. As I had requested, his mother had supplied khaki pants, dress shoes, and a blue oxford shirt. With a new closely cropped haircut, he looked like he belonged behind a rental car counter. The bulky bandage underneath his shirt would not be noticed by the jury.

He looked warily around the courtroom, squinting under the fluorescent lights. "So, did that witness show up?"

"Doesn't look like it. The judge will issue a warrant for his arrest, and hopefully we can find him." Darnell shook his head with a look of disgust.

Judge Ludlow took the bench. "Good morning. We are here for the People of the State of California versus Darnell Moore. Appearances, please."

"Nathaniel Winston Didery for the People of the State of California, Your Honor."

"Joe Turner for Mr. Moore."

"Gentlemen," the judge began with confidence, "We have discussed the trial schedule in chambers. Counsel are to file their motions, which I will rule on tomorrow. Jury selection to begin tomorrow." Then, turning to his clerk, "Cherlynn, please call the jury commissioner. We'll need fifty jurors for tomorrow morning."

"Only fifty, Judge?" the clerk asked, then attempted unsuccessfully to mouth a silent message to her boss.

Didery and I looked at each other. In most criminal trials, the attorneys had at their disposal ten opportunities to excuse jurors without regard to their ability to be fair. However, in trials where the potential punishment was life in prison, the law bestowed twenty such opportunities, known as juror challenges. So, Ludlow's request of only fifty total jurors would likely be inadequate to accommodate the trial. His error was not surprising, given that he had spent the past few years hearing traffic and misdemeanor cases.

"Your Honor," Didery began, sounding as officious as ever, "Perhaps the Court is not aware of the rules of court as it pertains to jury challenges. Pursuant to Penal Code section—"

"Mr. Didery," the judge's booming voice broke in. By now, I saw that Cherlynn's note had reached His Honor's desk. "I am fully aware of the Penal Code. And I intend to request one hundred jurors," he barked, jowls jiggling from the force of his words.

It was another of Ludlow's less than endearing traits. To mask his incompetence, he often lashed out at attorneys, hoping bombast would somehow obscure mistakes. Didery had just experienced it first-hand. I shared a smile with Cherlynn. We both knew the courtroom's capacity was ninety.

"Your Honor," the prosecutor stuttered, in full backpedal, "of course, I certainly, um, by no means did I mean to imply that you did not know..."

"Mr. Didery," the judge interrupted again, having regained his composure. "I'm sure it won't happen again. Anything else, gentlemen?"

I stood. "Yes, your Honor, I subpoenaed for this morning a William Jesse Wendell. He is a material witness for the defense and therefore I would ask the Court to issue a warrant for his arrest."

Ludlow's vacant stare told me he had no idea he had authority to do any such thing. "Your Honor," I continued, giving the judge an out. "I should have indicated this request is being made pursuant to Penal Code section 881."

"Ah, yes, 881," came the predictable response from the jowls. "In that case then, I'll sign the arrest warrant, Mr. Turner. Gentlemen, I'll see you two tomorrow. We have a murder case to try," he said proudly, fittingly capping off the morning's tour de force of incompetence with yet another gaffe.

It was a homicide case. It would be up to the jury to decide if it was murder. Although seemingly a minor matter to those outside the world of criminal trials, the difference was fundamental, and assiduously adhered to by all reasonably intelligent judges.

Before I stood, Darnell, perceptive as ever, leaned over, whispering, "Yo, uh, seems like this judge don't really know what he's doing."

"We'll just have to educate him," I whispered back. "See you tomorrow."

In fact, Ludlow was going to be much worse than I had thought. The first glimpse of the judge in action had me genuinely concerned he could keep the trial on the rails.

On the way out of court, Didery handed me a CD. Apparently, still shaken from his tongue lashing, he didn't request that I sign for it at his office. I was pretty sure it contained ballistics results from the shell casing comparison.

"This is bad for me, isn't it, Nate?" I asked as he stepped onto an elevator.

The gangly prosecutor stood with his fingertips together, hands at his chest, savoring his answer. "I wouldn't describe its contents as helpful to the defense, if that's what you are asking," he answered, breaking into a smile before the doors closed in front of him. I was beginning to dislike Nathaniel Winston Didery.

I walked to the office imagining myself explaining to the jury how it was that Darnell's gun had been used in the shooting.

"Nathan Didery called," Lawanda said, handing me two notes as I entered the office. "Something about signing for the CD he gave you. Also, some law student says he wants an unpaid internship. Free labor, right?"

"Yeah, it usually ends up being more trouble than it's worth," I grumbled, tossing my satchel on my desk.

"You're in a mood. Bad day in court?"

"Let me guess. You got Dudlow'd?" Andy called from his office.

"Yeah. That and the truckloads of evidence against my client lining up outside the courthouse. Jury selection tomorrow," I said as he reached my doorway.

"Well then you'd better pick some idiots. Just get

some of your old clients on the jury."

"Sadly, most of them can't vote. Being felons and all."

I collapsed into my chair and slid the CD into my computer, bracing for a ballistics report matching the shell casings found at the scene to Darnell's gun. Instead, the index listed only a video file labeled 466 9th Ave. The address was about a quarter mile from the murder scene.

I clicked and digital quality video of a parking lot filled the screen. It appeared to be the half-empty lot of a convenience store. The time in the left-hand corner of the screen read 5:58 p.m. I watched for twenty seconds before a very familiar vehicle entered the parking lot. The olive-green sedan parked in front of the store, centered in the surveillance video. The car had no front license plate, but there was no mistaking the lighter shade of green on the car's hood.

I paused the video, not exactly knowing why. I knew what was coming but I just didn't want to see it right away. "Anyone for a hotdog?" I asked, walking out of the office, hearing no response.

Alone on the elevator, I assessed. The good news was that it wasn't the nuclear bomb that the ballistics results would have been. Still, assuming Darnell was about to appear on my computer screen, driving his car less than twenty minutes before the murder, no longer could the jury realistically conclude that someone else had been driving Darnell's car at the murder scene. I supposed it was likely inevitable anyway, what with his admission that he may have been in the neighborhood. Still, another escape route had been sealed tight.

Also, to some extent, the video validated

Bedrossian's identification. He had been correct in his identification of Darnell as the driver. Now, I would be left to argue that he must have been mistaken about seeing him shoot out the window.

Back in the office, hotdog in hand, I grabbed a beer out of the office fridge, resumed my position in front of my computer, and clicked play. Within seconds, the driver's door swung open and Darnell hopped out, as big as life, carefree smile in place. He even seemed to pause in front of the camera before entering the store. Three minutes later, he emerged from the store carrying a small paper bag.

I played the video clip from beginning to end several times, trying to determine if there were occupants in the back seat of the vehicle, but it was too dark. I heard Didery's adenoidal voice in my head. "Ladies and Gentlemen, the defendant clearly purchased at least one item in the store. Does the video show him distributing items to the back seat or communicating with them? No, because he was alone in that car."

I walked home with considerably less bounce in my step than I had in the morning. While the air remained sweet with the smell of spring, my client seemed a little less innocent.

All in all—an opening day loss for the home team.

Chapter Twenty-Two

In an effort to ease the pressure on his handcuffed wrists, Jesse leaned forward in his hard vinyl seat in the back of the police cruiser. He rested his forehead against the steel mesh cage, cursing his rotten luck. He wasn't even going to get high today. He actually planned on going to court just to put the suits' minds at ease. But he wasn't going to testify. After all, this was Oakland—and he was a survivor. He'd go to court and he'd keep in touch with the old hippie investigator then disappear right before it was his time to testify. That was the play.

But now he was fucked. He'd overslept and then his ride to court had bailed on him. He knew if he showed up late, they would want to put him in jail until the trial was over. And he couldn't go back to jail, especially not as a witness to a gang hit.

In some ways, the juvy pen had been easier than life on the streets. It had been hard at first. Being away from Damon, mostly. Then having to fight to show you're nobody's bitch. But he'd figured it out. Got through his twelve years relying on his smarts and playing the angles. He'd peddled dope the guards would smuggle in, traded cigarettes, sold himself when he had to. For a while he had a racket renting out books that Damon would send him. The first of a series was free, then it was a dollar a book.

Out here on the streets, though, there was too much drama. Who owes who money? Who stole who's stash? Who snitched? One thing about prison, you damn sure knew what to expect every day. Out here, though, there were too many variables. Too much could go wrong. He'd been out less than two years and had already been back to jail three times.

Like today, after he missed court, he was just going to lay low. But Eva had called. She'd scored some weed, probably after rolling one of her johns. He didn't ask. Anyway, she wanted to smoke, so they got high in her motel room.

Still, everything had been cool until they got the munchies and he started craving pizza. Real pizza, not the ketchup and cheese on toast you could make in the pen. And not the cold dumpster pizza he and Damon had eaten growing up. Real hot bubbly pizza that burns the roof of your mouth. He'd only had it twice in his life. Once with Damon when he first got out.

So, he and Eva had ordered a pizza—pepperoni with extra cheese—and just like he'd planned it, he had waited for the delivery guy in the parking lot. He should have known, though, when he saw how athletic the guy looked. He should have called it off. But he kept thinking of that pizza.

He'd managed to surprise him from behind a car and snatch the box, but the guy was fast. That and being high had slowed him down. Anyway, he'd been tackled, the pizza lost. Of course, given his luck, a cop had been driving by.

Still, he was pretty sure the cop was going to just cite and release him. He'd be in Eva's room now, eating ramen off of her hotplate. But then he'd heard the radio chatter, then the rattle of the handcuffs. The cop found out about the warrant, and that was it.

Jesse lifted his head and leaned back in the cruiser, the steel of the cage cooling his skinned knee. He dreaded the phone call, but now he had a serious problem. He needed his twin brother.

****

"Hear ye, hear ye." boomed the voice of Deputy Hartag, as the great Ludlow ascended the bench with a flourish, robe billowing behind him. "All rise. Department 27 of the Superior Court of the State of California, County of Alameda, Oakland Hall of Justice, is now in session, The Honorable Douglas Latimer Ludlow III, presiding. Please be seated."

The judge paused slightly when he reached his perch and looked out across the courtroom filled with prospective jurors with a prideful smile, as if surveying his kingdom.

I had heard tell of Ludlow's over-the-top entrance and it certainly lived up to all expectations of absurdity. The call-to-order was left to the discretion of the individual judge. Most opted for "Ladies and Gentlemen, come to order, this court is now in session." Ludlow being short on discretion, his introduction more resembled a gaudy coronation.

Darnell sneaked a look behind him at the gallery and frowned. I read his mind. Watching the courtroom door as the jurors entered, I had counted only six African Americans out of ninety.

As a city, Oakland has one of the largest black populations in the state. However, jurors are summoned to court from throughout sprawling Alameda County. County wide, African Americans make up less than ten percent of the population. Also, juror lists are gathered from voter registration rolls, which do not include the many disenfranchised residents of Oakland.

The judge welcomed the venire and told them they were here for a criminal trial. Then he read the charge, always one of the worst moments in a felony trial. "The People of the State of California have accused the defendant, Darnell Jackson Moore, of a violation of Penal Code section 187, Murder, in that on or about March 22, 2021, Darnell Jackson Moore murdered Cleveland Barlow."

Darnell squirmed in his seat to my left as we felt the stare of every eye in the courtroom. "The charges themselves are not evidence, ladies and gentlemen," Ludlow said, reading from a script. But by now, the prospective jurors were probably no longer listening, instead wondering why Darnell had killed and how he had done it.

Ludlow reviewed the trial schedule. Didery and I were surprised to hear that we would be in session only four days a week. This was common for many departments, as they often handled motions calendars on Fridays. Since Ludlow couldn't be trusted with a motions calendar, his incompetence bought him a vacation day once a week. He certainly wouldn't give up that for our silly murder trial.

After the first twelve jurors were seated in the box, Ludlow began to question them, again reading from a script. There was the usual collection of teachers, software engineers, retirees, and office managers. Overall, not a bad group from a defense perspective, save for one crusty retired marine who looked like he was ready to convict Darnell before lunch time.

Things went smoothly until it was the marine's turn with the microphone.

"Mr. Eggers, I see you've served our country…"

"It's Captain Eggers," the juror cut in abruptly.

"I see, sir." Ludlow stared hard at the man, undoubtedly thinking, 'Didn't you read my name plate? I'm the God damned judge.' The judge began again, emphasizing the title ever so slightly. "Well, Captain, have you had any previous jury experience?"

"Yeah. Military Court. It's not the same though. We didn't go through all this unnecessary process."

"Sir, the trial process is hardly unnecessary. The trial—"

"Well, why don't we get on with it, then? There's clearly some pretty strong evidence that this guy did it, so let's just—"

"Mr. Eggers, stop interrupting me!" Ludlow bellowed, banging his gavel like a child. "You are on thin ice, sir. You're being disrespectful to me and this courtroom and this murder trial." For a moment, I thought the flustered judge would fling his gavel at the juror. "Counsel, approach."

When we reached the bench, Ludlow turned off his microphone and leaned down to whisper. "Gentlemen, it seems to me that my options are rather limited."

Didery and I both assumed that he was about to tell us his course of action, but instead, the judge just stared at us with searching eyes. He literally had no idea what to do.

Didery took the lead. "Well, Your Honor, as you are obviously well aware, one clear option is to rule that the juror can't be fair. Then you can excuse him for cause."

"Yes, yes," the judge said, nodding. I think I saw him taking notes. "I had considered that option." He shooed us back to the counsel table with a wave.

"Mr. Eggers, I am ruling that you cannot be fair. I am excusing you for cause," the judge said, likely reading his notes. "Good day, sir. We're in recess, fifteen minutes."

I texted Eddy during the break.

—*Hey there. Are you free Friday?* —

—*Nope! Plans with you. How's trial?*—

—*Tedious jury selection. Going to need to relax on Friday*—

—*Perfect. I know just the thing*—

Back in the courtroom, Ludlow summoned the attorneys into his chambers before the arrival of the jury. "Gentlemen, my court reporter, Arlene, is exhausted. I assume there'd be no objection to waiving the reporting of the jury selection?"

Like nearly all of Ludlow's suggestions, it was out of the question. In misdemeanor trials, jury selection was often not transcribed. However, in homicide trials, errors made in jury selection were occasionally the basis for an appeal. Waiving the reporting of the proceeding would be malpractice.

"I'm sorry, Your Honor. I can't agree to that."

"Joe," Didery chimed in, "I certainly would agree to it and I think the judge's suggestion is a good one, wouldn't you agree?"

I wanted to throttle the pissant jerk. Didery knew full well I couldn't agree to the waiver. Until now, we'd managed Ludlow's ineptitude in a joint effort but now he was seeking to benefit from it. I filed it away.

"Okay, Mr. Turner, I can't make you agree but I

had hoped we could be reasonable," he said, getting up and disappearing into his private bathroom.

I checked my phone before court began and saw a text from Chuck.

—*Guess who got picked up last night?*—

—*Are you kidding? He didn't make it one night?*—

—*For once, Oakland's finest helped us out*—

After another grand call to order, it was Didery's turn to question the jury.

Whereas the prosecutor was a poor interpersonal communicator, in front of a jury, his nervous ticks and fidgets dissolved, leaving a confident and assertive speaker. Even his nasal tone wasn't as off-putting, lending to his professorial affect. His questions to the jury were right out of the D.A. handbook. First, he focused on lowering the jurors' expectations of the upcoming evidence as well as the burden of proof.

"Mr. Alison, do you watch the show *Forensic Team* on television?"

"I've seen it before, yes."

"And how about you, Ms. Jennings," he asked, addressing a kindergarten teacher of twenty years, "are you familiar with the show?"

"Actually, I was a big fan, but its last season was three or four years ago."

"Wow, I need to update my material," quipped the prosecutor to laughter throughout the courtroom. Who was this breezy charmer, and what has he done with jittery Didery?

"My point is, ladies and gentlemen, in the real world, we can't obtain DNA off the head of a pin or trace a dust particle on the defendant's shoe to a crime scene. Does that make sense?" My mind went to the shell casings. Was it possible he had neglected to test them?

Jittery continued, smooth as silk. "Mr. Hernandez, you're a scientist, correct."

"Essentially, yes."

"Although the standard of proof is high, my burden is not to prove the case to a scientific certainty. As a person who deals in absolutes are you okay with that?"

"Yes, I would hope I could adapt to the law and decide accordingly."

"Ms. Overton, there is a jury instruction that tells you that you may rely on one witness to prove any fact. That means that if one witness tells you that Mr. Moore committed this crime, the law says it's okay to base your verdict on that witness."

I hated this line of questioning, as it tended to distort the law. Some judges would have explained to the jury that the rule was still subject to the beyond a reasonable doubt standard of proof. I looked at Ludlow who, at the moment, offered the proceedings a vacant stare. There was a better chance of him sprouting wings and flying to the ceiling.

The social worker from Berkeley frowned. "That doesn't seem right."

"Will you promise to follow the law even if you don't agree with it."

"Uh, yes. If that's the law, I will follow it."

Didery's questions continued after lunch and well into the afternoon session.

"Will everyone promise me that if I prove that Darnell Moore killed Cleveland Barlow beyond a reasonable doubt, you will return a verdict of guilty?"

The jury nodded in unison, and Didery sat down,

having ended with an expression of absolute confidence in his case.

"Good afternoon," I began, addressing the prospective jurors after the afternoon break. "My name is Joseph Turner and I represent Darnell Moore." I briefly rested a hand on Darnell's shoulder. "Ms. Jennings, I sensed some concern from you about the rule that you could rely on the testimony of one witness to prove a fact, including the fact that Darnell Moore committed murder?"

"Yes, it just doesn't seem right that one witness could prove the entire case."

"You are correct to be skeptical. The way the jury instruction was presented to you by Mr. Didery was somewhat misleading."

Jittery was not pleased. "Objection, your Honor."

"Mr. Turner, what are you getting at?" asked the judge, probably actually curious about the law himself.

"I was about to say that His Honor will instruct the jury that all of the instructions should be considered together."

The judge nodded his approval, no doubt because I had referred to him as 'His Honor'. "Continue, Mr. Turner."

"One very important instruction is that in order to find Darnell Moore guilty, you must find that he committed the crime beyond a reasonable doubt. It is the highest standard of proof we have in the law. So while the rule cited by Mr. Didery says that it is theoretically possible to prove the case with one witness, in order to rise to the level of beyond a reasonable doubt, that witness would have to be extremely persuasive.

"For example, imagine a nun with twenty-twenty eyesight is robbed in broad daylight by her neighbor whom she has known for fifteen years. If her testimony is the only evidence of the crime, then Mr. Didery's rule states that there is no rule that says you need more than one witness. Does that make sense, Ms. Jennings?"

"Yes, I feel much better about it now."

I addressed the jurors as a group. "If you're driving through your town's main street and you see a man in handcuffs next to a police car, do you wonder what he must have done, or do you wonder if he is guilty of anything?

"Mr. Choi, how about you?" I asked the middle-aged insurance executive.

"Well…" He paused, grinning sheepishly. "I'm afraid I'd wonder what he did."

"Yes, and that is a perfectly natural reaction. But as you can imagine that mindset is the polar opposite of how we operate here in Court. Rather than assume that Mr. Moore has committed the offense, he is presumed innocent. Right now, Mr. Moore is as innocent as anyone else in the courtroom.

"Mr. Edson, you look skeptical."

"Yeah," the beefy construction worker said. "It just seems like since we've gotten all the way to this point, there must be some pretty strong evidence against him."

"That's a good point, sir. Mr. Moore's name wasn't drawn out of a hat. But you said, 'we've gotten all the way to this point.' The reason that we've gotten all the way to trial is because Darnell Moore has been accused and he has said, 'No, I'm innocent.' At every stage, he has denied the charges and demanded his trial."

I concluded the inquiry with questions about how

they go about deciding if a witness is being truthful. Suggestions ranged from the consistency of the testimony to body language. My implied message to the jury was that I wanted the truth to win out. Also, I was subtly hoping to overemphasize the importance of Bedrossian's testimony, the weakness in the prosecution's case.

Ludlow called a halt to the proceedings at four-forty-five p.m. "Ladies and gentlemen, we have concluded the inquiry of prospective jurors. We will finish the jury selection tomorrow and then begin the trial itself."

I wanted to gently remind the judge of my motion to suppress the gun, but he was off the bench well before the last juror filed out. However laughable, the prospect of Dudlow's tiny brain trying to wrap itself around an actual legal issue, he was still going to have to try sometime.

My phone buzzed on the way out of the courthouse.

"Hi, Eddy," I said, fixing my earbuds into place for the walk to the office.

"Did you get a jury yet?"

"No. In addition to being a bundle of nerves, turns out Didery is also long-winded. It was interminable."

"So maybe you should try thinking of me instead?"

"Oh, trust me I have been."

"Yeah? Bikini and whip again?"

"Yes, standing atop Machu Pichu in stilettos."

"How professional of me."

"I thought so, too. And it caused a few embarrassing moments when I had to stand and address the jury, so dress appropriately next time."

"I'll try," she said, laughing. "Getting on the train. Bye, Turner."

Entering the lobby of our office, I was greeted by the stoic figure of Elijah Jakes, sitting motionless, one hand resting on top of the curved silver handle of a black onyx cane. My introduction was met with silence, but he shook my hand firmly and followed me into the modest conference room I shared with Andy. He leaned heavily on the cane as he went, limping on his left foot. Chuck was already there. It was a good policy to have a third party observe witness interviews on the off chance the witness said something helpful and denied it later.

"Mr. Jakes, you must have quite a collection of canes. I noticed your carved cane the last time I saw you."

"Thank you for noticing," he answered in a gravelly voice. "My favorite one is a hollowed-out carved walking stick. Holds two ounces of liquor. Hidden screw cap on top. Another one I got turns into a sword. But I don't suppose you want to talk about my canes, now do you?"

"Sir, I would be interested in knowing whether you saw the shooting."

Jakes looked down at the table briefly, rubbing his black, wizened face with a bony hand.

"Look here," he said, his eyes fixed on mine. "I don't have any intention of saying anything that would help out the young thug you represent or any of his kind."

I knew it was useless, but I had to try. "Mr. Jakes, if you could just—"

"Let me tell you something, Mr. Turner," he said earnestly. "Gang members just like your client have ruined our neighborhood. And if your client didn't do this shooting, then he'd do another one, taking someone else's life from them. Now the cops are finally gonna get one of them off the street, and you're asking me to help him?"

"You know," he continued, "I opened the E&J back in seventy-five. Back then, it was a damn fine neighborhood. Don't get me wrong, it was still Oakland. You had to watch yourself in a dark alley. But it was a fine place to live." He paused, looking at the table for a memory.

"We used to open after church on Sundays. Families would come to the store. Kids would come and get ice cream. We'd sit and visit with each other on the porch. Usually had a ballgame on the radio. Now..." He shook his head, his raspy voice gone dry.

After he'd gone, Chuck and I sat in my office, sipping beers from the office fridge.

"You can't put him on the stand, Joe. I believe him when he said he'll never help us."

"Yeah, but that would leave Jesse Wendell as our only witness." I shuddered at that prospect. "Even if Jakes describes the number of shootings in the neighborhood, maybe it can show that literally every member of the Iceboyz is a potential suspect." Chuck let my words hang in the air, withering away on their own. "I know. I'm reaching." I sighed, draining my beer before heading out.

"Speaking of the eye-witness Jesse Wendell. Can you believe that scrawny, skittish little guy killed someone?"

"Yeah, hard to believe."

On the walk home, a number I didn't recognize

appeared in my phone.

"This is Joe."

"Hi, Mr. Turner. I spoke to your assistant yesterday. I'm the law student at Cal, looking for an unpaid internship?"

"Oh, yes. I meant to get back to you. It's not a great time for me. I'm in trial and it would take some time for me to show you the ropes. Maybe try back in a month or so?"

"Actually, I know you're in trial, Mr. Turner." He paused before continuing. "I think I could be of some help to you."

Now I was confused. The trial hadn't gotten any press since Darnell's arrest. Who was this guy? "Really?"

"Yeah. I'm Damon Wendell. Jesse's brother."

Chapter Twenty-Three

After an evening at my neighbor's house, watching baseball over too much beer and tamales, I overslept and drove to court, using the time to think about my ideal juror. That meant categorizing people based on gross generalizations and sweeping stereotypes. Liberal social workers and therapists were good. Conservative law enforcement types were bad. So said the unwritten manual of jury selection.

Since a not guilty verdict seemed impossible, the goal was a hung jury, which meant I needed strong-willed jurors who would stand up for their beliefs no matter how unpopular. Given the state of the evidence, jurors who seemed a little wacky wouldn't hurt.

Assuming that Darnell managed to dodge the ballistics bullet, the evidence would remain strong but largely circumstantial. There was no DNA or fingerprints to deal with. That meant engineers and scientists, who are used to proving theories to an absolute certainty. Jurors with sons the age of the victim should be avoided if possible.

The gender question was a sticky wicket. On one hand, two strong women would testify for the prosecution. However, in speaking with jurors after trials, I found that female jurors were often more critical of their own gender. Race was also tricky since both the victim and the defendant were black. Also, recently I had found my most strident pro-prosecution jurors to be successful African Americans who resented gang members who gave their community a bad name.

The nature of the selection process made it impossible to select an entire jury of defense-oriented jurors. Didery had an equal say in the process and no doubt had his own agenda. While it was impossible to avoid every pro-prosecution juror, the trick was to steer clear of those confident and opinionated jurors who could persuade other jurors to convict.

I hustled into court less than a minute before the judge's grand entrance. Shortly, the juror selection took on a gameshow feel, with the prosecution and defense taking turns excusing jurors, their replacements taking their seats in the jury box. Generally, I tended to entertain suggestions made by my clients when it came to jury selection. It was their life in the balance, after all. So far, Darnell had been quiet, save one suggestion of keeping a young college woman, which I suspected had little to do with her worthiness as a juror.

At twelve-thirty p.m., Didery and I both relented, each side satisfied with the jury's composition. Seven men and five women would decide Darnell's fate. After three alternates were selected, Ludlow dismissed the rest of the relieved venire.

"Ladies and gentlemen, we now have a jury. After lunch, report to the jury room, and we will reconvene in the courtroom with opening statements. See you at two o'clock."

After the jury had left the courtroom, Didery addressed the judge. "Your Honor, did the Court plan to hear Mr. Turner's motion to suppress prior to our opening statements? I would prefer to know whether or not I can mention the gun to the jury."

Didery had a point. We were both fairly certain my motion would be denied, but even so it would be nice to know for sure before addressing the jury. It was unheard of to begin the trial prior to an *in limine* ruling, but Ludlow was clearly deathly afraid of such a hearing due to his ineptitude.

"We will hear the motion in due course, Mr. Didery. In due course," repeated Ludlow, ambling off the bench.

"What the fuck does that mean?" I whispered to Didery.

The prosecutor rubbed his forehead and grimaced. "Unbelievable," he muttered through clenched teeth.

I grabbed a hotdog and strolled to the park a block from the courthouse. Sitting on a park bench overlooking Lake Merritt, I thought about the defense of Darnell Moore. Although my confidence had been shaken lately, I still mostly believed in my client's innocence. I asked myself why and came up with the same nebulous answer. Granted, I didn't know him well, but I just didn't think he was capable of murder.

So, I would argue what I believed. Without Darnell testifying, the jury would have no basis to form that opinion on their own, but that had never stopped me before. Another looming problem was the aiding and abetting theory. Even if the jury concluded that Darnell wasn't the shooter, they could still convict him of murder for assisting in the crime as the driver.

But one problem at a time. If those shell casings were traced to Darnell's gun, his fate would be sealed. If they were not a match, Didery would be obligated to let me know. The D.A. was annoying, but he didn't strike me as unethical. If Didery had somehow forgotten to test them, the last thing I wanted to do was to call it to his attention. Still, I hated not knowing. As usual, I resorted to back-up.

—*Chuck, any chance you can check some backchannels for info on the ballistics?*—

—*I can try a few of my old contacts at the lab*—

—*Thanks*—

After a few flirty texts with Eddy, I began to make my way back to Department 27 where I found Didery, perched on the edge of his chair with both hands on the edge of the table, a bony raptor ready to take flight.

After Ludlow took the bench with the usual folderol, I flashed on the laughing fit I'd had with Eddy as we thought of suggestions to add to the entrance. She thought his rise to the bench should be accompanied by a soaring rendition of *Ode to Joy* or a royal procession of bagpipes. Maybe Ludlow should take a victory lap around the courtroom, stopping to shake hands with the gallery like the president before the State of the Union address. Perhaps a unison reading of All Hail, Ludlow.

Juror number nine, a free-lance writer, caught me recalling the memory and shot me a knowing smile, no doubt astounded by the charade that was repeated after every courtroom break.

"Mr. Didery," Ludlow invited from the bench, "your opening statement?"

Didery, Cherlynn and I all exchanged glances. Ludlow had forgotten to have the jury sworn. The clerk silently wheeled her chair to the side of the bench where, shielded from the jury's view, she discreetly passed her dull-witted boss a note.

"Actually," Ludlow said, pretending that the

thought just popped into his head, "I believe that now would be a good time to swear the jury. Ms. Robinson, will you do the honors?"

After the jury was sworn, Didery walked to the podium confidently. "It is March 22 of this year, around six-fifteen p.m., still daylight," he began quietly. I hated the overly dramatic first-person present tense crap. It was an opening statement, not a poetry reading.

"Cleveland Barlow is hanging out in the front yard of 454 West Eighth Street, here in Oakland, only about three miles from here. Cleveland is with members of a gang called Cashtown. He is seventeen years old. He is unarmed.

"Young Cleveland has no idea that a rival gang member from a gang called the Iceboyz is approaching. He has no idea," Didery said more loudly, walking toward our side of the counsel table, "that this man, Darnell Moore, will soon end his life."

Reaching his crescendo, the prosecutor pointed at Darnell from only a few paces away. Somewhere in some prosecutor's manual, it was written that pointing is required. Probably some bullshit about displaying your personal conviction. It usually comes off as an awkward gesture, at least from my biased point of view.

"You will learn that Darnell Moore drove his own car past his victim once, then minutes later pulled up in front of him and using a semi-automatic gun, fired two shots from his car before speeding away. One struck Cleveland in the head, the other in the chest. Cleveland's friends returned fire, striking the car, but Mr. Moore got away. He got away with his cowardly act, ladies and gentlemen, but he will not escape justice."

Didery went on to methodically summarize the investigation which led to Darnell's arrest—how his license plate number was captured on surveillance tape which eventually led to a witness identification. The District Attorney chronicled the evidence of Darnell's gang affiliation, showing photos on the courtroom flat screen of Darnell posing with other gang members, flashing guns and gang signs. Didery told the jury that Darnell had first told the police that he was home at the time of the shooting and then later changed his story, admitting that he had been in the area.

"The evidence will be clear and overwhelming," Didery said after forty-five minutes in front of the jury "and the evidence will lead you to one inescapable conclusion: Darnell Moore killed Cleveland Barlow in cold blood, and he is guilty of murder in the first degree."

"Mr. Turner, does the defense wish to make an opening statement?"

"Yes. Thank you, Your Honor," I answered, wishing I were somewhere else.

"Good afternoon, Ladies and Gentlemen. I should remind you that after that very eloquent summary by Mr. Didery, the judge will instruct you that in making your decision, you are to consider only the evidence. And thus far, you haven't heard any evidence. What the attorneys say is not evidence.

"Evidence," I said, emphasizing the word, "will show that Darnell Moore did not commit this crime. You will learn that he is himself only nineteen years old. He grew up here in Oakland, graduating from Franklin High School. The evidence will show that despite some run-ins with the law, Darnell Moore has never committed a violent crime."

Steering clear from the mountain of circumstantial evidence, I spoke about the presumption of innocence, the necessity that the jurors keep open minds, and the prosecution's burden to prove the case beyond a reasonable doubt.

"You will hear circumstantial evidence that will require speculation and will fall well short of that standard of proof. The prosecution's case will rise and fall on the eye-witness testimony referenced by Mr. Didery. You are all on this jury because in jury selection, you showed me that you have what it takes to properly evaluate that eyewitness and find the truth. When you do, I am confident that you will find Darnell Moore not guilty."

"Thank you, Mr. Turner."

Didery stood, ready to call his first witness.

"Ladies and gentlemen, it's been a long day," Ludlow pronounced at three-fifteen p.m., provoking some sideways glances in the jury box. "We'll be in recess until tomorrow morning."

The big man was off the bench with a furtive glance toward Didery, deftly avoiding another inquiry about the suppression hearing.

I drove to the office to find a smartly dressed clean-cut young man in the lobby, no doubt one of Andy's clients ready for a deposition. I was at my desk unpacking the Moore file when Lawanda walked in, ten minutes later. "Did you see the law student?"

"What?"

"Mr. Wendell is in the lobby."

With my mind consumed with the trial, the fact that Damon Wendell was a law student had completely escaped me. To me, the person I was meeting was the brother of my recently incarcerated star witness. So my mind's eye had pictured someone similar in appearance to the down-and-out street urchin I had met last week.

"Damon Wendell," he said pleasantly, shaking my hand.

"Hi, Damon. I apologize for walking past you. It's just that you look a bit different than your brother."

"Yeah, we're actually identical twins, but I know what you mean. We've lived different lives," he said with a compassionate smile. And now I saw it clearly, starting with the arresting green eyes. Apart from Damon being slightly heavier and healthier looking and his grown out blond hair, their features and builds were a perfect match.

"So, you're a law student?"

"Yes. I'm a second-year at Cal."

"Wow. Good for you." I'm sure he wanted me to ask why in God's name he was in law school when his twin was a petty criminal? And, by the way, a murderer.

"Jesse and I were raised in foster care. He's obviously made some bad choices, but he's also had it pretty rough." I assumed Damon knew I was aware of Jesse's murder conviction as a juvenile. If so, it was one of the few times I'd heard murder referred to as *a bad choice*.

"I'm sure his childhood wasn't easy. Yours either, for that matter."

"I got lucky. Got placed in a wonderful home and ended up being adopted."

"Well, my client and I really hope your brother will take the stand and tell what he saw."

"I talked to him briefly on the phone," Damon said. "He's scared. Says the gang will target him in jail just on the chance he'll snitch. That seems crazy."

"Unfortunately, he's right. My client is in the same boat. Won't name the shooter, but the gang won't take the chance."

"Of course, he wants me to try convincing you to release the witness hold," he said without conviction. "Says he'll appear if he's released." He sounded like someone who had heard such promises before.

"Sorry, we tried that."

"Yeah, I get it."

"Obviously, I feel bad that he's in custody and at risk, but my client's defense has to come first. I've spoken to the watch commander at the jail. They know the situation and have taken measures to protect Jesse. Did he say if he planned to testify? Right now, he's the only hope my client has."

Damon sighed, pausing to choose the right words. "Jesse has been incarcerated for more than half his life. He trusts me, and that's about it. With other people, he tends to assume they're using him."

"Sounds like it might be good for you to keep in touch and maybe be a go-between with him."

"I'd like that. Actually, I also thought I could help you out with trial prep if you need it. It would be good for my resume."

"Sure." I thought for a second, catching sight of the large box of files I hadn't reviewed yet. "After you familiarize yourself with the case, you can check these investigation files of other gang-related shootings. It's a long shot, but you might find something interesting."

I copied the police reports, copying being on

Lawanda's "doesn't do" list, and told Damon to feel free to use the conference room any time. He was there reviewing the files when I left.

After a run, I made myself a bean and cheese burrito and reviewed witness statements. Since Fridays were Ludlow's day off, I anticipated that Didery would want to get through as many witnesses as possible before the long weekend. I nodded off in the recliner then went to bed with trial thoughts swirling in my head.

I awoke to the sound of my own voice telling Damon that his brother was my client's only hope. "Good God," I said into my pillow, recalling the shifty-eyed, paranoid pothead devouring his cheeseburger. Even if he testified that Darnell was innocent, which was no guarantee, the jury would hear of his prior murder conviction. On my drive to court, I called to schedule a jail interview with my pathetic excuse for a star witness.

Needing a mental break from the case before court, I turned up my country music play list and belted out the lyrics in my off-key baritone until I arrived at the courthouse.

Inside Department 27, Didery, looking particularly insect-like in a light gray suit and black bow tie, stood at the counsel table, rapping his pen against his chair. He had picked up this annoying habit recently, and it was becoming intolerable. The D.A. asked Cherlynn if we could see the judge in chambers. The clerk picked up her phone and relayed the message.

"Mr. Didery," the clerk said with her phone still to her ear, "Judge Ludlow would like to know if this is about the timing of the motion hearing."

"Yes, it is," said Didery, with more than a tinge of frustration showing in his voice.

Cherylyn shrugged, hanging up the phone. "He said he'll address it later."

Didery's head sagged to his chest in frustration. "You've got to be kidding me," he said under his breath, and tossed his legal pad on the table.

This was getting ridiculous, even for Ludlow. He was actually hiding in his chambers. Surely, he realized that eventually he would have to hear the motion or risk an automatic appeal, but maybe this was giving him too much credit. Maybe he thought if he just closed his eyes it would go away.

Ludlow finally took the bench at nine-thirty-five a.m. Once there, he continued his campaign for laziest judge in the world. "Ladies and Gentlemen, today, due to matters beyond my control, we will be adjourning at twelve noon. There will be no afternoon session. Mr. Didery, please call your first witness."

"Your Honor, may we approach?" asked Didery, clearly struggling to contain his exasperation. For a meticulous master of minutiae like Didery, Ludlow's constant changes in the schedule were becoming torturous.

"Make it quick, Mr. Didery. We have to get this trial moving."

The D.A. took a few seconds to absorb the judge's oblivious comment, but wisely chose not to respond. "Your Honor, with all due respect, I have subpoenaed four witnesses for today and have another two on standby who believed they would be testifying yesterday. Is there any way we can be in session this afternoon?"

"As I said, Mr. Didery," Ludlow whispered, covering the microphone with one hand, "these are circumstances beyond my control. Step back."

"Very well then, The People call Sergeant Robin Severson."

The sergeant entered the courtroom looking even more serious than she had at the preliminary hearing. Her hair was stretched taut, appearing to pull her sharp eyes apart. Out of uniform, she wore a severe charcoal gray suit and blouse. She marched to the witness stand before a crisp about face to take the oath, her right arm forming a perfect L.

"Sergeant Severson, how are you employed, sir, I mean, ma'am?" Didery asked with a nervous laugh. I was happy to see that the personal communication required for examining witnesses had brought with it the return of jittery Didery.

"I am a police officer for the city of Oakland."

"And were you so employed on March 22, 2021?"

"I was."

"And were you dispatched to 454 West Eighth Street around six-twenty p.m.?"

"I was."

"When you arrived at that location, what did you see?"

"I saw a male black lying in the street, suffering from gunshot wounds. He was unresponsive."

I always wondered why officers used the term "male black" rather than "black male." To me, using the color as a noun rather than an adjective seemed vaguely racist.

The sergeant again described the precise location of Cleveland Barlow. "Sergeant Severson, I'm handing

186

you what's been marked as People's Exhibit 1. Do you recognize this?" asked Didery, showing me the photo before handing it to the witness.

I breathed deeply, bracing myself.

"I do."

"Your Honor, permission to publish the photo to the jury?"

"Granted."

Back at the counsel table, Didery pressed a key on his laptop and the image appeared on the court's flat screen. The courtroom was deathly silent as the prosecutor paused to allow the image to wash over the jury. It was Cleveland Barlow, splayed on his back in the street, arms and legs akimbo, his head resting on the sidewalk. Blood soaked his white T-shirt, obscuring the logo. His young face was fixed in distant sadness, a perfect black circle on his forehead.

Didery and I had haggled about which of the photos would be shown to the jury, neither of us trusting the decision to Ludlow. I had prevailed upon him not to use another, more gory side-angle shot that revealed the larger exit wound in the back of the victim's head.

Now, the young man gazed down from the flat screen in a faraway, sorrowful trance, as if mourning his own death. When I first saw the photo in my office, I had quickly looked away and for the most part blocked it from my memory. Now, the haunting misery of this image would stick with me long after the trial ended. If my own reaction was telling, I was certain I had made the wrong choice with the photos.

"Sergeant Severson," Didery's pinched voice broke the silence, "does the image accurately reflect what you saw that evening?"

"Yes, sir. That photo was taken after paramedics had pronounced the young man dead."

As she had done in the preliminary hearing, the sergeant described her actions in setting the perimeter, organizing the technicians, and dispatching a homicide detective to the scene. She told the jury how she had placed plastic bags around the victim's hands so that they could be tested for gunshot residue.

Finally, after giving the jury a cogent explanation on how shell casings are ejected from a fired gun, she described the cluster of casings in the front yard of the residence and the ten forty-caliber shell casings near the middle of the street.

"Just one more question, Sergeant. At some point were you able to identify the victim?"

"Yes, I found a wallet on the pavement, under the victim's legs. It appeared to have likely been dislodged from his person. After opening it, I found an identification card with a photo that matched the young man's appearance."

"What was the name?"

"Cleveland Barlow."

"And Sergeant, what type of identification card was it?"

"It was a student body card for Madison Park High School." It was a nice touch by Didery, as if there wasn't already enough sadness in the courtroom.

"No further questions."

There was a pause before Ludlow remembered his line. "Mr. Turner, cross examination?"

"No questions, Your Honor."

"Sergeant, you may step down. Ladies and

gentlemen, it's time for our morning recess. We'll resume at eleven-thirty-five a.m."

After the jury had filed out, I asked the clerk if I could see the judge in chambers. "Not about the motion," I hastened to add. "I would like him to sign an order that my client be allowed to shower and shave on trial days." It was a routine order that even Ludlow could understand.

My request granted, I entered to find Ludlow brushing powdered sugar from a half-eaten jelly donut off his robe. He grunted and reached for the order and commenced an inscription with an elaborate flourish that ignored the confines of the signature line.

As I turned to exit, I caught sight of a gym bag on the floor next to his desk, unzipped to reveal spotless white golf shoes, no doubt the "circumstances beyond his control" that were sending us home early.

Back in the courtroom, Didery was speaking to his next witness, Rocco Bedrossian, who cut a dashing figure in the army's midnight blue dress uniform. I approached and shook hands. "Ready for a scathing cross examination?" I joked.

"I'm actually pretty nervous."

"Piece of cake," said Didery. "Probably a total of five questions, all about the videotape."

"Nate, are you sure you don't want to just stipulate to the authenticity of the videotape?"

"No thanks, Joe. Since we have Mr. Bedrossian here to authenticate it for the jury in person, I think this is more thorough. Wouldn't you agree?" he said, smiling. We both knew he wanted the handsome soldier on his side.

"No, but okay," I replied with a shrug, mouthing, *I*

tried to Rocco after Didery turned away.

Once Ludlow retook the bench, the Assistant D.A. assumed a military bearing of his own, practically saluting his next witness. "The People of the State of California call Captain Rocco Ovsanna Bedrossian, Your Honor."

The witness walked up the aisle with perfect posture, noticeably limping on his right leg. Good God, now he was a war hero, too?

True to his word, Didery's direct examination was brief. Rocco verified that the video surveillance system was properly maintained and set to the correct time. At the request of an Oakland police officer, he had provided the relevant footage. The video now authenticated, the first week of trial ended with Darnell's car flashing across the big screen.

"How do you think it's going?" Darnell asked after the jury had filed out.

Answering questions like that was always tricky. On one hand, I didn't want to give my client false hope. On the other hand, as still the most watched person in the trial, I didn't want him projecting a belief of certain defeat to the jury.

"Your guess is as good as mine," I said, hearing the insincerity in my voice. "See you Monday."

Outside the courthouse, Rocco got my attention. "Joe, I couldn't talk to you in front of the D.A. I'm having real concerns about my dad testifying," he said, then suddenly focused on someone approaching from behind me.

"Hey! Why are you talking to him!" It was the unmistakable accent and staccato speech of an angry man. "Don't talk to him! He is helping the murderers!"

"Dad, I'm trying to help you," Rocco said. "You don't realize how much danger you're in."

"My son the soldier is a coward! These gang members have ruined our neighborhood, ruined my store. Someone must stand up!"

"Dad—"

"No!" Bedrossian the elder dismissed his son with a wave and turned his sights on me. "And you! Stop bothering my friend Elijah Jakes! He's a good man. He grieves the loss of his wife and you harass him!" He stalked off down the sidewalk, looking like he was spoiling for a fight.

I used the unexpected free afternoon to catch up on some billing before heading to the jail for a meeting with Jesse Wendell. I was escorted into one of the new interview rooms, equipped with a two-way microphone that allowed communication without phones.

As I sat on a metal stool waiting for him to appear on the other side of the glass, I wondered if my visit was too soon. I had planned to wait until after Damon had a chance to speak with him, but Jesse's public visiting day was Tuesday and I didn't want to wait that long.

Through the glass, a metal door buzzed open and Jesse sauntered into the tiny room. He closed the door behind him and rested a foot on the stool in front of him. He leaned against the wall, looking down at me, expressionless. A pale-yellow jumpsuit worn by the jail's general population hung from his spindly frame.

"Hi, Jesse," I said awkwardly. A full minute passed as he continued to look at me impassively, unaffected by the silence. I should have waited for Damon to visit.

Although I was certain I knew how Jesse felt about

his incarceration, on some level, it was clear that he was more comfortable in jail. Gone were the nervous twitches and furtive fidgets I had witnessed in the coffee shop. I thought about his brother's remark that he had spent more than half his life in custody. I could say the same about other of my clients in their forties, but Jesse had been raised in prison.

Finally, he shrugged, the gesture asking what I wanted.

"I know this isn't fair, Jesse, and I'm sorry you're in custody."

He slid down the wall onto his stool, a wry smile spreading across his face. "Look, man," he said disgustedly, "don't give me that shit. You wanted me in here, so you're guaranteed I'll come to court, so don't pretend any different."

I really should have waited for Damon. "Jesse," I said calmly, "think what you want, but I would have preferred that you had shown up to court like you promised."

"Look, Joe," he said, looking me in the eye, "You got a job to do. I get it. But just don't tell me you give a shit about me. You don't think the Iceboyz are gonna make a run at me while I'm in here? I'm in on a snitch warrant. You know how it works, and you don't care. Just don't pretend like you do."

I was surprised that he knew my name. I suspected that its use was by design, to try to connect personally so I would release the custody hold. Still, I did feel for him. I never felt good about witness warrants. Incarcerating someone because they chose not to risk their life to testify wasn't fair. I had also thought about the risk that Jesse would be attacked in jail. But now, seeing him locked inside, his fear and desperation seeping through the glass, made the danger real.

"Jesse," I said changing course, "I need you to tell me what you saw."

He stared at me, planning his next move. "No," he said, "you need me to say what I saw in court." This guy recognized his leverage. Also, his identical twin's career choice was beginning to make sense.

"True, but let's start by telling me here."

"Okay," he said after a time, looking around the tiny room reflexively, leaning towards the glass. "There was this car coming toward Maybeck. Older looking car. Green, I think. Right before the intersection, it stopped like suddenly. I saw the dude who got shot in front of his house with his buddies. Then there were all kind of shots and then I saw the guy on the sidewalk fall."

"Did you see anyone on the porch at the market across the street?"

"Yeah. Two older guys. Short white guy and an old black guy with a cane."

"Who was the shooter?"

He shook his head. "I'm not snitching," he said emphatically. "Your guy didn't kill anyone, though."

"The problem is, if you don't identify the shooter, you're not going to have any credibility with the jury."

He smirked. "Sounds like that's—how do you suits say it—in your issue box."

He stood and stretched, then sat down again. "How about this. How about you let me out of here then I'll tell you who the shooter is, and you can do some investigation on your own?"

"Sorry, Jesse. I can't risk it. You are really playing

the angles."

"You think I'm playing?" he asked earnestly. "Okay, then, maybe the D.A. will be interested in what I have to say about your client, know what I'm saying?" he said casually. "Maybe he was the shooter, after all."

I stared hard at his poker face, his threat hanging in the air. "You tell that lie and an innocent man goes down for murder."

"Been known to happen." He shrugged.

I wanted to yell but knew he was too important of a witness to alienate. "Jesse," I said after a deep breath, "my client would go away for the rest of his life."

"Yeah, well, this is my life!" he hissed, forcing his words through clenched teeth. He stared at the floor, forcing himself to calm down before continuing. "Besides, life's hard, Joe." His green eyes met mine, and I could tell he meant it.

We sat in silence for several minutes. "So, you know not to talk about the facts of the case on the phone with Damon," I said, not wanting to end the visit on a bitter note. "They tape all the phone…" I trailed off, seeing his deadpan stare. "Yeah, I guess you probably would know about that."

I stood to press the button to summon the guard.

"Hey, so I guess Damon is in law school?" he asked tentatively.

I sat back down. "Yeah, not just any law school. He's at Cal. Doing really well."

"Probably going to be a suit like you, someday," he said, staring into space. "Living in a big house, driving fancy cars. I sure am happy for him."

Then Jesse smiled. Not the smirk he wore like a hard mask but a genuine smile. At that moment, I saw the identical twin of the affable law student I'd met in my office. The tears and sweat of his youth spent in a cage, like water over sandstone, had etched his face with a bitter scowl. But just for a moment when he smiled his brother's carefree smile the lines faded, his face warming in the glow of his twin's happiness.

Chapter Twenty-Four

From my office, I heard the door to our lobby open. "I'm not saying it's hot out there," boomed Chuck, "but I'm pretty sure the thermometer reads 'Satan's balls!' " He stopped in mid-stride, mortified to find Eddy in my office, beaming.

"Oh." He covered his mouth with his hand. "I'm so sorry."

"Not at all," chuckled Eddy. "That's hilarious, and from what I've heard about you, it must be a movie line."

"Really, I'm so sorry," he repeated, his face reddening, "it's just so unusual for Joe to have a woman in his office."

"Very funny, Chuck. This is Eddy."

"Of course. Joe's been talking my ear off about you. Sorry to interrupt you two."

"Nice to meet you, Chuck. And no worries. I was actually just leaving. See you tonight around seven, Turner?"

"Yes, bye, Eddy."

She had stopped by after a business lunch nearby. Her company occupied a floor in the latest high rise in San Francisco, so I was a little self-conscious. On the other hand, I had survived her visit to my home. She had met Lawanda, who had since gone home, and Damon, who was working in the conference room.

"You, sir, have outkicked your coverage," my investigator said, after she was gone.

"Yes, Chuck, I'm aware. *Satan's balls?* Very nice. Any word on the ballistics tests?"

"No, I'm striking out so far, but I'll keep at it. All my old contacts in the lab are either dead or retired. I'm serious, Joe. She's a knockout."

"Again, I'm aware. And if you don't mind, I'm trying to feel less self-conscious about my relative attractiveness."

"Right. Can't help you there. How'd your meeting with Wendell go?"

"Well," I said shutting my office door so Chuck wouldn't say anything regretful within earshot of Damon, "it went." I explained to him about Damon and summarized my meeting with Jesse.

"I emailed you some invoices for the county. Happy trails." He introduced himself to Damon on the way out.

"Scanning? Emailing?" I called at his retreating back. "Who are you?"

Back in my office, I checked on the progress of the Armenian translator. Nothing yet. Next, I listened to Bedrossian's taped statements again, preparing for his upcoming cross examination. I sensed that I was hearing the words but somehow missing their meaning.

"Joe?" It was Damon in my doorway, carrying his open laptop.

"Yeah, Damon, what's up?"

"I think I may have something here." He had been in the conference room when I arrived this morning reviewing reports of other gang shootings.

"C'mon in. Thanks so much for all your help."

Seeing him up close on the heels of my visit with Jesse was surreal. It made sense that the more I was around each of them, the more their identical appearance became obvious. From their exact shade of sandy blond hair, to their sea green eyes and closed mouth smiles, they were dead ringers for each other. They even shared the same ambling gait and slight vocal twang. But their physical sameness made the difference in temperament all the more jarring.

Damon opened a file on his laptop and two photographs came on screen. I recognized them as two photos of the front of 454 West Eighth, one a closeup of the door, the other showing the entire residence from curbside. In each photo, the three bullet holes in the door and one in the door frame were visible.

"What am I missing?" I asked. "These are the bullet holes in the door, right?"

"Yes," Damon said with a gleam in his eye, "but the photo on the right was taken—" He paused for dramatic effect. "—three months before the shooting."

"No shit?" I asked, slapping him on the shoulder. "That's awesome! How'd you manage this?"

"I just searched the address because I was curious about where it was and out popped this real estate ad from January of this year."

"Good work. So that means," I said, thinking out loud, "that with the possible exception of the untraceable bullet lodged in the victim, none of the ten bullets fired at the scene are accounted for. "Strange, wouldn't you agree?" I asked, wishing Didery were around to hear it.

Despite my repeated suggestion to call it a day, Damon turned down my offer of a beer and was still at work in the conference room when I left for home at five o'clock p.m.

I went for a run before dinner, determined to flush the thoughts of Jesse Wendell that had danced at the edge of my mind since my jail visit. Instead, as I made my way into the Oakland hills, they flooded my brain.

Although I didn't believe he would follow through with his threat to send Darnell away, I was far from sure. I reminded myself that there was a time when I questioned whether Jesse was capable of murder. Since the jail visit, those doubts had vanished.

Jesse wasn't physically imposing, but the tenacity of his survival instinct betrayed a sad and painful past. At the diner, I had witnessed his nerves, laid bare and frayed from years of tension and misery. In jail, simmering under his thorny shell of protection, surveying his prey before striking with his cold, calculated threat, his prior violence as a child seemed much more believable. My guess was he had been pushed into a corner and had come out fighting.

After a shower, I drove to Eddy's.

"Another stellar wine choice, Turner," she said, taking the bottle from me with a kiss.

"Okay, answer me this, my seductive sommelier. I'm in the grocery store, walking down the wine aisle, paying attention, as instructed, to the vintage, whether or not it was estate bottled, and all the rest."

"You have been paying attention!"

"So, then I read about this rating scale for wine that's fifty to one hundred, fifty being an F and one hundred an A."

"Extra reading. Now you're just sucking up to the teacher."

"Of course, I'm trying to get laid. Seriously though, I thought it would help me but every wine in the store was between an eighty-six and ninety-two? Have you ever heard of a class of five hundred all getting either a B-plus or an A minus?"

"Truly absurd. Can we order in and watch a movie instead of going out? I feel like Thai food," she said opening the wine.

"Perfect."

And I meant exactly that. Time with Eddy had become the highlight of my week, and I had begun thinking about seeing her again as soon as we parted. Her presence was an electric current that charged my soul and a warm wave that calmed my mind. Somewhere in a recess of my brain I was wary as I watched myself tilting slowly into her, but it was a whisper amid a soaring orchestral symphony of bliss.

Thai food and two episodes of a British comedy was followed by another night of lovemaking, each foray more free and instinctive than the last.

"Thanks for the coffee." She set her cup on her nightstand and draped her warm body over me, resting her head on my chest. "It keeps getting better, doesn't it?"

"The coffee? Yes, I'm really getting the hang of your coffee maker."

"You dork," she laughed. "I knew you were going to say that before the words were out of my mouth. Soon we'll be completing each other's sentences like me and my twin."

I thought of the Wendell twins. "So, you met Damon. His twin is our star witness."

"The homeless, criminal witness who's in jail?"

"Yeah, and Damon's totally squared away. It's crazy."

"Actually, I was going to tell you I got sort of a weird vibe from Damon."

"Really, how so?"

"Hard to explain. His eyes just look sort of hollow or dead or something. Like there was a lot of sadness in his life."

"You should see his brother. He's basically been in jail since age ten. Horrible life."

"Maybe Damon was feeling his twin brother's pain."

"Do you ever feel it when Rose is in pain?"

"Good memory on the name. Not telepathically or anything, but if I know she's in pain, I feel a real, like visceral need to make it stop. There's something about seeing someone who looks identical to you suffering. Or if I think she's in danger, instinct takes over and I have to keep her safe."

"Good lookin'," I murmured to myself.

"What?"

"Nothing. Damon and Jesse just seem so different."

"I'll bet they're not," she said looking up to kiss my lips.

"Well, you're the twin. I'm sure you're right."

She rolled on top of me. "I'm happy to straighten you out," she whispered, and trailed kisses down my stomach.

****

After a Sunday of trial preparation, I walked into Department 27 on Monday morning to find Didery unpacking his trial box and Ludlow already on the bench. I frowned a question at Didery, who shrugged.

"Well, gentlemen, I was under the impression that we were litigating the motion to suppress this morning at eighty-thirty a.m. Obviously, given both of your late arrivals, there's no time now. We'll have to take it up later in the week." The judge plodded down off the bench as Didery and I sat, dumbfounded by his transparent remarks.

It was becoming embarrassing and awkward. Everyone in the courtroom—the clerk, the court reporter, the attorneys—saw through Ludlow's childish deceit. And this time, even Ludlow himself had to have known that we knew.

After another triumphant return to his throne by the judge, Didery resumed his relentlessly thorough and deliberate prosecution. He first called the proprietor of the convenience store to authenticate the videotape that would show Darnell in his car less than twenty minutes before the murder.

Again ignoring my offer to stipulate to the authenticity of the tape to save time, Didery was intent on sealing Darnell's coffin shut with a thousand tiny nails. Maybe there was value in his approach. Perhaps on a subconscious level, the greater number of witnesses who testified for the prosecution, the more likely that the jury would ascribe greater strength to its case.

To whatever effect, the prosecutor spent most of the morning session painstakingly reviewing with the store manager how the surveillance video camera operates, how the system is maintained, and how the digital information is stored. Next came the police officer who obtained the video from the store, meticulously documenting the requisite chain of custody. By the time similar testimony had authenticated the 911 tape, the jurors' eyes were glazed.

After I declined to question the witness, the courtroom waited for Ludlow to excuse the officer and mercifully order a recess. But the courtroom was silent.

The judge was fully reclined in his chair, facing the ceiling. Even though his eyes were not visible, no one doubted that he was dozing. Darnell snickered to my left. Cherlynn looked at me and blinked slowly, then looked down. Soon the soft buzz of the judge's phone could be heard somewhere near the bench. He sat up suddenly, looking startled before getting his bearings.

"Your Honor, I am at a good stopping point if the court wishes to take the noon recess," said Didery, throwing Ludlow a lifeline.

"Indeed. Yes. Well, ladies and gentlemen, let's take our noon recess. We'll resume at one-thirty p.m." He staggered off the bench, no doubt to resume his nap.

I walked to the office over the lunch hour, enjoying the sunshine. I arrived to find Damon finishing up his review of the files and asked him to follow up with the translation service. There had to be an Armenian translator somewhere.

Back in Court, the action picked up with Didery's playing of the 911 tape. I was pleased when juror number one, an insurance agent from Hayward asked if they would be provided a translation of the first few words uttered by Bedrossian.

"That will be up to the parties," answered Ludlow, for once getting it right.

Next, Didery played the video from the convenience store. The jury leaned forward in their seats as the big screen showed Darnell's car entering the parking lot. Didery stopped the video with Darnell's face centered on the screen as he entered the store.

The image was a haunting parallel to the one the jury had seen last week when they saw the victim's sad face in repose. I was sure they thought of Cleveland Barlow, and how this young man on the screen stopping for a snack was about to end his life.

Next, police lab technician Melissa Wu took the stand. A veteran expert witness, she made Didery's job easy. After listing her credentials, Didery asked her to explain gunshot residue to the jury.

"When a gun is fired, the explosion that propels the bullet also expels particles into the air and often onto the hands of the shooter. These elements, mainly from the bullet's explosive primer, include nitrates, barium, and lead. If deposited on the hands of a gunman, the elements can be identified through a process called atomic absorption spectroscopy."

"Can you summarize this procedure, Ms. Wu?"

"Yes. Essentially, a subject's hands are swabbed to collect samples. Then, a flame is used to create light. The wavelength of that light is then measured to determine the specific element found on the sample." Wu went on to tell the jury that samples from Cleveland Barlow's hands tested negative for gunshot residue, thus indicating that in all likelihood he had not fired a shot before being killed.

The technician's testimony was irritating in one respect. On two separate occasions over the years, I had used a lack of gunshot residue as evidence of my client's innocence. In those cases, Wu had testified for the prosecution, noting that wind gusts or rain could explain a negative test, or the defendants could have rubbed off the residue. But she was a formidable witness, and I needed to choose my battles. If the jury believed Darnell was the shooter, then whether or not Barlow was armed wouldn't matter.

The afternoon session wrapped up with the testimony of detective Ed Acuna, who showed the jury a satellite image of West Eighth street superimposed with the crime scene photo to depict the exact placement of the shell casings in the street, aligned as they did with the victim's dead body and the door of 454 West Eighth. Unnecessarily, he used a laser to "interpolate" the flight path of the bullets.

I was pleased that Didery assumed that the bullets dug from the door were fired from the car. I had made the same assumption before Damon's discovery. My only question on cross examination was to confirm that there were only four bullet holes, leaving no wiggle room for Didery to explain the missing bullets. I could tell he wondered about the purpose of my question. I would wait until the defense case to reveal the photos of the bullet holes taken prior to the murder.

On my ride home from court, Damon called from the office, interrupting my off key but enthusiastic rendition of rock songs from my '80s play list.

"So what's up with the translator service?"

"They can't help us. Turns out Bedrossian wasn't speaking Armenian. He was speaking a language called Kurmanji. It's only spoken by an ethnic minority in Armenia called....um, here it is, the Yazidi. I can try to track down a translator if you want but sounds like they are few and far between."

"That would be great. Thanks. Unless you want to just learn the language in the next week."

"If I can manage it, I'm seeing Jesse tomorrow on his visiting day. I'll let you know how it goes."

"Okay. What do you mean if you can manage it?"

"Jails sort of freak me out. I visited him a lot in the pen. I never got used to the idea of being locked in."

"Yeah. Not my favorite either. I think they have video conferences you can do from the lobby now."

"No, I want to see him in person. I'll be all right."

"Thanks again." The kid was really helping. I turned up the '80s rock and thought about my next date with Eddy.

****

Jail was bad enough, but LuAnne Epperson hated Mondays. She hated her worthless, gangbanging, baby-daddy for getting her into this mess. It was six p.m. and soon she would hear the ominous echo of the fat deputy's black boots on the cement floor.

It had started as a one-time hustle for dumbass Skeets to buy her some protection in the Dungeon while she did her nine months for pedaling his dumbass' dope. Fucking Skeets and his Iceboyz punks. She'd done her share of hookin' when she was younger, but the blade was one thing. She got paid for one, and she could choose her johns and turn down pigs like this.

The one-time thing had turned into every Monday. He would pop open her cell door and escort her out of the pod to a small room filled with janitorial supplies. And now it was expected. She was trapped between the deputy and the gang. One could end her life and the other could make it miserable. The deputy had made clear that any mention of their meetings would find her in the hole. It was one of the few things he had ever said to her.

She was getting better at numbing her body and transporting her mind to a different place as he writhed on top of her. Now though, the nightmares and the dreading were almost worse. In her cell at night, she heard the jingle of his keys as he shoved himself inside her, felt his grotesque belly on her back, smelled the beef jerky on his breath.

"Only one this week," he said, fishing the kite out of the front shirt pocket of his ill-fitting uniform after he yanked up his pants. No bigger than a quarter, she took the tiny folded note from his pudgy fingers and put it in her bra without reading it. She wanted to know as little as possible.

Now that the kite was in the inmate population, the rest would be easy. Back in her pod, LuAnne would turn it over to Ivy, the big bitch who ran the F-pod for the Iceboyz. She would send the kite on its way, usually routed through trustees or orderlies who had access to both the men's and woman's sides of the jail, then through one of the endless networks of inmate bribes and side hustles to its eventual destination.

****

"Welcome back to Department 27, ladies and gentlemen." Judge Ludlow greeted the jurors sporting a fresh dye job, its tawny hue not found in nature. "Mr. Didery, your next witness please."

"The People call Detective Mike Jameson."

I had spoken to the detective in the hallway before court. He had been cordial but had resisted my invitations to talk about the case or his testimony. He would be Didery's expert witness on the Iceboyz gang. In his mid-thirties with clean-cut good looks, he took the stand wearing a sport coat and tie.

T. L. Bequette

"Detective, how are you employed?"

"I am a peace officer for the city of Oakland," he said smiling a greeting at the jury, his eyes pausing for a moment on juror number eleven, an attractive pharmaceutical saleswoman.

"You've reached the rank of detective quickly. How many years on the force have you served?"

"This is my eighth year. I've been very fortunate." This guy was going to have the jury eating out of his hand.

"What is your current assignment?"

"I serve on the city's gang task force, primarily investigating homicides in gang-related cases."

Didery had the witness review his expert witness qualifications. In classic Didery fashion, he addressed the detective's curriculum vitae line by line. The prosecutor was now rapping his pen on the podium after every question as if calling an orchestra to attention. Finally, he asked the court to declare Detective Jameson an expert witness, qualified to render opinions in court in the area of criminal street gangs.

"I so declare," said Ludlow, forgetting to ask me if I wanted to question the witness or object.

Didery shot me a glance but I waived him off. There would be no benefit in refuting the witness' expertise. "Detective Jameson, are you familiar with the Iceboyz gang?"

"I am. The Iceboyz is a criminal street gang operating in west Oakland. It was founded in the late eighties by members of the Crips Mafia prison gang. Its members are predominantly but not exclusively African American." The detective went on to describe the gang's territory in Oakland, its rivalry with Cashtown, and the gang signs and tattoos common to their members.

In some ways, the next testimony would be the trial's most devastating to the defense. Along with the murder charge, Darnell was accused of committing the crime for the benefit of a criminal street gang. Although the sentencing enhancement would mean another fifteen years tacked on to Darnell's life sentence, the real problem was what that meant for the trial.

As part of his burden of proof, Didery would have to prove the existence of the Iceboyz as a criminal street gang. In so doing, he would have the opportunity to present evidence of other crimes committed by the gang, irrespective of Darnell's involvement.

For the next two hours, he paraded evidence of three of the most violent murders committed by Iceboyz members. First was a drive-by murder of a fourteen-year old member of Cashtown as he sat on his front porch. Next came a highly publicized murder of a mother of three, felled by a stray bullet in a gun battle as she tried to scuttle her children to safety. To my left, Darnell sighed and rubbed his face.

As the courtroom flat screen filled with bloody images, the mood in the courtroom again turned somber, the jurors averting their eyes from the gore. The last was a triple murder of three Oakland high school football players, executed as they sat in their car in a drive-through line after a game. By the time the carnage inside the car hit the screen, the jurors were visibly stunned. Juror number two, a first-grade teacher from Fremont, sat clutching her handbag to her chest with both hands and staring grimly at the floor.

The detective concluded his remarks by identifying Darnell as a member of the Iceboyz gang and rendered the opinion that the murder of Cleveland Barlow was committed for the benefit of the gang.

Thank goodness Ludlow had the sense to take the morning recess. The jurors needed it, and I had no interest in beginning my cross examination of the superhero on the heels of the avalanche of atrocity.

I walked around the courthouse outside to clear my head and was back at the counsel table when Darnell got my attention with a whisper. He met my eyes and gestured with his head toward the counsel table. His left sleeve was pushed up so that his bare forearm rested on the table in front of him. On top of his forearm, prominent against his light brown skin, was a very noticeable tattoo of a large "G".

I looked at him and frowned. I hadn't seen the tat before. In fact, his lack of visible gang tattoos had counted as a positive. I frowned at him and stared straight ahead. "Where'd that come from," I said out of the side of my mouth.

"Been having this for two years," he said softly, moving his hands under the table. "Check the car video."

I felt Didery staring at us, and I didn't trust Deputy Hardass sitting five feet behind us. "We'll talk about it later."

Ludlow made another grand entrance, vaulting out of his chambers, his robe flowing behind him. "Mr. Turner, cross examination?"

"Thank you, Your Honor. Good afternoon, Detective Jameson."

"Good afternoon."

"Just to be clear, these awful crimes that you've just described, you are aware Darnell Moore is not responsible for those crimes in any way."

"As a member of the Iceboyz, the gang that committed those murders, I would say he is responsible."

I cursed myself for my careless question and decided to take out my frustration on this nauseating huckster. "Detective, you're familiar with Operation Ice Out? That was an extensive investigation of the Iceboyz members in all three of those murders, correct?"

"Yes."

"The investigation was a colossal undertaking, utilizing surveillance, wire taps and search warrants, correct?"

"Yes."

"Among the enormous amount of information gathered, was there a single piece of evidence that Darnell Moore shot those victims?" I asked tersely.

"No."

"Any evidence he helped plan the murders?"

"No."

"Any evidence that he assisted in the murders in any way?"

"No."

"Any evidence that he knew the victims?"

The detective's smile had faded as the speed of my questions increased. "No."

"Any evidence that he was anywhere near the scene of the murders?"

"No."

"Any evidence whatsoever that he was even aware of the murders?"

"No." He was spitting out his answers now.

"And yet, Detective, you just testified under oath, that in your expert opinion, Darnell Moore is responsible for those murders."

He scowled. "I stand by my opinion."

"Detective, isn't it true that not all gang members are violent?"

"I would say that is not a correct statement. If you're in a gang, at some point you will be asked to participate in violence to show your worthiness as a gang member."

"At what age do gang members typically join their gang?"

He didn't know where I was going, so he was being vague. "I would say it varies."

"Thirteen, fourteen?"

"Typically, about that age, but sometimes younger."

"Darnell Moore is nineteen years of age, correct?"

"Yes."

"And how many times has he been convicted of a violent crime?"

"Zero. We don't catch them all," he added, smiling for the jury. This guy was the consummate prick.

"And prior to his arrest in this case, how many times has he been arrested for a violent crime?"

"Zero, prior to this case, but I'd say murder counts as a violent crime."

"I see. So you know Darnell Moore is a violent gang member because he committed this crime and you know he committed this crime because he is a violent gang member."

"Objection, argumentative." Didery probably

objected to prevent the detective from leaping down on me from the podium.

"Withdrawn," I said, walking back to the counsel table. "No further questions."

Over the lunch hour I visited Darnell in his cell adjacent to the courtroom. It was possible that I had not previously noticed the tattoo on his forearm. Were that the case, we would be on to something. I wouldn't have to "check the video," as Darnell had suggested. I had seen the surveillance footage of his green sedan turning left in front of the E&J enough times to recall that there was no tattoo on the bare forearm that rested on the top of the door.

He was finishing up his bologna sandwich when I walked in.

"So, Darnell," I said after Deputy Hartag left us alone, "you can tell that the driver of that car does not have a tattoo on his forearm."

"So, then we're in business!" he said punching my arm.

"The problem is, you and I both know that you can get tattoos in jail."

"No, Mr. Turner, I..."

"Hear me out, Darnell. There is police body camera footage of your arrest. There is video inside the police car you rode in. You were being filmed during your interrogation and for the five hours you spent in the box before they spoke to you.

"Darnell," I said, looking him in the eye, trying to will him to be honest, "if your forearm appears in any of that footage without a tattoo—and believe me, if it exists, Didery will find it—then your plan backfires. Getting a tattoo in jail in order to avoid prosecution would look like the work of a very desperate, very guilty man."

He bowed his head, and shook it slowly, staring at the floor. "Guess I was desperate," he said quietly.

"Why a "G?" I asked.

"It's for my mom, Glenda." He smiled. "She's still gonna kill me for doing it."

The afternoon session was another Ludlow special. After Didery's brief re-direct examination of Detective Jameson, he called to the stand Dr. Eugene Haverfaller, the pathologist who would describe Cleveland Barlow's gunshot wounds. Didery's painstaking review of the doctor's qualifications took the trial to the afternoon recess, after which Ludlow dismissed the jury.

I checked my phone after court, finding a text from Chuck.

—Turns out the shell casings were only submitted to the lab yesterday. Didery must have finally remembered. Results likely next week—

—Thanks. I thought all your old friends from the lab were retired or dead—

—I've always relied on the kindness of strangers—

—You're dating yourself—

****

After it left F-pod, the tiny scrap of paper had been passed through four sets of hands in less than twenty-four hours. From an orderly, who complied out of fear, delivering it to a cafeteria worker, who had extracted three cigarettes and passed it on to a trustee, parting with a can of fruit cocktail in the process. The trustee kept it overnight then delivered it to an Iceboyz captain in the exercise yard.

The gang member scanned the yard, then

summoned one of the newer recruits who lived in C Pod. "Time to do work," he said, dropping the kite in the younger man's back pants pocket as he brushed past him. It would remain there until that evening when the recruit called Turbo took it out in his cell, unfolded it, and ate it after reading two words: "Jesse Wendell."

Chapter Twenty-Five

Wednesday's trial session began with an announcement by Ludlow that we would not be in session on Thursday. With Friday already declared a day off by the judge, I began to wonder if the jury might lose the threads of evidence, which wouldn't be a bad thing for the defense. Beside himself, Didery's fidgeting and tapping reached new heights.

Back on the stand, Dr. Haverfaller described the path of the two bullets that killed Cleveland Barlow. After more than thirty years on the job, the Chief Pathologist for the Oakland Police Department was not about to change his ways when it came to visual aids. His testimony would not include three-dimensional depictions on the flat screen or animated re-enactments of the bullet paths. Instead, he brought with him a bald, white mannequin and thin wooden dowels to use as directional aids.

A tall, thin man with an unhealthy pallor, the pathologist appeared straight out of central casting. He was bald on top, and longish wisps of white hair ringed his head, reaching the shoulders of his outdated tweed sport coat. "I cannot determine which bullet struck the victim first. I can tell you that either on their own would have been fatal." His tone was matter of fact.

Didery asked the doctor to describe the path of the bullet that entered the victim's chest.

"The bullet entered the bottom portion of the chest, left of center, passed through the liver then through the bottom portion of the left lung. The bullet then travelled out the back of the body though soft tissue."

The doctor spoke as if he were describing a subway route, then unceremoniously pierced the soft exterior of the mannequin with a dowel and shoved it through the body at the angle he described. A woman in the gallery, whom I had guessed to be Cleveland Barlow's mother, left the proceedings, dabbing a tissue to her face.

Oblivious, the doctor continued, now describing the bullet that "entered the right forehead, through the skull, into the brain at a slightly downward angle, then lodged at the base of the skull." Now the expressionless mannequin stood next to Dr. Death, impaled through the chest and the head with the wooden rods, lending a ghoulish aura to the already morbid proceedings.

After concluding with the rather obvious pronouncement that the cause of Cleveland Barlow's death was gunshot wounds, it was my turn for cross-examination. For everyone's sake, I wanted to be brief. "Doctor, the bullet that entered the chest of the victim was travelling at a downward angle," I said, steering clear of his creepy visual aid.

"Yes, at about thirty degrees."

"And the same with the head shot?"

"Yes, approximately the same angle."

"And common sense tells us that a bullet fired from, say, twenty feet away that entered the body on that downward angle would have to be fired from a position substantially higher than the body."

"I would say that is accurate. Although, sometimes bullets ricochet off of bone in the body and change course. In this case, it is possible that the bullet's contact with a rib or the skull may have changed its angle."

Thankfully, I had researched this area. "In your experience, if a forty-caliber bullet fired from approximately fifteen feet away met human bone in a direct hit, isn't it true that it would likely not ricochet?"

"Correct, it would more typically shatter the bone if it were a direct hit on the bone. In order to ricochet it would have to be a glancing blow to the bone."

"So that would mean that both bullets in this case would have to glance off bones."

"Yes."

"And both would have to glance off bones and happen to ricochet at the same thirty-degree angle."

"Yes."

"And that would be quite a coincidence, correct."

"It would be a coincidence for sure. I'm not a mathematician, so I don't know precisely how much."

"No further questions."

After Ludlow dismissed the jury for lunch, I grabbed a hotdog from the stand outside the courthouse. The morning had been bad, but at least my cockamamie sunroof theory was still intact, the fatal shots having been fired by Darnell's imaginary friend. Such was the state of the defense. Since neither my client nor my star witness would tell me what happened, I was flying blind, scrambling to preserve theories that may well be destined for failure.

Maybe Damon had made headway with his twin. I texted him.

—*How'd it go yesterday with Jesse?*—

Back in Court, a police video technician testified in

unnecessary detail about how the video surveillance had been enhanced, and the new version of the surveillance was played for the jury on the flat screen.

After the afternoon recess, Detective Bosco took the stand. A veteran in the courtroom, he was forthright and direct, pleasant, without the smarminess of Jameson.

He told the jury how he had obtained the license of the green sedan from the enhanced video and traced the vehicle from Department of Motor Vehicle records to Darnell Moore. "Mr. Moore was arrested without incident and transported to the police department for questioning."

"And was Mr. Moore cooperative in the interview?" asked Didery, punctuating his question with a rap of his pen.

"He was. We told him of his right to remain silent, but he agreed to speak with us."

"What was his demeanor?"

"He was cooperative, but generally evasive. He told us that he thought he was there to address some unpaid parking tickets."

"Did you find this believable?" I could have objected, as the witness's opinion as to his believability was technically irrelevant, but I just wanted it to be over.

"No. We had introduced ourselves as homicide detectives, so I did not find that statement particularly credible."

"And what did he tell you about the murder?"

"First, he denied any involvement or knowledge of the shooting. We told him his vehicle was on video and we had a tentative identification from a witness."

"And what was his reaction?"

"He maintained his denial. He said he was at home at the time of the murder."

"Eventually, Detective, did Mr. Moore change his story?"

"Yes. We created a ruse in which we told him that we had cell phone records placing him at or near the murder scene."

"And what was his reaction?"

"May I refer to the transcript of his interview?"

"Yes, Detective, if that would refresh your recollection."

Detective Bosco removed papers from his black leather portfolio and flipped to the appropriate page. "He said, 'I guess I might have been in the area,' but continued to deny his involvement in the shooting."

"No further questions, Your Honor."

"Mr. Turner?"

"No questions, Your Honor."

Ludlow dismissed the jury for their four-day weekend and hurried off the bench before Didery could ask about scheduling the hearing on the motion to suppress the gun. As the Deputy D.A. meticulously packed up his file and color-coded pens, I asked again about the surveillance video from inside the E&J.

"Yeah, nothing yet. I'm not sure what the problem is. I'll have my inspector check on it."

"Thanks."

On my way out of court, I read Damon's return text.

—*Sorry. I wasn't able to make it to the jail. I will visit him next Tuesday for sure*—

Eddy and I had moved our standing Friday date to

Thursday due to Ludlow's decreed vacation day, so I headed home, took a run, and headed to Bill and Nick's. It was becoming our place.

"Hi there!" She greeted me at the bar with a kiss and a fizzing Gin and Tonic. "How's trial?"

"Dreadful. My client is afraid to testify, my witness is afraid to name the shooter, the prosecutor's nervous fidgets are a constant pebble in my shoe, and the evidence is coming in by the truckload. Other than that, peachy. How's your week been?"

"Brilliant compared to that. Actually, though, I'm souring on corporate life. I think I mentioned I've applied for some professorships."

"Good for you. Professor Busier has a nice ring."

"I'm glad you like it because I'm going to make you call me that in bed."

"Really?" I said laughing. "I think I can do that."

"So, back to your trial. Let's put our heads together. I'll bet we can solve the case."

"Love where your head's at, Busier. Let's assume Darnell's innocence and figure out the killer. Wild speculation is welcomed." I summarized the crime scene evidence as she sipped an Aviation, her favorite cocktail.

"Great," she said with enthusiasm. "From my experience watching cartoon detective shows, the bad guy is in our midst, already introduced at the beginning of our story."

"Is that right?"

"Yes, only to be unmasked at the end of the episode as the gang says together in astonishment, 'Mr. Ridley!' "

"I don't think we have a Mr. Ridley here."

"How about the shop owner, Bedrossian? It's always the grumpy old guy introduced at the beginning of the show."

"Ah yes, the one who would have gotten away with it if it weren't for those meddling kids."

"Yes! And that reveal at the end would be classic. 'Mr. Bedrossian!' "

"Not a bad guess. I think he wishes he shot the kid, but if he did, I get the feeling he'd own up to it. Also, how would he have known when Darnell was planning the shooting?"

"Or how about his son, the army stud?"

"Sorry, Busier, he was out of the country."

"Okay, how about the guy on the porch?"

"Same problem with the coincidental timing of Darnell's drive-by. With respect to your cartoon analysis, my money is on a gang member in his car. Someone he knows, hence the attempt on his life in jail."

"You're no fun."

"Time for another round," I said, heading to the bar. When I returned with the drinks, she gestured toward the flat screen on the wall opposite our seats.

"I got the ball game on for you."

"What would I do without you?" I asked, feeling starry-eyed.

"Is that you or the alcohol talking?"

"It's me talking to the alcohol."

She punched me in the arm. "Good one, Turner. Okay, how about if the shooter was Damon?"

"Damon Wendell, the law student who agreed to help me on the murder he actually committed? Your cartoon analysis is losing credibility."

"I told you I got a weird vibe from him. Maybe that's why Jesse doesn't want to name the shooter?"

"It's creative, I'll give you that," I said laughing.

We strolled back to her place, arm in arm, leaning together as we went. Our time was becoming more of everything—at once more exciting and relaxing, intense, and carefree.

Inside her house, she melted into my arms, her forearms behind my head.

"I have so much fun with you," she said, staring into my eyes. We kissed softly at first, then dived in, our greedy mouths hungry.

"You ain't seen nothing yet, Busier," I panted between kisses.

"That's Professor Busier to you, Turner."

****

"So, how in God's name are you and Eddy still a thing?"

Andy was in my office early on Monday morning, doing his best to ruin my good mood. Eddy and I had spent Saturday together. Sunday, I prepared for cross examinations while reliving my time with her. "Surely, you'll screw things up soon," he said with a wicked grin.

"Thanks again for all the support, and don't call me Shirley."

"How goes the trial?"

"Not well, so far. Damon's brother is likely our only hope, and he's not exactly rock solid."

"Damon is awesome. He's helping me with deposition summaries."

"He is. Hard to believe the twins are twins. Makes you tend to take the side of nurture over nature."

Cherlynn sent an email that due to a juror conflict, trial wouldn't commence until two p.m. After paying some bills, I walked to the jail for a visit with Darnell. I had managed to get through to him about the tattoos, and I hoped to ride that momentum into convincing him to come clean with me about the shooting.

I opted for a "contact" visit with Darnell. I had never completely trusted that my conversations with my clients through the glass were confidential. The same phones were used for family visits, which were frequently recorded. It would be easy for the Sheriff's Department to record my conversations if they were so inclined.

I waited in the very room where that maniac Dunigan had succeeded in convincing me of my imminent death. The windowless rooms at least gave the illusion of privacy. The small window in the door was opaque glass. An oversized video camera from the nineties pointed down from its mount in a corner of the low ceiling.

When Darnell took his seat across the table, I could see the stress of the trial was wearing on him. His effervescent smile had been permanently replaced in court by a look of concern as he concentrated on the evidence. His boyish cheeks were gone, victims of the jail food diet, and he'd developed a facial tic, his eyes spasming in rapid blinks. "Hey, Mr. Turner."

"Hi, Darnell. I wanted to speak to you about testifying."

"Look, no disrespect but…"

I raised a hand. "Please, hear me out."

He smirked. "Sure. I got nothing but time."

"Thanks. It's not because you need to tell the jury

who did it, although that would be nice. If the D.A. asks that, you can just refuse to answer. Technically, the judge could hold you in contempt, but you're already in jail. The real reason is this. Everyone on that jury will be thinking, 'If I was accused of a crime, and I was innocent, I would damn sure take the stand and deny it.' If you don't, it's almost like a signal to the jury that you're guilty."

He sighed and stared down at the table. "It's like this, though," he began, "the moment I even take the stand, it don't matter what I say. At that moment, it's over. I'm a snitch for the rest of my life, in custody or out. I've seen how these fuckers work. My mom and my brother would be in danger, and I'm not gonna do that to them."

I sat there, thinking of his impossible predicament. I respected his decision and knew I wasn't going to change his mind. "Will you at least tell me who else was in your car?"

"So you can have your investigator go snooping and have them find out? No," he said looking me in the eye. "I ain't talking about what happened."

I nodded in acceptance, then hit the buzzer and we sat in silence. "Oh, Darnell," I said, hearing the footsteps of the deputy in the hallway, "be sure to keep that tattoo out of sight as much as you can."

"Yeah, thanks." For the first time, I saw sadness in his eyes.

My phone rang on the short walk to the courthouse.

"Hey, Joe, it's Rocco Bedrossian."

"Hi, Rocco."

"Hey look, I'm getting really worried about my dad testifying. The market got shot up late last night. Thank

God we weren't there, but this is crazy. Is there anything that can be done?"

"Rocco, unfortunately, I'm the wrong guy to advise your dad on this. It wouldn't be ethical. Have you tried calling Didery? I'm sure he could probably get your dad moved to a hotel during the trial, or at least get patrols in the neighborhood increased."

"Okay, thanks. He's just so stubborn, he probably would refuse to move anywhere. I'm thinking about making him leave the area. I really think testifying is a terrible idea. I have to go back overseas next month, and he'll be here alone."

"Sorry I can't be more help."

"Thanks anyway."

Damon texted as I entered the courthouse.

—*Hey, still no luck with the translator*—

—*Thanks for the update. Please keep trying*—

It was shaping up to be a boring day in Court. Didery planned to call an officer who seized Darnell's car and a Firespotter technician, presumably to needlessly establish the exact time of the shooting.

I arrived in Department 27 to find Didery pacing back in forth in the empty courtroom, twirling his pen in one hand. "This is fucking ridiculous," he mumbled to himself. "We should be giving our closing arguments by now."

I toyed with the idea of telling him about Rocco's concerns but thought the added stress would be cruel.

"By the way, Joe, I think you'll like the next witness." Didery's tone was cocky.

Fuck it, then. "Hey, Rocco Bedrossian called me. Says he's thinking about taking his dad out of town." Didery's confident expression faded and the prosecutor began typing on his phone frantically, no doubt alerting his inspector to the potential issue.

Before court began, Didery managed to talk his way into a chambers conference. "Your Honor, Mr. Turner and I were hoping we could litigate the gun motion this week. Perhaps Friday?"

"Friday I'm afraid I'm otherwise engaged," the big man said, no doubt referencing a tee time in his mind. "Let's do it Thursday. And no more delays, gentlemen. We need to get this litigated."

Ludlow took the bench to a particularly resounding call to order at two-thirty p.m. and Didery finally called his next witness, Officer Gabe Lucero, who had supervised the seizure of Darnell's car. The witness identified photos of the vehicle, its driver's side riddled with bullet holes. He told the jury that a search of the vehicle had revealed mail on the floorboard, parking citations, and old pay stubs, all bearing the name Darnell Moore.

"One more question, Officer," Didery said, glancing my way. His tone was smug. "Did you have occasion to test the power windows in the vehicle?"

"Yes, they were operational."

I felt the nauseous wave of revelation just before his next question.

"How about the sunroof, Officer? Did you check to see if it functioned?"

"I did. The sunroof was closed and would not open. It was nonfunctional."

"No further questions," Didery said with a smile of satisfaction. So much for my lame sunroof theory.

Technician Emily Bradshaw took the stand next and explained the Firespotter technology to the jury in needless detail, concluding that the first shot fired at the murder scene had been fired at six-seventeen-o-five p.m.

"Technician Bradshaw, did I ask you to check Firespotter records for the previous two years for any gang-related shootings?" Still reeling from the death of my sunroof theory, I felt queasy again, this time with the feeling that I had missed something important.

"I did."

"And what did you find?"

"I found that there were shots fired two days prior to Cleveland Barlow's homicide, on March 20, 2021. Police responded to the scene and found possible bullet holes in a wooden fence surrounding a residence. There were no witnesses, no victim, and the case was closed without an arrest."

Didery's pen taps on the podium were punches to my stomach. "Officer, what was the location of those shots?"

"According to Firespotter, those shots were fired in front of 483 Clement Street, in west Oakland."

"Does that residence have any significance to you?" asked Didery theatrically, feigning true curiosity.

"Yes. That's the home of the defendant, Darnell Moore."

After Ludlow dismissed the jury for the day, I stalked out of court, cursing my own lack of preparation. During the testimony of the technician, a "Clement" word search on the entire case file had pulled up the report of the shooting. It had been buried amidst the two thousand pages of reports reviewed by Damon. It wasn't his fault. He wouldn't have been aware of Darnell's address to make the connection. In giving him the assignment, I had been lazy.

I was also pissed off at Didery. At the time the mountain of reports had arrived, I had wondered about their relevance. Absent a connection among the homicides, reviewing every Iceboyz-related murder for the past two years seemed like overkill. I had chalked it up to Didery's profound thoroughness, but now it seemed that he had purposely hidden the one very relevant report in the massive stack.

—Hey Chuck, could you go to the murder scene and take about 400 random photos?—

—Uh, sure (????)—

—Tell you later—

What I assumed would be a rather benign day in court had turned out to be devastating. The sunroof theory had been rife with speculation anyway, but combined with the angle of the bullets, it had been something.

But this latest blow—that there had been shots fired outside Darnell's home only two days prior to the murder—was much worse. Now there was evidence that Darnell, separate and apart from every other gang member, had motive. It was yet another coincidence that would require an explanation. Another drip on the defense forehead in Didery's relentless prosecution by Chinese water torture.

"And heaven forbid my client would give me a heads up about the shooting," I complained to myself once inside my car. I put in my earpiece for cover and yelled over my heavy metal play list.

"Can someone please tell me the truth about this case?"

****

Turbo didn't know when he would get the weapon or what it would be. That was for the O.G.'s to sort out —the "Original Gangsters", veterans of the pen who knew how to make weapons in jail. He figured it would be some kind of shank fashioned from metal: a bed spring, a nail, a piece of chain link fence. He'd heard the O.G.'s tell stories of lots of elaborate weapons—a ping pong ball filled with lighter fluid, a toothbrush handle melted and sharpened, a toothpaste tube filled with feces and urine to squirt on your enemy. But he figured his would be the standard metal shank.

He had seen the target, a skinny white kid, in his pod. He didn't look hard, but you never knew here in jail. He'd heard he'd done time for murder but had no idea if it was true. One thing he'd learned in his six months in the Dungeon, there were more rumors here than at his mom's hair salon. Whatever was true, he had a job to do. He knew what happened to members who disobeyed orders. He wouldn't do that to himself or his family.

****

Damon Wendell hated jails. For one, his twin had suffered in one for twelve years, keeping him from the only person in his life that mattered. But it was more than that. He had spent one night in juvenile hall when he was eight and he never forgot it. He and Jesse had been caught trying to break into the rec league snack shack for candy and hotdogs. Even now, he could conjure the smell of the dank air of juvy, the feel of the damp cement, and the echoing sounds of metal doors that had kept him up all night.

To think his first instinct as a kid when Jesse went away was to somehow break *into* the prison. When that seemed impossible, he thought about committing a crime, but he figured he would probably have to kill someone to get sent to Jesse's jail. He remembered doubting that he could do it unless he really hated them.

Sitting in a tattered chair in the crowded lobby of the North County jail, Damon snorted at his childhood thoughts. Memories like those made him realize how young he and Jesse had been back then. It was true they had seen more than most ten-year-olds. Still, they were children when Jesse had been taken away.

He hadn't been able to visit his twin in juvenile prison until he was fifteen. They had written letters, of course. Every day at first, then weekly for every week of those twelve years. He still had the letters. Jesse complained about the food and told funny stories about messing with the guards, but Damon knew he kept the really bad things from him. He could tell. Damon also undersold his good fortune of being placed with the Swenson family. He was sure Jesse could tell that, too.

He recalled his first visit with Jesse like it was yesterday. After a trip through a metal detector, he had been escorted into a large room filled with families sitting at round tables. One inmate sat at every table, distinguishable by their orange jumpsuits with "PRISONER" across their backs.

He had seen the "no contact" signs and the armed guards but hadn't cared. He hadn't seen his twin in five years. He and Jesse had embraced, clinging to each other desperately until pried apart.

Damon had begun to notice the changes, first in his letters and then on his visits. Jesse had been the cock-eyed optimist, a joke always at the ready. They both had been, really, taking turns helping each other through difficult times. Slowly, he became less resilient, his buoyancy weighted down by the relentless burdens of prison.

By the time of his release, Jesse was constantly on edge, a frightened animal set free in strange surroundings. He had lived with Damon for a while and later showed up from time to time, usually to borrow money. But Damon could tell he hated to ask, and he seemed happier by himself.

Last Tuesday, Damon sat in his car, sweating, and chomping on the nicotine gum he hadn't needed since he was fourteen, trying to muster the courage for the jail visit until it was too late. Now, he was filing inside the Dungeon with the other family members. By the time he arrived at the long row of stools bolted to the floor and facing windows of thick glass, Damon was a wreck, flinching with every clang of a metal door.

Then his twin brother appeared on the other side of the glass.

"Am I ever happy to see you," Jesse said with a tired smile.

"Me too. Obviously, I wish it wasn't here," Damon said, looking around.

"Yeah, this side of the glass ain't no day at the beach either. We just finished lunch. The food here is worse than the pen."

"Is it better than dumpster pizza?"

"That's a close one," Jesse said, smiling. "Those were some fun times though," he said after a time.

"They were," Damon said quietly, knowing they were sharing the same memories.

"Hey, remember the time we were dumpster diving at Vinnie's, and we got a salad dumped on our head?"

asked Jesse.

"A salad? More like the entire salad bar. We had lettuce 'fros.' " Watching each other laugh, they were taken back to happier times.

"Hey, any luck with the suit on maybe springing your bro out of here?" Jesse asked after the laughter died down.

"He won't budge."

Jesse bowed his head. "Yeah, I figured it was a long shot."

"Hey, I dropped some books off for you at the front. I remember you liked *Flames of Sorcery*, so this is the next one."

"Oh, thanks. I actually read the rest of the series in the pen, but I like to read them again. Helps pass the time in here."

"It really sucks that you're in here. I mean, you didn't do anything this time. Just happened to have witnessed the shooting. Doesn't seem fair."

"Yeah, well..." Jesse said, a sheepish grin spreading across his face, "even if I was on my way to buy weed in a stolen car, it was rotten luck."

Damon laughed and shook his head. "I did wonder what you were doing in west Oakland. Jesse, you are unbelievable."

"So, this attorney, Joe. I told him I'd say that his client wasn't the shooter, but he's after me to testify about who I saw shoot that kid."

"Yeah, he is. And I know that's easier said than done."

"Yeah. It's hard for me to explain to someone who ain't in this world, D. For people who have done time, snitching is like the worst thing you can do. It's more than being afraid to snitch. It's like I don't never want to be the reason behind someone doing time, no matter what they did."

"Yeah, but I guess Joe's point is that if you don't say who it is, the jury might not believe you and an innocent guy will be in there."

"Yeah, I get it." Jesse nodded.

"My concern is your safety in there. It seems crazy that you're in danger even though you aren't going to snitch."

"Yeah, the thing is, these guys don't want to wait to see if you're gonna snitch. You take the stand, it might be too late for them. So they just take care of business."

"Isn't there some sort of protection in here for you?"

"Yeah, don't worry about me. I know how to take care of myself."

Damon didn't believe him but knew it was no use to ask Jess to go into the protective custody section of the jail. They had had that conversation before when he was in prison.

"So Jess, I know you've heard this from me before, but I'd really like to see you turn it around when you get out. I know you got your GED in prison. You should go to the local junior college. I'll pay the tuition."

Jesse sighed, nodding. "Yeah, okay. It is probably time I got it together."

"You should. Your grades were always as good as mine."

"Yeah, who knows, we might be law partners one day."

"There you go. Wendell and Wendell."

"Hey, how's your schooling going, D? I hear you're kickin' ass."

"Oh, it's no big deal. I'm doing okay."

Jesse looked his twin in the eyes with a serious expression and sighed. "Listen, Damon. This is something I've been meaning to tell you, really, for a long time now." He looked down for a few seconds, gathering his thoughts.

"Here's the thing, D. You doing well, going to law school, having parents and nice things, it is a big deal, and I don't need you pretending that it's not. I tell damn near every person I meet about you. Just five minutes ago, I'm walking here from C-pod with a deputy, telling him that my twin brother drives a nice car and goes to school at Cal and is going to be a lawyer. Not one of them dump truck public defenders, neither, but a real successful one," he said, smiling for a second.

"And I know you think when you talk about yourself it might make me feel bad or something. But it don't. It makes me feel proud. And even though I don't have those things, I feel like part of me does and I can enjoy them. Not like you can, course, but hearing about them makes me happy.

"I'll never forget one time you visited me in the pen. We'd just turned sixteen and you were telling me about this birthday party your new family had for you. I could tell you didn't want to talk too much about it. But you said there was cake, ice cream, and presents, and the whole family sat at a big table and sang. I remember you said you even got to choose what kind of cake it was. You had them write 'Happy Birthday Damon and Jesse' in blue frosting." He paused to look down and swallowed hard. "That day, hearing about all that…it was one of my best days since they took me away from you. Inside or out."

Jesse re-focused on Damon, looking his twin in the eye again. "Anyway, D, I want to hear about all that. What law school is like, what it's like to drive a car, have a steady girlfriend. All of it. Got it?"

Damon blinked away tears. "You got it, Jess."

"Good. That's settled. So, D, let me ask you something." They both heard the buzzer, signaling the visit's end. "If I don't say who the shooter was, will that kid go down?"

"Hard to say, really."

" 'Hard to say.' Typical fucking suit answer," he said smiling at his brother. "Take care, D. Love you."

"Love you, too."

Chapter Twenty-Six

"Mr. Bedrossian, do you see the man who shot out of the car in the courtroom?" Didery's direct examination had taken the better part of the day to reach its climax.

The squat market owner scanned the courtroom for dramatic effect, his small, dark eyes falling on Darnell. "Yes. He is there," he said, pointing, "sitting next to his attorney in the blue shirt."

"Your Honor—" *Tap tap tap.* Didery was at it again. "—will the record reflect that the witness has identified the defendant?"

"It will so reflect," said Ludlow, keeping up with the proceedings.

Bedrossian wore a new looking charcoal gray suit and a red tie for the occasion, his deck shoes a give-away that it wasn't his normal attire. When Didery asked how certain he was about his identification, Bedrossian smiled at the prosecutor. "I am very sure." If I wasn't mistaken, his accent seemed thicker now. "It is, how do say here in America, 'as plain as the nose on my face.' " The comment drew smiles from a few jurors.

I rose to begin my cross examination. Although I had plenty of ammunition, I remained convinced I was missing something. I had spent last night reviewing Bedrossian's preliminary hearing testimony, listening to his 911 call and his recorded statement to the police. There was something there.

"Good afternoon, Mr. Bedrossian. Your store has been severely impacted by gang violence, hasn't it?"

"Oh yes. Many shootings, especially at night. Of course, people don't want to be outside. It used to be, people would gather at the store. Buy a soda and talk. Now, because of gangs—" He gestured toward Darnell, disgust in his body language and tone of voice. "—no one comes."

"And when you hear shots outside your store, what do you do?"

He smiled at me like I was an idiot. "Of course, you get to the floor. Right away if you're inside. If you're outside, you get yourself inside and get down."

"Mr. Bedrossian, did you see the car first or hear the shots?"

The market owner's eyes shifted to Didery, as if asking for help. "I heard car, shots, then looked up and saw shooter."

"Mr. Bedrossian, have you ever heard the term 'profile'?"

He looked quizzically. "I'm sorry. My English is not too good," he said, smiling at the jury.

"Your English is fine, sir. Certainly better than my Armenian." I picked up the preliminary hearing transcript. "Do you recall that in the preliminary hearing, you testified, 'Profile. I saw the shooter's profile'."

"I don't recall," he said, shifting in the witness chair.

"Prior to your testimony at the preliminary hearing, you met with Mr. Didery, correct?"

"Yes."

"Is that where you got the term, 'profile'?"

"Objection, Your Honor, argumentative." Didery was out of his chair, glaring at me.

"Move on, Mr. Turner," said Ludlow, again dodging an actual legal decision.

"So, Mr. Bedrossian, assuming the shooter was looking where he was shooting, he must have been looking away from you, correct?"

"I saw his face," the witness said with finality, crossing his arms over his paunch.

"Mr. Bedrossian, when you heard the shots, you were on the porch."

"Yes. I was in the store sweeping then went out to sweep the porch. I heard the shots."

"And as you told us earlier, if you're outside and you hear shots," I paused, flipping back a page on my legal pad. "I wrote it down. If you're outside, 'you get yourself in and get down'."

"Yes, but—"

"So when you heard shots on March twenty-second, that's what you did. You didn't wait to look and see who was in the car, you got inside, correct?"

"No!" Bedrossian pounded the witness stand. "No! I saw your client!"

"Mr. Bedrossian," Ludlow broke in. "Please remain calm and only speak if you are asked a question. Continue, Mr. Turner."

I had walked to my computer during Bedrossian's outburst. "Sir, this is a photograph of a sports car, correct?" I asked, presenting the image on the big screen.

"Yes," he replied gruffly, boring a hole through me

with his eyes.

"Now, Mr. Bedrossian, please tell me which one of these photographs looks the most like the sports car." The big screen showed a large sedan and a truck.

"Four-door car," he said holding his stare. He had had enough of me.

"Now, Mr. Bedrossian, at the Oakland police department, before you gave a description of the shooter, you were shown a group of six photos, correct?"

"Yes."

"And you circled two faces, one of Darnell Moore and one of someone else," I asked, displaying the photospread on the screen.

"Yes. You see on the screen. Why do I have to speak?"

"And you told the officer that these two photos looked the most like the shooter, didn't you?"

He smiled, as if planning my painful death. "Yes."

"Then after you were shown the photographs, you were asked to give a description of the shooter, weren't you, sir."

"Yes."

"And the description you gave was, quote, 'young black man, light complexion.' "

"Yes."

I paused, looking up at the six photos, all of young African American men with light complexions. "No further questions."

"Re-direct, Mr. Didery?"

"Mr. Bedrossian, prior to the shooting, did you have anything against Mr. Moore?"

"No."

"Had you ever seen him prior to that day?"

"No."

"And sir, you realize the seriousness of the charges against Mr. Moore?"

"Of course."

"Are you quite sure this is the man that you saw shoot out of his car?"

"No question," he said earnestly. "Mr. Turner can try to change my wording. Doesn't matter. And I'm sorry for his family. But this is the person who shot."

Before Bedrossian was excused, I asked that he be made subject to recall in case I found a translator and needed to ask him further questions. Or if I finally found what I was missing…

On my way home, Damon called.

"Hey there. Did you make it in to see Jesse?"

"Yeah, I'm not sure that he's going to go as far as naming the shooter. He's in a tough spot. One thing he asked me is would your client get convicted if he didn't name the shooter. I told him I didn't know."

"I don't know either, but I'd hate to find out."

"Yeah. Joe, in your experience, how much danger is Jesse in?" I heard the concern in his voice.

"Honestly, it's very possible that his life is in danger. The bad guys know he's in there on a witness warrant. That's why I suggested protective custody, but I understand that has its own disadvantages."

"Joe, what if you agreed to his release and—"

"Sorry Damon, I—"

"I know. Hear me out. I know he'll come to court. He could stay with me and I would make sure he'd be there."

"Damon, I feel horrible about this. But Jesse

already failed to appear once. I wouldn't be doing my best for my client if I agreed to his release."

He sighed into the phone. "Okay. About his testimony, I think I could maybe make some headway with him if we were in the same room. The phones make it difficult to really talk to him. Is there a way I could get a contact visit?"

"Sorry, they're only for attorneys. I can set you up with a video conference with him. Best I can do."

"Okay, thanks."

"Any progress on the interpreter?"

"Yeah, I think I found one in Fresno. Apparently, it's an Armenian hub."

"Okay, thanks Damon."

"See you."

****

Turbo felt the shank drop in the back pants pocket of his jail jumpsuit while in line for chow. He knew the rules. It had to happen within twenty-four hours, and he couldn't get caught with the weapon before.

Turbo didn't know that his shank was a shank. Before its current usage in prison parlance, the word originally described a metal piece inserted in the sole of leather work boots just below the arches. Turbo's shank had been dug out of a guard's extra pair of boots, stolen from his station by a trustee. The five inches of metal had been filed to a sharp point on the jail cement floor. One end was wrapped thickly in plastic tape to form a round handle.

Back in C pod, it was "pod time", when the inmates were allowed out of their cells and into the common areas. Turbo had noticed that the skinny white kid usually stayed in his cell reading. Another Iceboy made eye contact and gestured toward Jesse's cell. It would be standard procedure. Turbo would enter and take care of business while his partner stood in the cell door, preventing intervention, and acting as a lookout.

He gripped the smooth ball of tape in his palm, the sharp dagger protruding between his middle and fourth fingers. He walked from his corner cell across the pod with his partner in tow. The cell door was open. The kid was on his bed in the bottom bunk, reading.

****

Eddy and I had dinner and a movie planned for Thursday night, so after a workout, I got a head start on the cleaning. Next, I prepared for the hearing on the admissibility of the gun and began assembling the jury instructions. I was not looking forward to the conference with the judge on jury instructions. In deciding the correct instructions for the jury, Ludlow would have to have paid close attention to the facts, then apply the law correctly. He may as well be asked to bend spoons with his mind.

The aiding and abetting instruction was a problem. Even if I somehow convinced the jury that someone else in the car was the shooter, Darnell's role as a driver would have him convicted of murder.

My phone alerted to an email at nine that evening. I knew the odds were good it was Didery, probably sitting with perfect posture still in coat and tie somewhere in a spotless home office. My stomach turned when I saw the subject line: "Ballistics Tests."

I opened the email attachment and scrolled to the report's conclusion: *"Given the matches of both unique striations and impressions left on the sample shell casing and the specimen shell casings, the specimen*

243

shell casings found at the scene of the shooting were fired by the firearm found in the residence of the defendant."

I stared at the page and re-read it, hoping for a different outcome. The evidence was now overwhelming. It was Darnell's car, Darnell's gang, Darnell's motive, and Darnell's gun. Bedrossian's identification was window dressing. It was time to fold the cards.

I emailed Didery: *Second degree murder for fifteen to life?*

His response was almost immediate: *Yes, but the offer is tomorrow only, prior to our hearing. Once the gun is in evidence, the deal is off the table.*

I would visit Darnell before court. It was time for a come-to-Jesus moment. I was opening a bottle of wine when Eddy called.

"Hey, Busier, how was the pedicure with your sister?"

"Very fun. She was sorry not to meet you but only had a few hours in town." She sounded more serious than usual.

"No problem, what's up?"

"Well, remember how I told you I'd sent off some applications to colleges?"

I felt a knot forming in the pit of my stomach. "Yes."

"Turns out, I just got an incredible offer from a university in Rome."

"Wow," I said, trying to muster excitement in my voice. "Rome, that's awesome."

"Yeah, I mean, I had no idea it would be this soon, but they want me to start in the summer term." Her sentence hung in the air.

"Well, I mean, it's Rome, so obviously you have to take it."

"Yeah, I think I do. It's sort of the home of archaeology. I mean I wanted to tell you in person, but I just felt like I should let you know and…"

"No, no. No need for that. That's really exciting, Busier," I heard myself say in a monotone. "Hey, listen, I should get back to this, you know, stuff I'm doing."

"Oh, sure. Okay, I mean we're on for tomorrow right? I want to talk about—"

"Uh, I'm pretty busy. I'm going to have to, um, pass."

"Look, Joe, this doesn't have to affect us, I mean it's…"

"Uh, yeah it does," I snapped, surprising myself with my own terse tone. "I mean, let's be real, Eddy. It sure seems like it does. You're moving to Italy, so that's kind of it for us." My words escaped out in a torrent, as if damned up before their release.

"Well, if you'd just let me—"

"That's why you called, right? So you wouldn't have to do this in person."

"Joe, why are you doing this?"

"Why am I? Sorry, I have to go."

"Okay, goodbye, Joe."

I sunk down into the recliner and stared into space, feeling hollow. After a time, I tried to process the conversation. She said she wanted to see me tomorrow, but she couldn't have meant it. That's why she had shared the news on the phone, and I was thankful. I was better at wallowing on my own.

I went to the kitchen. Ice, gin, a splash of tonic and

two gulps. Why had I allowed myself to think we could be an actual match in the long term? Part of me knew she would eventually end it. She was too perfect. God was she perfect—the way her blue eyes gleamed when she thought of a joke, our smiles sharing an unspoken language of our own. Two more gulps. I already missed the feel of her lips on mine, the sight of her hair spread on the pillow. Ice, gin, tonic, repeat.

Sure, she thought I was funny. "I have so much fun with you," she had said the last time we were together, her depthless comment a tinny voice in my ears. For Eddy, I had been an entertaining little fling, nothing more.

Andy, Chuck, everybody saw it but me. Except that I had seen it. Deep down, I had been expecting it. Our end had been my nighthawk, circling high over the edges of my consciousness, its dark shadow flickering across my mind, always when we were apart. Ice, gin, repeat.

****

After two coffees and a large bottle of water, my head stopped pounding somewhere during the drive to the jail. On the way, I had second-guessed my handling of Eddy's news. Her mention of Rome had somehow tripped a switch, and words had tumbled out without thought.

Arriving at court, I shook thoughts of Eddy away and headed in to speak with Darnell and convey Didery's offer.

"I already know what you're gonna tell me," he said as I sat down in the windowless cell just off the courtroom.

"Yeah, Darnell, you probably do. They matched

the shell casings at the scene to your gun." I didn't have the energy to lecture him about telling me the truth. Besides, that ship had sailed.

"Look, Mr. Turner." He looked up with tears in his eyes. "I know you don't believe me, but I didn't do this. If I did, I'd take the deal, but admitting something I didn't do…I just can't do it."

"Then tell me what happened, Darnell. It's your only chance."

He sighed deeply, wiping his eyes. "I was supposed to do it," he began, staring into space. "They said I needed to kill me a Cashtown or I wasn't one of them…that I wasn't down for the struggle, a soldier, all that mess. One of them was in my backseat. I ain't giving a name. I don't care, I'll die in here before I do that to my family.

"So, I'm driving over there and I'm, you know, having second thoughts. Like am I really gonna kill some dude I never met, who never did nothing to me? But I'm driving there, and I got dude in the back."

"Were you both armed?"

"Yeah. So I drive up on 'em and my gun is out. I put it out the window, but I couldn't do it. I just fired straight up in the air. Emptied the clip."

"So your partner in the back did it?"

"I don't know. I guess so. I just drove off, dropped him off."

We sat in silence for several minutes while I digested his words. Firing in the air would explain the missing bullets and obviously mean that someone else killed Barlow. His partner's shell casings weren't at the scene, but they could have been ejected inside the car. Without Darnell's testimony, though, the theory lacked even a shred of evidence.

Finally, his voice interrupted my thoughts. "There's no way out, is there?"

"You never know," I said. "Let's keep fighting."

"Hey, Mr. Turner, you okay?"

"Yeah, why?"

"Just seem like you're having a bad day or something."

"I'm good, thanks."

Back in court, Didery was at the counsel table. "I assume no deal?" he asked without looking up.

"No deal."

"I figured. Some guys just need to be convicted." I missed the old Jittery Didery. The prospect of a quick guilty verdict was turning his nervous insecurity into a nerdy swagger. "By the way, I'm calling a jailer this morning who processed your client on the day of his arrest," he said casually. "His body camera shows his forearms. Not that I need the extra evidence, of course."

"Listen, asshole, keep your needle nose out of my confidential communications with my client."

"Temper, temper, Joe," he chastised in a creepy tone.

Whether it had been him or Bailiff Hardass who had overheard Darnell, I wanted to slam his smug smile into the counsel table.

"Hear ye, Hear ye…"

The elaborate call to order interrupted our tussle, and soon Deputy Evan Santoro was on the stand, educating the jury about how inventive inmates manage to give each other tattoos in jail. "Inmates are quite resourceful. For the tattoo gun, they take the motor out of a beard trimmer and attach it to the shell of a pen.

For the ink, they burn cotton balls doused in baby oil and collect the soot. For the needle, I've seen guitar strings or straightened springs from inside a pen. It's not safe but they don't seem to care."

"Deputy Santoro," said Didery, after a pen tap, "let me know if you recognize the video I'm about to play on the screen." The screen filled with a shaky video of Darnell being led down a hallway in the jail on the date of his arrest. His handcuffs were removed behind him as he faced the camera. Didery slowed the video as Darnell brought his hands in front of him and rubbed his wrists. The prosecutor stopped the video with Darnell's left forearm clearly visible on the screen. There was no tattoo on the forearm.

"Yes. I recognize this as a video from my body-worn camera on the date of his arrest and the subject as the defendant, Darnell Moore."

After I passed the witness, Didery tapped his pen twice on the counsel table then strode to the well of the court like a peacock, centering himself in front of the jury. "Your Honor," the prosecutor started solemnly, "at this time I request that the defendant be ordered to stand and reveal his left forearm to the jury."

Ludlow looked like he'd seen a ghost, sensing a legal issue at hand.

"No objection, Your Honor," I said, easing his mind.

While a defendant could not be made to testify, it was a well settled legal precedent that showing a body part or even saying a phrase for the purpose of voice identification was not "testimonial" in nature.

"Very well," said Ludlow, "Mr. Moore, please stand and show the jury your forearm." Darnell complied. The black "G" showed prominently on his light skin. Juror number five, an African American software engineer from Berkeley slowly shook his head with a crooked smile of disdain. He, for one, was ready for his ballot.

"Your Honor, I have one more witness," Didery said, beaming. "He is not available until Monday. I thought we could take up our legal issue this afternoon."

The judge dismissed the jury until Monday and said he'd be back on the bench in fifteen minutes to address the motion to suppress. Still feeling the effects of my sad bender, I drained another water bottle and wolfed down a hotdog before returning to court.

Ludlow took the bench in the empty courtroom wearing a scowl. "Gentlemen, litigating a motion at this late date indicates a failure of the parties to reach a resolution." This was a uniquely stupid assessment, even for Ludlow. Never mind that he and he alone was the only reason for the delay, it was not a "negotiable" motion. Didery wanted the gun in evidence and I did not.

"Mr. Turner, please recite your argument for exclusion of the firearm."

"Thank you, Your Honor. As the Court is aware, I have moved to exclude the firearm based on a violation of my client's right to privacy. Specifically—"

"Mr. Turner, in my courtroom, I expect the attorneys to support their arguments with citations." I had expected to have to spell it out for Ludlow, but this was extreme.

"Yes, Your Honor. I'm referring to my client's right to privacy as guaranteed by the Fourth

Amendment to the United States Constitution. 'As warrantless searches of homes are unreasonable, the search of—' "

"Mr. Turner! Again, if you'd like a ruling on your motion, I must insist on clear citations!" I caught sight of Didery to my right, silently chortling to himself, reveling in my frustration. Ludlow didn't care about citations. He was trying to find a non-legal reason to deny my motion.

"Okay, as the Court is aware," I said, losing my patience, "the search clause of the Fourth Amendment to the United States Constitution protects warrantless searches and the exclusionary rule renders inadmissible any evidence seized—"

"Counsel, citations!"

"The exclusionary rule?" I asked, exasperated. "You want me to cite the exclusionary rule?" No one had cited it since law school because everyone knew the rule. "Um, I believe that would be Mapp v. Ohio, Your Honor. Since the gun was seized from a closet—"

"Mr. Turner, I don't appreciate your tone," the judge began calmly. "More importantly, that is not a proper legal citation!" he bellowed. "Since you continue to flout my clear instructions on citations, I have no choice but to deny your motion."

"Excuse me, Your Honor?" This was a new low for Dudlow. "You're denying the motion? Would the court care to articulate on what legal basis?"

"I've made my ruling."

"Your Honor, with all due respect, I haven't even—"

"I told you I needed citations in my courtroom!" he boomed into his microphone.

I'm not sure what made me snap. It wasn't just Ludlow's incomprehensibly ignorant bluster. Maybe it was the trial, sliding as it was, inexorably toward a guilty verdict. Maybe it was Didery's snooping or his pen-tapping that continued unabated. More than likely, my stupidity with Eddy played a role.

"Okay, Your Honor, you want citations? Let me start again. Joe Turner for my client, Darnell Moore. I think therefore I am!"

"You'd better watch your tone, Mr. Turner! I'll hold you in contempt," he yelled, jowls quivering.

"Please do," I yelled back. "I have nothing but contempt for this Court, so it'll be your first correct ruling of the trial!"

"Mr. Turner!"

"You need the citation for contempt, judge? P.C. 166. The P.C. stands for Penal Code!"

"Don't test me! I will find you in contempt!"

"Judge, you couldn't find your ass with both hands!"

"Contempt! I hereby find contempt!" the judge shouted, banging his gavel like a child. "That is, I, err, find you in contempt! Deputy Hartag, take him away. Bail is one thousand dollars. Enjoy your ride to the jail, Mr. Turner."

The deputy sprang into action like he'd been dreaming of the opportunity all his life, cinching the cuffs until I flinched in pain while my client stared, wide-eyed. "Pretty stupid move, counselor," he said in his best tough guy voice while shoving me into the holding tank.

"Go practice your 'Here ye's,' asshole."

Soon I was joined in the tank by Darnell.

"Damn, Mr. Turner, that judge wouldn't even listen to you."

"He's an idiot."

"Well," he said, "I appreciate you fighting for me."

"That's my job, Darnell. So what happens now?" I asked after I had calmed down.

"Bus back to the jail. Usually leaves in about an hour."

We sat there, discussing the case until the bus arrived. I continued to be impressed by his understanding of the evidence and the nuances of trial strategy. "Hey, Mr. Turner," he said before we were loaded on the bus.

"Yeah?"

"Guess you're having a bad day now."

Chapter Twenty-Seven

Until I feared I would lose it, I never loved to read.
One does not love breathing. —Harper Lee

Once at the jail, I was put in a large holding tank filled with new arrestees, all misdemeanants from the looks of them. Lots of future DUI clients, but I wasn't exactly in the mood to drum up business. It was eight p.m. before I got access to a pay phone. Thankfully, Andy picked up.

"You're where?" he asked in disbelief. "Ludlow?"

"Ludlow."

"Sorry, partner, I'm in Tahoe," he said trying to contain his laughter. "Let me make some calls. I'll find someone."

It was an hour before the jailor called my name. I walked to the door, smelling freedom, but was denied at the door. "You have a visitor," he said, gesturing to an interview room to my left.

"Are you sure?" I asked, walking in.

It had crossed my mind that Andy might call Eddy, and there she was on the other side of the glass with a phone to her ear. "Thanks so much for coming," I said after picking up the receiver on my side.

"Listen, Turner," she said, cutting me off. "I haven't posted the bail yet. You want out, you need to answer some questions."

254

"Okay."

"Do you want to be in a relationship with me?"

"Yes."

"Okay, I feel the same way, but can you grow a pair and get over your ridiculous insecurity. Because if you can't, tell me now."

"Yes, I can."

"I mean, would you ever not date someone because they were slightly less attractive than you?"

"Of course not."

"Well, do you think I'm that shallow?"

"I guess I just assumed…"

"I know what you assumed. But I'm not fifteen, Joe. If I don't want to be in a relationship with you, I'll tell you. I called to tell you about the Rome thing because I was excited about it and I wanted to share it with someone I care about. I wanted you to be happy for me and all you thought of was yourself."

"I know that now. I'm sorry, Eddy. You mean a lot to me…really a lot. I just thought I had lost you."

Her features softened. "You know you're going to owe me. This place is disgusting. What happened?"

"Uh, Eddy?

"Yes?"

"Will you please bail me out now?"

"C'mon, I already did. I just needed to get your attention."

Two minutes later, we were walking out the front door of the jail, my first stint in custody over. "You don't mind if I don't kiss you, I hope," she said finding my hand as we walked through the crowd of protestors outside the jail.

"No, I need a two-hour shower."

She drove me to her place where we shared a pizza after my shower.

"So…" I said tentatively, sipping my Pinot Noir next to her on the couch.

"Spit it out, Turner."

"About this Rome thing. You're going, right?"

"Yes, and what I was trying to tell you was that the position was only for a semester. I thought you could visit?"

"Wow. That would be great." I felt relief wash over me. "I mean, would you want me to?" I asked, just wanting to hear her say it again.

"Yes, Joe." She took my hands in hers. "I feel like we're on to something here."

"Me too."

"Yeah?" She sipped her wine. "When do you think you knew?"

"Oh, easy. First date, I asked about your profession. You said, 'I'm a shepherd.' A great line. And yes, I'm just that shallow."

"Hmm. After I drove to the jail, rescued you, poured out my heart, and saved us, I was expecting a little romantic soliloquy. I mean, I was thinking about suggesting make-up sex, but if that's the best you can do, I'm not sure," she said with a coy smile. "I mean, you do talk for a living, after all."

"Okay." I thought for a second or two, then looked into her eyes. "When I get up in the morning, if I'm going to see you it's a good day. My coffee tastes better, the air smells sweeter. If I'm not, then I make it a better day by thinking of you. I think of what you might be doing right then or imagine you bored at a meeting at work or leaning into me as we walk down the street. If something good happens or I see something funny, the first thing I think of is telling you. I picture your reaction—the way your eyes widen when you inhale just before you laugh, the way your lips part in a triangle when you're about to say something to make me smile."

"You *do* talk for a living," she said, kissing me on the lips.

"Well, make-up sex...the stakes were high." She inhaled a little, her eyes widening before her laugh. "So, Eddy, when do you think you knew?"

Her lips made a triangle before widening into a smile. "You had me at 'Wow. So like, digging.'"

****

I was tiptoeing back into her bedroom on Friday morning with coffee and a bag of donuts from the shop down the street when my phone buzzed. It was Damon.

—Hey Joe. I hope you're out of jail by now. I found a Kurmanji interpreter. I sent him the 911 transcript. He's available for the trial if necessary—

—Great news. Thanks—

"Yum." Eddy stretched and sat up in bed, taking her coffee. "Thanks. And who are you texting with at this ungodly hour?"

"Damon. He found an interpreter."

"Oh, for the market owner's statement at the beginning of the 911 call."

"Great memory."

"So what do you think he said?"

"Hopefully, something like, 'It's too bad I didn't see the shooter.'"

"Or better yet, 'Did you see that? I shot him twice.'"

"Now you're talkin', Busier. But I doubt if he would have said that to the 911 operator in any language."

She sat pensively, chewing a glazed old fashioned. "Did you ever get the video from inside the store?"

"No, Didery promised it by Monday."

"But I assume Bedrossian claims he was alone."

And just like that, it clicked. All those hours of listening to Bedrossian's taped statement to the police and reviewing his preliminary hearing transcript, and the missing piece finally fell into place. As I had predicted, the elusive subtext of the market owner's story had been hiding in plain sight. It had taken Eddy's question to reveal it.

"You are sexy and smart and perfect." I kissed her before hustling into the shower.

"Is that the donut talking or you talking to the donut?"

****

That afternoon, I arrived at the office to find Damon making copies for Andy. I asked about his video conference with Jesse.

"He didn't feel too secure talking on the video conference, so I don't think I made much progress." Damon seemed distracted, probably concerned for his twin's safety.

"Any new information?"

"Same story. Wouldn't tell me who the real killer is, if he knows him, or if he could recognize him if he saw him again. He saw the two old guys on the porch. One white guy, one black guy waving his cane around. The green car stopped in front—"

"Wait, Damon. Back up. Did you say the black guy

was waving his cane around?"

"Let me check my notes," he said, pausing. "White guy, black guy on the porch," he mumbled. "Here it is. Yeah, black guy was waving his cane around. Is that important?"

"Hadn't heard that before." I recalled Elijah Jakes leaning heavily on the cane in my office. It wasn't a prop. "Seems odd that when shots were ringing out, Jakes would be using his cane for anything except for getting himself off that porch?"

"Good point, I guess."

"Hey, Damon. You've really been an asset in the office. If you'd like to work on other cases, Andy and I can probably scrape together some slave wages for you."

"Thanks. I'd, uh…" He paused, looking down at the copier buttons. "I'd probably be better suited for Andy's cases. This was kind of a one-time deal because of Jesse's involvement."

His answer surprised me. "Sure, criminal defense isn't for everyone."

"Yeah," he said, still looking down, "I know everyone deserves a defense, but people who bully or abuse…" When he looked up, his jaw was set, his eyes, empty and flat. "I tend not to react well to them," he said deliberately, imparting a massive understatement.

"Totally understand." I looked away from his icy stare and tried not to shudder. These Wendell twins were something else. So much seemed to be going on beneath the surface. One thought had flipped Damon's switch, and I could almost feel the rage pulsating through him.

Later in the day, he was back to his pleasant self.

"Thanks for the offer," he said, poking his head in my office on the way out. "I'll talk to Andy."

"Sounds good. And let me know when you hear from the interpreter."

"Will do."

I texted Chuck as he left.

—Can you find out how Elijah Jakes' wife died?—

—I'm on it—

After another round of miniature golf with Eddy on Saturday, I spent the rest of the weekend preparing for the final trial push. The prosecution was likely to rest on Monday after the shell casings evidence, Didery's coup de grace. I would call Chuck to testify the bullet holes found in the door pre-dated the murder and then Jesse—not exactly a tour de force for the defense.

Jesse was obviously the key. If he took the stand and merely said Darnell wasn't the shooter, I didn't think the jury would believe him. He hadn't reported the crime to the police and his credibility would be suspect, especially given the tiny matter of his prior murder conviction. But if he would just reveal the actual shooter, or even describe him, we might at least have a fighting chance.

By Sunday evening, I needed an Eddy fix, if even just a text.

—Hey, good lookin', thanks again for the bail out—

—You mean bail outs, plural—

—Good one, Busier. Yes, thanks for setting me straight. And BTW, I know what you mean about Damon. Something's maybe a little off—

—Yeah. I think he feels all his twin's pain. So my theory that he's the murderer???—

—Ha-ha. Still nuts—

****

Jesse loved escaping into the magical worlds of fantasy novels. The books let him slip through the bars of his cell to lay in a lush shire or soar among the spires of medieval castles. Still, it was jail and his guard was never completely down.

The squeak of the cell door had him on his feet before his attacker reached the bed, two hands on his book, a hardback copy of *Daggers of Sorcery*. He saw the flash of metal and blocked the first punch with the book but not the second, the jab piercing the flesh of his left shoulder.

Another wild slash to his face dodged, but now Jesse was pinned against his bunk by the larger man, who jabbed at him relentlessly as Jesse tried to block the blows. A thrust to his midsection hit his book but not a chop downward, the shank plunging deep into his left thigh. The pain was starting to register, but he kept his wits as he endured two more sticks, one high on his arm, another puncturing his ribcage. Losing blood but propelled by adrenaline, he knew he would collapse soon, exposing his vital organs to his attacker.

Jesse caught the next blow to his thigh with the book, the sharp metal sticking into its cover for a moment. He coiled downward clutching the book, and ripped upwards with all his strength, catching his assailant under the chin, and sending him against the opposite wall. Jesse heard the knife clatter against the bars of his cell door and dove toward it. His hands groveled frantically for the weapon as his attacker leaped over him and out of his cell before the guards arrived.

****

"Your Honor, for its last witness, The People of the State of California call James Burns," Didery announced grandly. The more the evidence mounted, the more insufferable he became. And here was none other than Burns, every Alameda Assistant D.A.'s favorite witness. He was at the top of his field, beyond reproach, and spoke with a clipped high-brow British accent that would make him sound smart ordering a cheeseburger.

"Mr. Burns, good morning. How are you employed, sir?"

"Good morning to all," he said nodding to Didery and the jury. "I am employed as Chief of the Alameda County Crime Laboratory," he said, using the British pronunciation of his final word while the female jurors swooned.

"Mr. Burns, please summarize your educational background."

"Yes. I hold an Honors Degree and a PhD in Physics, both from Shraffordshire University, in England."

"And prior to your current employment, where were you employed?" And here it came, for my money, the coolest part of his resume if not the most impressive.

"I was employed as Vice Constable at Scotland Yard, in London."

Didery strutted in front of the jury as if he, himself, were the ex-Scotland Yard employee, guiding the witness through a summary of the field of ballistics before describing the testing conducted on the shell casings. The witness wove a video presentation seamlessly through his testimony, demonstrating how identifiable and unique marks are left on shell casings as they pass through a firearm before being ejected.

It was nearly noon before Didery asked his last question. "Mr. Burns, in your considerable expert opinion, is there any doubt that the shell casings found at the scene on the street were all fired by People's Exhibit twelve, the firearm recovered from Mr. Moore's residence?"

The witness turned to face the jury, as if considering the question for the first time. "No," he said in a classically British understated tone. "I haven't a doubt at all."

"Mr. Turner, cross examination?"

"No questions, Your Honor." Strangely, my initial exchange with the judge didn't feel awkward. My opinion of his incompetence could not have been a mystery to him before my outburst but now that it was out in the open, the air was clear.

At the lunch recess, I checked my messages. Chuck asked me to call.

"What's up?"

"Jesse Wendell was attacked in jail last night."

"Oh God. Is he all right?"

"Multiple stab wounds but no vital organs hit. Sutures and stitches but no surgery."

"Damn it. I feel awful. Does Damon know?"

"Yeah. I called him first. Seemed pretty shaken up. And another thing. Julissa Jakes died six months ago in the crossfire of a shooting in west Oakland."

"Interesting. Any way you can get Elijah subpoenaed for tomorrow."

"Just did it."

"You're the best. Are you on your way? You're on at two p.m. and Dudlow wants to break early again."

"On my way. You know I hate testifying."

"Piece of cake. Just relax and tell the truth."

"You can't handle the truth."

"See you soon."

I called the infirmary at the jail to check on Jesse. After receiving stitches and sutures, he had refused further medical treatment and had demanded to go back to his pod. He could testify Thursday if necessary but not sooner.

I called Damon, not sure what I was going to say. I felt terrible about Jesse and second-guessed my decision to keep him in custody. I could have agreed to his release. He could have stayed with Damon. What if he'd been killed? I got Damon's voicemail and left a stuttering, awkward message of apology.

Back in Court, I asked to speak to Ludlow. I knew he would jump at the chance for a mid-weekday off.

"Gentlemen, I hate to delay this trial again, but I understand it's out of our control. I suppose we could take Wednesday off and resume on Thursday."

Didery spoke up, knowing he couldn't change the judge's mind when it came to having a day off. "Your Honor, perhaps we could utilize the time and meet briefly on Wednesday morning for our jury instruction conference?"

Ludlow scowled at the thought of his free day taken away. "Why don't we meet briefly tomorrow after testimony to deal with jury instructions? Briefly, mind you. I expect you two to consult beforehand." *So I don't have to make any legal decisions.* He dismissed us with a wave of his hand.

Out in the courtroom, I barely recognized the distinguished middle-aged man in the dark suit. Chuck's radical transformation from aging hippie surfer to corporate investigator never failed to surprise me.

After another of Deputy Hartag's rousing calls to order, Ludlow addressed the prosecutor. "Mr. Didery, do you have further witnesses?" The Assistant District Attorney strode deliberately to the podium with his chest out. "Your Honor," he said solemnly, trying desperately to communicate the momentousness of the occasion, "The People of the State of California rest."

I even thought I detected the slightest of eye rolls from Ludlow. "Very well. Mr. Turner, do you wish to present evidence?"

"Thank you, Your Honor, the defense calls Chuck Argenal."

Chuck walked to the witness stand looking uncomfortable, no doubt because he wasn't wearing flipflops.

"How are you employed, sir."

"I am a private investigator, retained in this case by your office."

"As part of your duties, did you review photographs taken by the arresting officers in this case."

"I did."

"Directing your attention to the video screen in the courtroom, do you recognize that photograph?"

"Yes, it is a photograph taken by technicians investigating this case. The photo shows the front of 454 West Eighth Street. A pattern of four bullet holes is depicted in a half-moon pattern on the front door and door frame."

"I walked to my computer and pulled up a slide of the same photograph, this time with another photo of the door though shot from a slightly different angle alongside it."

Out of the corner of my eye, I noticed Didery shuffling though his file. After his stunt of burying an important piece of evidence in a stack of thousands of pages, I had delivered the old real estate photo to Didery amidst a file containing four hundred-fifty of Chuck's random crime scene photos. I had been dragged down to his level, but it felt good.

"You see the photo you just identified on the right. Do you recognize the photo on the left?"

"Yes, that was a photograph of the residence showing the same pattern of bullet holes in the front door."

"Do you know the source of that photograph?" If I had had a pen handy, I would have rapped the podium and glanced at Didery.

"That photograph was published in a magazine called 'Baytown Real Estate' in March of 2019, more than two years prior to the shooting in this case. If you look closely you can see the caption of the magazine's letterhead on the photograph in the upper right-hand corner."

"No further questions, Your Honor."

"Mr. Didery, do you wish to cross examine?"

The prosecutor smirked for the benefit of the jury. "No, Your Honor."

And with that, the defense had landed its first punch of the trial. Given the current state of the evidence, it was more of a tap. The prosecution could easily argue that Darnell had killed Barlow with two shots, then fired wildly, missing the house entirely as he drove away. Still, it was something. Personally, I liked the fact that it rendered the prosecution's silly laser show worthless.

After Court, per our tradition, I bought Chuck a beer at the Armory, a bar a block from the courthouse that overlooked Lake Merritt. Elijah Jakes would testify tomorrow. I wasn't sure why I was putting him on the stand, but I was certain he knew more than he was letting on.

"Never ask a question you don't know the answer to," I told Chuck, repeating the golden rule for trial attorneys. "With Jakes, I'll be violating that rule with every question."

"Yeah, as you might imagine, he wasn't thrilled to receive the subpoena. He's a bitter old dude. Wife shot, store he founded gone to hell. Maybe you can get him to confess on the stand."

"Ah, the Perry Mason moment. I'd like just one in my career."

"How's our boy, Jesse Wendell?"

"Stitched up and back in his pod."

"The kid's got more guts than you can hang on a fence. He knows the culture, too. In that world, if you show weakness, you'll be a victim all your life."

"It's sad." I understood Jesse's motivation, but the premise was that he had resigned to being "in that world."

"It is sad," Chuck said, finishing his IPA, "and I can't help but think the attack won't exactly motivate him to help us in court."

"Damon thinks his twin will do the right thing. We'll see."

"I wouldn't hang your hat on it."

Damon returned my call on the way to my car.

"Hey, Damon, I feel terrible about Jesse. I—"

"No," he said cutting me off. "You were doing your job. Jesse put himself in jail by not showing up."

"Thank you for saying that."

"I just can't believe he's back in that cell. I know it's his choice, but isn't there something that can be done? I spoke to him on the phone last night. Everyone knows who did it but, of course, no one's talking."

"I'm with you, but as far as I know, if he doesn't want protective custody, it's his call."

"That's my stubborn twin. I really need to see him in person to talk some sense into him. Isn't there any way I can get in a room with him?"

How could I say no? "Yeah, I'll call the jail and designate you as my investigator. If you can meet me in court, I'll give you the jail pass."

"Thanks. Hey, the translator finally got back to me. Says he'll email a transcript first thing in the morning."

"Thanks again."

I had almost forgotten about the translation, which also reminded me to follow up on the in-store video I'd been after for weeks now. It was my turn to shoot Didery a late-night email. There were two witnesses left and the trial was still a tangle of loose ends. Given the state of the evidence, only an eyewitness naming a shooter other than Darnell would prevent a guilty verdict.

Darnell, Jakes, Jesse—someone had to have the courage to tell the truth.

Chapter Twenty-Eight

Sometimes it's better to bend the law a little in special cases.—Harper Lee

"Good morning, Mr. Jakes." My next witness was waiting outside Department 27 in a dark blue pinstriped suit and gold tie. I sat down next to him on a bench.

"I don't know why you need me here. I already told you everything I know."

"Frankly, sir, I don't think you did. I think you told me what you wanted me to hear."

"Is that right? And what makes you think I'm gonna say anything different on the stand?"

"Well, I'm hopeful you care about justice."

"Ha!" His reaction was genuine bemusement.

"Thanks so much for coming," I said, trying to lighten the mood.

"Justice. That's what you're after?" he asked, his gravelly voice dripping with sarcasm. "Justice for who?" He sat staring straight ahead, his hand resting on the brass eagle-head handle of his blue metal cane that matched his suit.

"Mr. Jakes, I'm sorry for your loss. I wasn't aware last time we spoke that your wife had died recently."

He nodded silently and continued to face forward.

"Is this the cane that holds whiskey?" I asked.

"No. Left that one at home."

"Amazing how they can make canes to be anything."

He turned to look at me, a sly smile spreading across his face. "Mr. Turner, you'd be surprised." Was this guy taunting me?

"Okay, you'll be the first witness. I'll come and get you when we're ready."

Damon caught my eye on my way into the courtroom.

"Hey, so Jesse is not scheduled to testify until Thursday morning now?"

"Yeah. Ludlow signed the removal order. He'll be transported from the jail. Here's your jail pass," I said fishing it out of my wallet.

"Thanks, Joe. I really appreciate this. I'm going to do my best to convince him to get out of that pod, even if I have to put him back in the infirmary myself."

"Good luck."

Just before Ludlow took the bench, I checked my email and read the translation, considering my options. I was developing a theory that was short on evidence. It would involve going after nice old Mr. Jakes and risk alienating the jury. On the other hand, it was my only theory, and he did seem like he was taunting me.

The judge reminded the jurors that we would hear one witness today, take Wednesday off, then conclude the case with the last defense witness and closing statements on Thursday.

"Mr. Turner, your next witness please."

"Thank you, Your Honor. The defense calls Elijah Jakes."

The witness made the long trek down the aisle of the courtroom and up to the witness stand, leaning heavily on his cane with every step. After he took the oath, he settled himself in the witness seat in his customary position with his right hand atop his cane, as if ready to leave on a moment's notice.

"Good morning, Mr. Jakes." He nodded a reply.

"Sir, you are quite familiar with the E&J Market, aren't you?"

"You could say that. I opened it in seventy-five." Christ, he sounded like everyone's favorite grandpa. This wasn't going to be easy.

"Yes, and you still spend a lot of time there."

"I do. Spend most days there on the front porch of the market. I'm friends with the current owner, Vardan."

"That'd be Vardan Bedrossian?"

"That's right."

"You two sit there most days, on the porch talking."

"Yes."

"You're even learning some of your friend Vardan's language."

"Yes." The witness's eyes narrowed as he paused, surprised by my knowledge. "He's taught me some phrases," he said cautiously. " 'Hi. How are you. Goodbye.' That type of thing."

"Mr. Jakes, when you opened the store back in seventy-five, can you describe the type of place it was?"

The witness adjusted his position in his seat, sitting taller as he faced the jury. "The E&J, when it opened, was a nice little store," he said with pride. "It became sort of the hub of the neighborhood. Families would come by after church. The First Baptist is just down the block. In the summer, people would congregate on the porch. The kids would play ball in the street. Couples would have a visit..." Jakes moved his focus to the floor for a moment, clearly immersed in a memory. "It was a nice little market," he said, his voice trailing off.

"How would you describe the market now, Mr. Jakes?"

He smiled and shook his head. "Now, in that neighborhood, people are afraid to be on the street. Gunshots night and day. The market today basically sells liquor, cigarettes, some rolling papers for the youngsters to smoke their dope. That's about it." Jakes was speaking in an easy manner and I was sure the jury could picture him sitting on a porch, spinning a yarn.

"And on March 22, 2021, you were on the porch at about six-fifteen p.m."

"Yes, I was."

"Were there any customers inside the store?"

"No, it was empty, as usual. Vardan was sweeping out the store."

"Sir, tell the jury what you saw that evening."

"Same as I told you earlier. Car pulled up. I heard a bunch of shots. That's it."

"And you didn't see anyone actually shoot."

"No. It all happened too fast."

"Mr. Jakes, you sit there most days at that market, like you said, with those gunshots going off day and night. Do you ever have a gun with you?"

For an instant, he stiffened, but then smiled, "No."

"It would make sense, for your protection, right?"

"No."

"Sir, are you ever bitter about what these young thugs have done to your neighborhood?"

"I am, but I don't need no gun."

"The gang members have ruined the neighborhood, right?"

"Yes."

"Ruined your store."

"They have."

"And Mr. Jakes, these young violent men who ruined your store are also responsible for your wife's death."

The witness stared hard at me, and I was glad he wasn't armed now. "Yes, that's true."

"Sadly, she was struck by crossfire on—"

"November 3, 2020," he spit out the words, cutting me off.

"Gang members again, right?"

"Yes."

"You opened the E&J with your wife, correct? Named it the E&J. Elijah and Julissa."

"Yeah, so what's your point?"

"My point, Mr. Jakes, is that on March twenty-second of this year, you had a lot of anger inside you directed at those gang members who rode into your neighborhood and shot up the place, ruined the store you founded and killed your wife."

"I understand," the witness said, smiling. "Your client is guilty. You got to do something, right?"

"I get to ask the questions, Mr. Jakes. Now, if a person were to shoot a gun off that porch at someone across the street standing near the sidewalk, you'd be shooting at a downward angle, correct."

"I guess so," he said smugly.

"Well, don't guess, sir. Look at these photographs," I said taking the photos of the E&J off the Clerk's desk. "People's Exhibits fifteen and sixteen. That's the E&J, right?"

"Yeah."

"And you have to climb four steps up to the porch to the front door, correct?"

"Yes." He was barely listening now, the smug smile still in place.

"So, the porch is about four and a half feet up from the street, right?"

"If you say so."

"So a shot across the street would have to be at a downward angle."

"If you say so."

"You own a great many canes, don't you, Mr. Jakes."

"What does that have to do with anything?" He was becoming agitated, looking at the judge for help with his palms up, then sitting in silence, shaking his head.

"Your Honor," I said after twenty seconds of silence, "I would ask the witness to be ordered to answer the question."

Ludlow arose from a mini-slumber, clearing his throat. "Mr. um, Jakes, is it? You are ordered to answer the question."

"Yeah, I got canes. What of it?"

"You have a cane that holds two ounces of whiskey, correct?"

"Yeah."

"You've seen a cane sword, right?"

"Yes."

"Before Court today, in the hallway, you said to me, with a smile, that it was amazing what they could do with canes, nowadays, didn't you?"

He stared daggers at me, nodding, like I had betrayed a sacred trust.

"Do you own a gun that's disguised as a cane, Mr. Jakes?"

He forced a laugh, shaking his head.

"I'm sorry, Mr. Jakes, did you not hear the question? Do you own a cane that shoots?"

"You got it all figured out, don't you?" he said with a sneer. The forced smile was gone.

"I'm starting to, Mr. Jakes."

"Objection!" Didery sprang from his seat. "Your Honor, Mr. Turner is testifying."

"Withdrawn," I said quickly, not wanting to kill the momentum.

"Mr. Jakes, you say you heard these shots," I said, using air quotes. *I was all in now, after all.* "You must have run into the store with Mr. Bedrossian."

"No, I told you, I got off that porch and hobbled my ass down the street." He glanced at the jury, smiling at his joke.

"Now, Mr. Jakes, the only way off that porch is down the steps toward the street, correct?"

"Yeah."

"So you heard these shots coming from the street in front of you and what you decided to do was run toward the shots?"

"I told you what I did."

"Sir, the truth is you went inside the store with Mr. Bedrossian."

"No."

"Mr. Bedrossian saw you shoot, so when you got inside, he said, 'Go! You have to leave. Now!' "

"No!" yelled Jakes angrily through clenched teeth. He had finally lost his cool.

I paused, walking from the podium to my computer, letting the jury digest his rage while I cued up the 911 call. "Mr. Jakes, I'd like you to listen to Mr. Bedrossian. This is once he's inside the store, having already dialed 911." The jury listened as the market owner spoke in his native language for less than ten seconds.

"Mr. Bedrossian, speaking his language is telling you, 'Go! You have to leave. Now!' isn't he?" I said, reading from the transcript on my phone. I noticed that Didery didn't object, which meant the weasel already had the translation.

"How would I know what he said?" The witness had regained his composure.

"Well, you had been learning the language, right? You told us that earlier in your testimony."

"I told you I knew phrases. Not words like that."

"Well, Mr. Jakes, you said yourself, the store had been empty, right? So when Mr. Bedrossian said 'You have to leave. Now!' was he talking to himself?"

"Objection, argumentative."

"Sustained. Save the sarcasm, Mr. Turner," chimed in Ludlow.

"Mr. Jakes, after you heard the shots, you used your cane to get off the porch, correct?"

"I always use my cane when I walk. Yes."

"So you would have no reason to wave the cane or point it at anybody, would you?"

"No."

"And if a witness says that they saw that, they would be mistaken?"

"Yes, they would." The witness was back to smiling, with a "get a load of this guy" look to the jury.

"No further questions, Your Honor."

Didery matched Jakes' relaxed smile as he arrived at the podium for cross examination.

"Mr. Jakes, I'll be brief. We've taken enough of your time today. Can I get you a drink of water?"

"No, thank you."

Didery was in full smirk for the jury. "Sir, do you own a cane gun?"

"No."

"Have you even heard of one?"

"No."

"Did you have any idea what time Darnell Moore was going to drive through that intersection that day?"

"No."

"When you said you had learned some phrases, does that mean that you understand the spoken language when someone is speaking to you?"

"No."

"How many shots did you hear, Mr. Jakes."

"I heard two. They seemed really loud. Then I heard a bunch of other shots that were not as loud."

This guy was unbelievable. Was he taunting me again? Were the first two shots louder because he fired them? This would make sense. First the two shots that killed Barlow, then Darnell's ten shots in the air.

Didery clearly didn't know what to make of the answer. "No further questions, Your Honor."

As Jakes hobbled down from the witness stand, I had no idea what the jury was thinking. The cross examination had gone well enough, but I knew my theory was Swiss cheese, especially compared to the prosecution's case against Darnell.

"Ladies and gentlemen," began Ludlow. "The defense has one more witness. As we discussed, we will not be in session tomorrow. We will reconvene Thursday morning, complete the evidence and hear closing arguments. Thank you."

****

Damon's heart pounded in his ears, a cadence syncopated with echoes of his footsteps on the tile floor of the long jail hallway. He couldn't believe he was heading back into the jail, but he needed to do this for Jesse. His twin had almost died, and he was mad at himself for not taking action sooner. He should have pressured Joe to let him out. He had asked politely, but he hadn't pleaded. And what had he been doing working on the case? The case was the reason why Jesse was in custody in the first place. He'd been selfish —trying to impress the attorney while his brother suffered in jail. It had almost cost Jesse his life.

And now his twin was back in that pod, a sitting duck for his assassin. Jesse would be in there at least another two nights, even longer if there was another delay. Damon owed his life to his twin: his family, the fun in college, his career. Everything.

And Jesse was right. Damon didn't understand why he wouldn't seek protection in jail, but that didn't matter. He needed to get him out of that pod. Damon didn't look forward to what he knew was coming. He'd never laid a hand on Jesse, not in anger. He knew he was still healing from the attack, but these were desperate times.

He arrived at the door with "Contact Visit" painted in black stenciled letters and pushed a button to its right. The door with the small window of opaque glass buzzed open and he went inside the windowless room, took off his jacket, and waited for the arrival of his twin.

Jesse entered the interview room followed closely by a deputy. As twins, they had always sensed each other's feelings—joy, sadness or, like now, pent up hostility.

"What the fuck are you doing here?" Jesse looked menacingly at Damon, while the deputy removed his handcuffs. "Ain't you supposed to be a law student. How is it you can't get me the fuck out of here?"

The deputy looked at Damon. "You all right in here?"

Damon nodded, and the deputy was gone, his footsteps fading as he retreated down the hallway. Jesse stood rubbing his wrists, then walked behind Damon, smiling as he removed his twin's jacket off the back of his chair.

"Let's do this, D. I know you've wanted to smack me around before," he said with a twinkle in his eye. "God knows I have."

Damon stood, hands at his sides, and approached his twin. He was shaking and felt a pit in his stomach. Jesse turned away and tossed the coat upwards with both hands, hanging it over the video camera mounted in the corner of the ceiling. Damon's hands were still down when Jesse spun around, his fist catching his twin flush in the nose.

****

After the jury was excused, Ludlow announced a fifteen-minute recess before the jury instruction conference in his chambers. I texted with Eddy. We were planning a getaway in the wine country after the trial, and I had left the details to her. If there was a guilty verdict, I wondered if I could go.

"Gentlemen," Ludlow said, waving us in from the doorway of his chambers. "I've read your requested jury instructions. Let's make this brief." Didery and I sat on the leather sofa as Ludlow collapsed in his chair behind his desk, reclining to stare at the ceiling. "I didn't see any discrepancies except for one of you asked for the Aiding and Abetting instruction."

"That was me, Your Honor," said Didery. "Obviously, it applies. I assume Mr. Turner must have just neglected to include it in his proposed instructions."

"No, actually, I don't think the instruction is appropriate." I knew full well the instruction was appropriate. If given, it would allow the jury to convict Darnell of murder even if he wasn't the shooter. Now, it was my turn to take advantage of Ludlow's incompetence.

"You can't be serious, Joe. You know the instruction applies," Didery whined, then addressed the judge. "Your Honor, if the jury finds that Moore was the driver and someone else was the shooter, then he's guilty on an aiding and abetting theory." Didery shot me a plaintive look, knowing that quoting the law to Ludlow was a losing battle.

"Your Honor, the prosecution's theory from the beginning of the trial has been that my client was the shooter. The prosecution is now, all of a sudden, switching theories? It's an ambush!" I said dramatically, slamming my legal pad on the floor.

Didery rolled his eyes. "You've got to be kidding

me, Turner. You know full well that the instruction applies."

Ludlow was losing patience. "I warned you two to sort this out before today!"

"Your Honor. Let's be real," I told him. "The prosecution's case is airtight and unfortunately, my client will be on his way to prison soon whether or not you give the Aiding and Abetting instruction. But if you do give the instruction, there will certainly be an appeal. Frankly, I'm surprised that Mr. Didery believes the instruction is worth jeopardizing his conviction."

My argument would have been valid if there was any chance of a successful appeal. Where the likelihood of conviction was strong, judges often shied away from jury instructions that might form the basis of an appeal for the defense. In this case, however, an appeal would be unthinkable because the instruction applied. But I was preying on Ludlow's incompetence and insecurity. His decisions had been reversed on appeal in record numbers, so he was vulnerable to my argument.

Didery began to panic, realizing that Ludlow was actually contemplating not giving the Aiding and Abetting instruction. "Your Honor, please. This is absurd. It is perfectly appropriate for me to argue to the jury that Mr. Moore was the shooter, but on the off chance that he was merely the driver, he's still guilty of murder. It's called arguing in the alternative. It happens all the time!"

"Your Honor, if you give this instruction, I will begin drafting the appeal now."

Ludlow put his elbows on his desk and covered his face with both hands. His worst nightmare was at hand. A legal decision. After several seconds, he stood. "Mr.

Didery, as Mr. Turner points out, this instruction is not essential to your case. You've proven that Moore was the shooter six ways from Sunday."

"Your Honor, please. Let me brief the issue this afternoon. I'll spell it out for you." I cringed, as his words hung in the air. Didery had gone too far. We knew Ludlow was incompetent; he knew that we knew. You just couldn't say it. The prosecutor hung his head, knowing he had no chance to win the argument now.

The judge stood, glaring at Didery. "I need nothing spelled out for me! I've made my decision. I will not be giving the Aiding and Abetting instruction. Now if you gentlemen will excuse me, I have some work to do," he said, grabbing a random book from his bookshelf.

"Tough one," I chided Didery, as we packed up our files in the courtroom.

"That was a joke, Turner, and you know it."

Joke or not, it was a significant victory. Now, to convict Darnell of murder, the prosecution would have to prove that he was the shooter.

****

The two deputy sheriffs were playing poker in their guard station when they heard the panic buzzer from the interview room. They hadn't noticed the camera to the room had gone black. They arrived to find Damon and Jesse grappling on the floor, cursing each other as they wrestled on the cold cement.

The deputies pulled them apart, flinging the inmate against the wall before handcuffing him. Jesse's body was sore. He was pretty sure the wound in his side was seeping, but he was determined not to show it.

"You don't fight bad for a suit."

"Go fuck yourself."

The twins traded a quick smile as Damon was escorted out of the room.

****

As I sat at my desk after court, I admitted having secretly harbored high hopes for the E&J market's long-anticipated surveillance video that captured the inside of the market. Perhaps Bedrossian would be caught on the video, saying, "I couldn't see a damn thing without my glasses," or in light of recent events, Elijah Jakes would be caught reloading his cane gun.

But it was not to be. The footage showed only the area surrounding the counter. At one point, what looked like the top of Bedrossian's head was seen in the foreground flashing across the screen after gunshots rang out.

I heard the office door open in the lobby. "Hi, Damon, Joe's in his office." I heard Lawanda's greeting shortly before my door was pushed open.

I glanced up. "Have a seat, Damon. I'm just finishing up here. Hey, nice hair-cut."

I looked up from my files, focusing on him for the first time. If it weren't for his eyes, I may not have noticed. If I would have looked closely, I may have seen that his button-down fit more loosely in the shoulders and that his khakis had to be cinched at the waist. Physically, though, the discrepancies would have gone unnoticed. But it was his sad, sunken eyes that had the realization washing over me moments before he spoke.

"Hi, Joe. It's Jesse."

Chapter Twenty-Nine

A man can condemn his enemies, but it's wiser to know them.—Harper Lee

As Chuck and I rode out to the crime scene on Wednesday afternoon, I thought back to Damon's request for the contact visit and wondered how long the twins had been planning this. I'd been careful not to ask Jesse how they'd pulled it off. As a rule, the less I knew about felony escapes, the better. I had simply treated Jesse as a witness who appeared in my office preparing for trial. And as it turned out, he had been remarkably forthcoming.

"Okay, here's what happened," he'd said simply, before describing exactly what he had seen on the day of the shooting.

Chuck eased Ma to a stop across the street from the E&J on Eighth Street, two houses down from the murder scene. I had filled Chuck in last night and we had agreed that Jesse's story could be supported by confirming a few facts with some photos at the crime scene.

"Keep your head on a swivel, Chuck." We sat in the jalopy with its top down, surveying the area. If Jesse was right, there was a potential for real danger.

"Joe, there's something I've got to tell you," he

said dramatically, peering out through his car's filthy windshield. "I've never shot anybody before."

"You're quoting movie lines at a time like this?"

Apart from a homeless man and his shopping cart, moving along the sidewalk toward the E&J, the area was deserted. The market's front door was closed, a makeshift "Closed" sign hung from a nail on the boarded-up front window.

Across the street at 454 West Eighth, the blue Victorian appeared vacant. Chuck and I walked to the sidewalk where Cleveland Barlow had perished. I had spent so much time staring at photos of the yard, I felt like I recognized every weed. The yard was still strewn with empty malt liquor cans, bottles, cigarette stubs and rolling papers. A strand of yellow police tape, probably left over from the murder, its end wrapped in a slat of the picket fence, fluttered in the breeze.

Chuck had set up on one knee, directly across the street from the E&J, his camera pointed toward the market when two shots cracked the afternoon silence, their fire-cracker pops merged with a metallic ricochet off a street sign not two feet above our heads.

I dropped to the ground on instinct, but that didn't seem right, so I was up again, sprinting to the car with Chuck. I dove in the back seat and Chuck was on the gas, plowing through plastic garbage bins in a sweeping U-turn as I buried myself in the floorboard. I stayed there for several minutes, catching my breath as we slalomed through the streets of west Oakland.

"That was awful," I called from the backseat once my breathing had returned to normal.

"Yeah, if he wanted us dead, we'd be dead," Chuck said, with a dry mouth.

"Yeah. He hit the street sign as a warning."

We rode in silence until we reached my office. "Looks like Jesse told the truth," Chuck said, parking on the street behind my car.

"Looks that way. Did you happen to get any photos?"

"No, but I'll figure something out. You know Churchill said nothing in life is more exhilarating than being shot at without result."

I just shook my head. "See you tomorrow, Chuck." Still shaky when I got home, I poured myself a stiff gin and tonic, outlined a direct examination of my star witness, and outlined my closing argument. Assuming Jesse showed up to Court and managed to seem reasonably credible with the jury, he would give the defense hope.

Before bed, I considered my professional ethical duties. I certainly had no obligation to report Jesse's appearance in my office. For all I knew, the jail had mistakenly released him. Even if I assumed an escape, I had no affirmative duty to report the crime.

I telephoned the jail, cancelling "Jesse Wendell's" transportation for his court appearance tomorrow morning. Jesse wasn't there, after all, so it wasn't necessary. The witness warrant would be withdrawn after he testified, then presumably the jail would release him, or rather, the inmate who was occupying his cell.

I thought of Damon, about to spend his second night in jail. I assumed he was in there, anyway, having taken the place of his twin. I recalled how much he hated jail and thought about how much he must care for his twin brother.

Chuck greeted me in Department 27 when I

arrived. "I didn't get any photos taken because, well, I was being shot at, but through the magic of the GPS on the Internet..." he said, presenting me with a folder of color images. "I emailed them to you so you can pull them up on the big screen in court."

"I'll never call you a Luddite again. Thanks!"

"I saw our boy outside. Good luck."

I realized I hadn't been the least bit worried about Jesse showing up.

Three weeks into the trial, dozens of calls to order had done nothing to mute the exuberance of Deputy Hartag's morning rendition. There was a spring in Ludlow's step as he ascended the bench, his crimson face betraying his previous-day's activity.

Didery stipulated to the translation of Bedrossian's remarks on the 911 tape, so I entered the transcript into evidence.

"Mr. Turner, your final witness," Ludlow said after saying good morning to the jury.

"Thank you, Your Honor. The defense calls Jesse Wendell."

The courtroom's double doors opened, and Jesse strolled down the aisle, cautiously peering about. Didery, immersed in his notes, did a double take upon seeing the witness in civilian clothes. *What the fuck*? he mouthed.

I gave him a shrug as Jesse took the oath.

"Mr. Wendell, where do you reside?" I asked from the podium.

"I live in Oakland. Currently, I'm homeless. I usually stay with friends."

"And for how long have you lived in Oakland?"

"I was raised in the foster care system all over the

bay area. Mostly in Oakland."

"Have you ever been convicted of a crime."

"Yes. When I was ten, I was convicted of murder."

I didn't look at the jury but felt them shifting in their seats. "And how old are you now?"

"I'm twenty-three, sir."

"How about other criminal offenses?"

"Since I've been out, some drug offenses, petty theft."

"Do you recall the events of March twenty-second of this year?"

"Yes, sir."

"Do you recall seeing a shooting?"

"I do."

"And where were you when you witnessed the shooting?"

"I was on the corner of Eighth and Maybeck in Oakland."

I cued up the E&J surveillance video of the intersection that showed Jesse at the intersection just before the green sedan drove past him. "Do you recognize yourself in that video?"

"Yes."

"What were you doing in the area, Mr. Wendell."

"I, uh, was going to try to buy some weed."

"And what did you see?"

"I saw a green car coming toward me on Eighth. It was an older model sedan—the one you saw in the video. I saw some young guys on the sidewalk in front of the house across the street from me on the corner. When the car got to the intersection, I heard shooting and saw one of the young guys fall."

"From your standpoint, could you see if the driver

of the green car had a gun?"

"Yes, the driver had a gun."

"Did you see the driver shoot his gun out of the car?"

"Yes. He stuck the gun out of the car and fired a lot of shots straight up in the air."

"What happened next?"

"The green car drove past me on Eighth."

"Mr. Wendell, did you see anyone else shooting that day?"

Jessed looked down at me from the witness stand. Then I saw his green eyes shift to his right, in line with Darnell behind me at the counsel table. The courtroom was silent as he sighed audibly into the microphone. "Yes, sir. Right before the driver shot up in the air, I saw someone shooting out of the second-floor window of the market across the street. He had a rifle."

I pulled up Chuck's satellite images on the big screen. On my previous trip to the E&J, I had been so focused on the front porch of the market, I hadn't bothered to look up, where a dormer window looked out on the street. The window was centered above the porch in what must have been a small attic. Likewise, none of the police photos taken from street level had captured the window.

"Is this the window where you saw the person shooting a rifle?"

"Yes."

"How many times did you see the person fire from the window?"

"I heard two really loud shots and saw the dude across the street drop. Then right after, I saw the driver shoot up in the air a bunch of times."

"Did you recognize this person you saw shooting out of the window."

"Yes, sir. I had seen him a couple days before in the market. I had gone in to buy rolling papers."

"Can you describe him, Mr. Wendell?"

"Big guy. He was in shape. It looked like he helped out at the store."

"May I approach, Your Honor?"

I pulled a photograph from a file Chuck had obtained from DMV records.

"Your Honor, I would ask that this photograph be marked as defense's next in order," I said, handing Cherlynn the photo. "I'm showing the photo to Mr. Didery." The prosecutor glanced at the photo and pretended not to care. "May I approach the witness, Your Honor?"

"You may."

"Mr. Wendell, is this the man you saw shooting out of the window on March twenty-second?"

"Yes," Jesse said. "That's him."

"Your Honor," I said, walking to my laptop, admittedly drawing out the suspense for the jury, "I will now publish the photo to the jury." The driver's license photo of Rocco Bedrossian filled the courtroom screen.

"Mr. Wendell, once again, is there any doubt that the man you see on the courtroom screen was the man who shot out of the window of the E&J Market?"

"No doubt."

"No further questions."

Didery sprang from his seat, not waiting for an invitation to cross examine. "Mr. Wendell, you not only committed murder, you did so by bludgeoning the victim with a barbell, isn't that right?"

"Yeah. That's right."

"Were you mentally ill?"

"No, sir."

"Were you having delusions?"

"No, sir."

"Well, Mr. Wendell, you're asking the jury to believe you today and I'm just wondering if you had any explanation for your committing this incredibly irrational, violent act?"

"I don't make any excuses for what happened." Jesse said, breathing deeply. He was overtly calm, but I sensed he was struggling to hold it together. "Obviously, sir, if I had it to do over again, I would handle it differently."

"Meaning, you may not have bludgeoned your father to death?"

"Sir, he was a foster parent," Jesse said, his voice shaking with emotion. "And he was..." His voice trailed off as he looked to the floor for several seconds.

Finally, he looked up at the prosecutor with moist eyes and a quivering bottom lip. Gone was the sullen face and permanent smirk. Something about Didery's question had reached Jesse's core. As he looked furtively at the prosecutor, the jury saw the witness as a helpless, whimpering boy.

After allowing Jesse to recover, Didery skillfully questioned him about whether he was high on the day in question, his vantage point, his ability to recall Rocco's appearance, and his decision not to contact the police. It was difficult to read the jury's reaction.

"Mr. Wendell, you saw Rocco Bedrossian one time prior to the day of the shooting?"

"Yes."

"And when you described him today for the jury, you said, quote, 'big guy, in shape,' correct?"

"Yes, sir."

"Is that the extent of your recollection of his appearance."

"No, he looked like he did in his DMV photo."

"Recalling when you saw him on the previous occasion, can you point to anything about his appearance that you recall as distinctive in the least? Facial hair, tattoos, anything?

"No."

"Nothing at all?"

Jesse rubbed his face and looked toward the ceiling, concentrating. Then he shifted his focus abruptly down and to the side. He began to nod.

"No further questions, Your Honor."

"Excuse me, Your Honor," I broke in. "I believe the witness is still contemplating an answer to the last question."

Ludlow looked at Jesse. "Sir, do you have an answer?"

"Yes," said Jesse, still nodding to himself. "I remember when I saw him in the store, when he walked, he had a pretty noticeable limp."

To my left, I saw Darnell clench his fist and whisper, "Yes!" under his breath. A few jurors nodded in recognition while others wrote notes on their pads.

Ludlow excused the jury for the morning recess. After a brief word with Chuck, I grabbed a hotdog and reviewed my closing, knowing that the case would likely turn on the jury's impression of Jesse.

Back in court, Didery's closing argument began with a predictably detailed review of every piece of evidence against Darnell. Finally, he walked in front of the podium to address the jury.

"Ladies and gentlemen, this has not been a trial where the prosecution's case has been proven with one dominant piece of evidence like a video of the actual crime or a signed confession. Instead, there have been lots and lots of pebbles of evidence. Darnell Moore had motive to kill Cleveland Barlow. Not only was he a rival gang member, his own house had been shot up just two days before he got revenge.

"Mr. Moore's car was used in the murder. His gun was fired at the scene. He confessed to being there. Mr. Bedrossian identified him as the shooter. And on and on. Eventually, you look over at all the pebbles and they have formed a pile. A big, undeniable pile of evidence that Darnell Moore committed this crime.

"And Darnell Moore knows that he is guilty. And he knows that you know. Why else would he give himself a tattoo in jail? He knows he's guilty, and he was desperate. He was hoping you all would fall for his trick.

"And against all this evidence—this huge pile of pebbles, the defense has submitted the testimony of one witness—an unreliable prior felon who has made an outlandish accusation against a war hero.

"Who in the world is Mr. Jesse Wendell? Does he have a relationship with the defendant? We know he grew up in Oakland, so it's entirely possible. And, ladies and gentlemen, where has Mr. Wendell been for the last four months? He didn't go to the police. There's no evidence he said anything to anybody about witnessing a murder. And now, at the eleventh hour, he strolls into court and expects you to disregard all the evidence to the contrary.

"That's not the way it works. You must make your decision based on the evidence. And when you do, I have no doubt you will find Mr. Moore guilty of murder. Thank you."

I approached the podium to address the jury for the final time. "Ladies and gentlemen, we have people on juries rather than computers for a reason. As I mentioned during jury selection, the truth is found not by adding up the number of witnesses, but in the nuance and subtlety of testimony and evidence.

"When I heard Mr. Vardan Bedrossian testify last week, a detail struck me as odd. He emphasized to you that on March twenty-second, he was alone in the store. Then I reviewed his statement to the police," I said, playing the audio for the jury:

This is Officer Zuckerman. I'm here with Mr. Bedrossian. It is March 24, 2021. I'm here at the Oakland Police Department. The time is one-twenty-four p.m. Sir, what did you observe on Monday?

I was alone in the store.

"So when asked what he saw, Mr. Bedrossian said that he was alone in the store. Then I reviewed Mr. Bedrossian's testimony in the preliminary hearing in this case." I opened the file and the transcript appeared on the courtroom screen.

Mr. Didery: Sir, what did you observe that evening?

Mr. Bedrossian: I was alone in the market, sweeping.

"Ladies and gentlemen, it was imperative for Mr. Bedrossian to convince everyone he was alone in the store. Now we know why. He was protecting his son.

"The prosecutor would have you consider Mr. Wendell's testimony in a vacuum—an unreliable, drug-addicted felon who can't be trusted. But I'm asking you to consider his testimony in the context of the trial.

"Mr. Wendell told you he recognized the shooter, Rocco Bedrossian, in part, because of his pronounced limp that we all witnessed here in Court when he took the stand. He told you he saw Rocco Bedrossian shoot from the upstairs window, and this would explain the downward angle of the shots as described by the pathologist. He described the two louder shots of the killer's rifle followed by others, which matches Mr. Jakes' description.

"Jesse Wendell told you that he saw Darnell Moore fire up in the air, which is why the ten shell casings were in the street, but no bullets could be found. Mr. Wendell's identification of Rocco Bedrossian explains his father's statement in his native language captured by the 911 call. 'Go! You have to leave. Now!' he told his son.

"And finally, I'd ask you to use your common sense. Does it make sense that Darnell Moore, who had never been convicted of a gun offense in his life, could fire two precision kill shots with one hand while operating his vehicle? Or does it make more sense that those shots came from a trained army marksman, firing the deadly accurate shots from an elevated, stationary position?

"Certainly, there are unanswered questions. How did Rocco Bedrossian know that Darnell Moore was coming, or was the timing just fortuitous for him? But these are questions, perhaps, for a future trial of Rocco Bedrossian." I closed, as I usually did, discussing the legal standard, "beyond a reasonable doubt"—the highest in the law.

I told the jury it was natural to want justice for Cleveland Barlow, especially seeing the heart-rending photos of the young man. I told them that it was obvious that Darnell Moore was not a saint—that he had been up to no good that day, and probably had thought better of his bad intentions at the last minute.

"But your question is discrete. It's not whether young Darnell Moore is a gang member or a bad guy. It's whether he shot Cleveland Barlow. The answer is no, and the only just verdict is not guilty."

I was greeted back at the counsel table with a subtle fist bump from Darnell. Exhausted, I half-listened to Ludlow's jury instructions and tried to read the jurors' faces and predict who among them would be elected foreperson. At three-forty-five p.m., the jury filed out to decide the fate of Darnell Moore.

My phone buzzed. It was Eddy.

—*How'd it go, Counselor?*—

—*Glad it's over*—

—*Can't wait to see you. Free for lunch tomorrow? I'll be in Oakland*—

—*Goodness yes!*—

On the way out of court, I found Jesse waiting at the bus stop.

"Hey, Jesse. I want to thank you. You were great."

"Thanks, Mr. Turner. That D.A. is kind of a prick."

"Kind of, yes. You know, you had me worried for a while that you'd testify for the prosecution."

"Naw," he said with a smirk. "I was just playing the angles. I know what it's like to do time for something you didn't, uh…have planned."

"Well, thanks."

"Sure. Hey, Mr. Turner. Can you tell me when there's a verdict? I'd like to be there."

"Sure."

I went to my empty office and began the long process of catching up on my other cases that followed every trial. Cherlynn texted at five p.m. to tell me the jury had gone home, and I did the same. After pizza and most of a bottle of an expensive Cabernet recommended by Eddy, I was drifting to sleep in the recliner by nine p.m. with Darnell, Didery, and Ludlow crashing my thoughts of Eddy and the wine country.

I awoke early, went for a run, and convinced myself not to try to speculate about the jury. Years of trying had proven useless and stressful. After more work in the office, I walked to the courthouse to see how Darnell was holding up.

"Hey, Mr. Turner," he said, shaking off the effects of a mid-morning nap. "Sorry, they got me up at four-thirty a.m. this morning. Any news?"

"No. Just came by to say hi. You doing okay?"

"Whew," he said shaking his head. "It's like whenever I walk into that courtroom, I'll either find out that tonight I'll be with my fam eating my uncle's barbeque or I won't ever taste that again."

"I know, Darnell. I wanted to sort of prepare you for either scenario, though. You know, if you're convicted, there's a path to the quickest parole. It will involve you renouncing the gang and doing a good program in prison. With your youth, you'll have a good chance at parole after twenty-five years."

"Yeah, I'm prepared for the sentence and all. I'll be strong for my family. But if I'm in prison, the gang will be my protection, so I don't know."

"Yeah, Darnell, I get it."

"Now, if it goes our way, I'm not messing with them anymore."

I smiled, knowing that keeping his word would be difficult. On the streets, having kept his mouth shut in the face of murder charges, his standing in the gang would be at an all-time high.

"We'll see," he said reading my mind.

I walked back out in the courtroom to find Didery reading the paper at the counsel table.

Cherlynn hung up her phone. "They have a verdict," she said calmly. "The judge is at lunch, so we'll convene at one-thirty p.m."

Didery practically skipped down the aisle on his way out of the courtroom. There would be no hung jury, so I was sure he was brimming with confidence and no doubt off to recruit his colleagues for the grave dance. The D.A.'s office kept up the somewhat morbid tradition of attending each other's verdicts, which usually involved reveling in the victory amidst the defendant's family's devastation. I tried not to let Didery's reaction influence my thoughts. We still had a chance.

I had already texted Darnell's mother, Chuck, Jesse, and Eddy. They were all present, along with a dozen D.A.s when Deputy Hartag belted out the call to order for the last time in the trial.

"Juror number five, Mr. Samuels," Ludlow said, "I understand you are the foreperson?"

The software engineer from Berkeley was not my favorite juror. "Yes."

"Have you reached a verdict?"

"We have."

As it was purely ceremonial in nature, it was no surprise that Ludlow knew the drill. "Then please hand your verdict form to Deputy Hartag." The deputy took the form and handed it up to the judge without looking at it. Ludlow then read the form to himself. Expressionless, he handed it to his clerk. "The defendant and his counsel will please rise. Ladies and gentlemen, please listen to the reading of the verdict."

I stood next to Darnell and heard his heavy breathing. His stress was unimaginable. Cherlynn cleared her throat. "Ladies and Gentlemen of the jury, please pay attention while I read your verdict. In the sole count of the criminal complaint, we, the jury, find the defendant, Darnell Jackson Moore, not guilty of murder."

Darnell collapsed in his chair, his head in his hands. I sat down and turned behind me to see his mother, sobbing tears of joy. Ludlow was droning on to the jury about the importance of jury service when Darnell looked up, his face streaked with tears.

"Thank you, Joe," he said, showing the smile he wore the day I met him, still collapsed on the table. "Thank you so much."

I patted his back. "Enjoy that barbeque, Darnell."

When the jury had filed out for the last time, I turned to find Jesse behind us in the first row. "Congratulations, Joe."

"Thanks again, Jesse."

Darnell stood and turned to face Jesse, greeting him with a slight raise of his chin and a look of respect. "Good lookin'," he said quietly. Jesse returned the gesture as Darnell was escorted away uncuffed for his ride back to the jail where he would be released.

Eddy greeted me with a kiss, my first ever in the courthouse, and Chuck walked with us to the Oaktown Brewery to celebrate.

"So, your truth detector instincts are still intact, babe," she said, as I set a pitcher of beer on our table.

"Thank goodness. I was beginning to doubt myself."

"Well," Eddy said with a smirk, "I believe I recall telling you that I thought the killer might be Rocco?"

Chuck frowned. "Really? This is the first I'm hearing of this."

"It's true," I said, clinking her glass. "You called it. And as long as we're passing around 'I told you so's,' I believe that I happened to question who travels half-way around the world without a suitcase."

"Very true." Chuck tipped his glass toward me. "He was obviously already in town."

"But it's not quite the same as naming the killer, now is it?" Eddy chided.

"Well, not to throw shade on your prediction," I said, still smiling because she had called me 'babe,' "but I believe as part of your ode to cartoon sleuths, you basically accused everyone."

"I don't remember that," Eddy deadpanned.

"Yeah, remember your theory that Damon was the killer? You said his eyes were hollow and creepy."

Chapter Thirty

People generally see what they look for and hear what they listen for. —Harper Lee

Damon Wendell was living his worst nightmare. He sat on his bunk holding his knees to his chest, rocking back and forth, desperate to calm his frayed nerves. The air in the jail was heavy with a film of body odor and disinfectant, the tension among inmates, constant. Knowing he was now a target, he hadn't slept much either of his first two nights in custody. He wouldn't have anyway.

Jesse's cellmate hadn't noticed the switch. Or if he had, he hadn't said anything. Last night, Damon had spotted the one they called Turbo who had tried to kill his brother. Cell Two L in the corner of the pod, bottom bunk. Jesse said Turbo skipped breakfast and stayed in his cell sleeping most days. Yesterday morning, though, he had gone to breakfast.

Damon stopped rocking and rubbed a hand across the stubble of his fresh buzzcut. "So here he was," he thought to himself, with a disbelieving smile. Thirteen years after formulating his plan, he had actually broken into a jail for his twin brother. God knows he owed it to him.

At seven a.m., he flinched as a heavy door to his cell buzzed open. He was rocking again, his wide eyes watching as inmates filed out for breakfast. Only a few of the forty inmates remained in their cells. Turbo didn't leave his bunk. Damon reached under the mattress and felt for the heavy lead pipe while staring straight ahead. Jesse had traded two weeks' commissary for it. It looked like a piece of plumbing, probably from one of the jail's industrial washing machines.

Just as Jesse had predicted, there was no one in the common area of the pod. The inmates who stayed in their cells for breakfast wouldn't snitch. He would be back in his cell before the guards arrived and be released later that afternoon. He trusted his twin.

Even if he got caught, he was prepared. Jesse wouldn't be around to take the blame for him this time. He would do his own time. Part of him even hoped that would happen. If he was in custody, he knew Jesse would straighten his life out and be happy. Jesse would owe him that, and he would do it for him, just as he had done for his twin.

As Damon waited for the stragglers to clear out of the cell block, his thoughts turned to the clothing swap with Jesse. It had been stressful and somewhat painful, but typically, the twins had found a way to have fun together. They'd bet on whether or not Jesse would be handcuffed—he wasn't—and had laughed at his pathetic attempt to tie Damon's necktie.

Jesse had resisted the idea at first but the twins both knew he had to agree. Neither twin could deny the other's visceral need to look out for one another. It had always been that way, and now, more than ever, it gave their lives purpose. So Jesse had relented to the clothing swap, just as Damon had given up his blood-spattered shirt to Jesse all those years ago.

Damon scooted to the edge of his bunk. "I got this, brother," he whispered, repeating his ten-year-old brother's words to him before the police had arrived on the worst day of their lives. He stood and walked through his open cell door wearing Jesse's jail clothing. He held the end of the foot-long pipe in his cupped right hand, pinning it to his side with his forearm. Cell Two L was ten paces away, a diagonal walk across the pod. Approaching, he could see the guy who had attacked Jesse dozing on his bunk, alone in his cell.

Damon's breathing shortened. "You've done it before, Damon. Just breathe," he told himself, reciting the silent mantra in his head. "Plan your work. Work your plan." He pushed silently through the open door and stood at the edge of the bunk. Then he jostled the bed with his knee and waited for the look of fear he needed to see.

A word about the author...

T.L. Bequette is a criminal defense attorney in Oakland, California. Most of his practice involves defending those accused of murder. He holds degrees from The University of the Pacific and Georgetown Law School and serves annually on faculty of the Stanford Law School Trial Advocacy Clinic. He is also the father of twin boys. This is his debut novel.

Thank you for purchasing
this publication of The Wild Rose Press, Inc.

For questions or more information
contact us at
info@thewildrosepress.com.

The Wild Rose Press, Inc.
www.thewildrosepress.com

CPSIA information can be obtained
at www.ICGtesting.com
Printed in the USA
BVHW031757201122
652385BV00014B/493